EXILE

SARAH BOURNE

The Train

Ella's War

InVisible

This book is for Neil, with love and thanks.

'The man who is in love is bound in a hard kind of slavery.'
Andreas Capellanus
De Arte Honeste Amandi
(The Art of Courtly Love)
12th Century

'Or the woman.'
Kirstie Bligh, 2019

1

———

EXILE

It was a Monday when first I came to this place, a week before Christmas. Selling my business and leaving most of my possessions behind, I left my London life, bringing with me a few clothes, some books, writing materials. After two days on trains and ferries I found what I had been hoping for – a secluded cottage on a hillside some way from the nearest village. It had belonged to my mother's parents but when they died no one took it on and it was allowed to sit empty in this gaunt landscape. I had just turned forty-four years old and in the last couple of years had managed to break apart a family, lose the man I thought I loved and leave destruction in my wake. Moving to Yell, this remote Shetland island, was my exile. My sentence.

The wind blustered from the south, which I would learn meant warmer weather. But that day there was no warmth to be had. Squalling rain worked its way through my clothes and dripped down my neck. The driver unloaded my suitcase and the food I had bought at the local shop. I'd told the shopkeeper I needed to recuperate from an illness and required absolute quiet. She had looked me up and down as if trying to find any trace of this malady and then nodded, one eyebrow raised in a disbelieving arc. Now, shielding his face from the rain, the driver nodded towards the cottage as if to say, 'Are you sure you want me to leave you here all on your own?'

Giving him a small smile, I looked around, noting the outhouse to one side, and made my way to the front door which rattled in the wind. The rough planks from which it had been crafted had shrunk away from each other leaving gaps for the weather to blow in. When I pushed, it groaned as if it didn't want to admit anyone after so long. The hinges were stiff from disuse, shedding rust that swirled before sinking to the floor in fine Titian trails as they finally squealed and allowed the door to open.

As I entered, the acrid smell of animal urine was so pungent I had to cover my mouth and nose with my sleeve and still didn't want to breathe deeply. The scurrying of tiny feet alerted me to the fact that rodents of some sort had their homes here and were none too pleased at the idea of being discovered. Dust motes danced on rays of light that squeezed through windows thick with dirt and crusted with salt. My heart lurched and for a moment I questioned my sanity. Escape from the world, yes, but to this? I took a deep breath and dug into my resolve.

Inside, the cups and plates on the shelves were covered in years of dust. Blackened pans hung over the range. The few utensils in the cottage were discoloured with age and the bone handles were coming away from the blades of the knives. I wondered about the people whose hands had held those items – my grandparents. I didn't even know their names but they had lifted the cups to their lips and sipped, had eaten years' worth of meals off the plates. Who else had lived here with them? I knew nothing about my family. A sadness settled over me. I hadn't met my ancestors and never would, but I would be living among their belongings, using their possessions. I hated my mother for not letting me know them.

The cottage was primitive – not a stove or fridge in sight. An old fiddle leant against the wall in the corner, the spiderwebs draping it almost as thick as the strings. Who had played it? My grandfather, perhaps even my mother? Someone's fingers had left their trace on the neck so its lustre revealed itself shyly when I wiped away the coat of grime. Two armchairs faced each other across the hearth and I wanted to believe this had been a happy home, a place where people spoke and people listened, where music filled the long winter nights.

There was an alcove with a faded curtain hanging across it, a wooden bed pushed back against the wall with an old crate beside it. The only internal door led to another room just large enough for a double bed with a blanket box at its foot filled with yellowed, musty-smelling sheets and mouse droppings. A small chest of drawers squatted beneath a picture of Mary and baby Jesus that looked like it might have been torn out of a book or a magazine. Opening the top drawer and seeing it contained coarse underwear I closed it again, unready for the intimacy of rifling through the clothes my grandparents had worn. Wooden planks had been knocked together to make a blind. A naked bulb hung from the ceiling but a flick of the switch by the door proved there was no electricity.

It was a poor place but a home that would have seen love as well as loss, joy as well as sorrow, some of each seeping into the marrow of the cottage, the stone walls strengthened by the lives that had been lived within. This was the perfect place – indeed, the only place – for me now. I would get used to the whispers from across the years.

The driver had followed me in, watching my exploration. He now placed my possessions at my feet and held his hand out. I gave him my shopping list for next time and a small tip. He clicked his tongue against his teeth, perhaps the only sound he could make, for it was the same noise he had used in his car as we made our way up the track, as if it was a horse needing encouragement. Then he walked away, not towards his car, but to a mound of turf cuttings. He gathered a basketful and brought it back, dumping it in the corner and pointing to the range. Peat for burning.

I watched him go, guiding the car along the rutted way, never once looking back. I was relieved to be of so little interest to him and given my history, more relieved that he was of so little interest to me.

I spent the next few days cleaning and bringing order to my new life. Rising early, well before the nine o'clock dawn of this far north place, I'd light a fire and put the water on for washing and for tea. I'd never cooked over a fire before, never been a Girl Guide on camp. I was trying to get the range going one morning, fingers numb with cold, when a gust of wind blew down the chimney and the ashes from the night before covered me. On another day, as I lay the fire, the embers from the previous day caught and a tongue of flame burst forth, catching alight the sleeve of my fleece. I ran outside and rolled in the turf, crying tears of shame and fear in the wind and the sleet. Then I went in and threw water on the fire, filling the cottage with smoke, making me cough and run out again, shivering in my ruined clothes.

The sludge that trickled out of the tap above the deep stone sink was the colour of the parquet flooring in my London flat, so I collected water from the spring that ran just below the cottage. My back ached from the weight of the bucket and several times I sloshed so much water over myself I had to dry my clothes out in front of the fire or risk freezing to death. The one time I hung my clothes outside after washing, they froze, and cracked loudly as I pulled them off the line, crystals of ice falling to the ground like a mini snowstorm. There was nothing dignified in the way I learned to accomplish these dreary tasks and the words that escaped my lips with every failure would have made a sailor blush. I was glad time and again there was nobody there to see how hopeless I was.

In the evenings I sat as close to the range as I dared, swatting the sparks from my clothes and read by the light of a hurricane lamp. Even in front of the fire, though, I never felt warm in those first days. I'd nailed an old blanket over the gaping boards of the door, but the wind whistled in through other cracks I couldn't see and found gaps between the layers of my clothing, chilling me to the bone.

In addition to my journals, I had brought several books with me. I'd read them all several times before, but they held special significance for me, and I considered them too precious to leave behind with the trappings of my old life. My favourite was the Austen; how often had I longed for a man like Colonel Brandon to whisk me away from my baleful existence? A gentleman, honourable through to the marrow in his bones. A man like him might discover something in me to love and cherish, might admire my reddish, rather unruly hair and broad, high cheekbones. He might run a finger lightly over my full lips, along the line of my jaw, stare passionately into my grey-green eyes and declare me beautiful. If my five feet seven inches brought my eyes level with his, he'd be pleased not to have to look down at me as he would have had to when gazing at the diminutive Marianne Dashwood. He would delight in my intellect, the conversations we could have. It would be a meeting of equals.

As if.

The light wasn't good in the cottage, the dark corners sucking it into themselves and many a night I was driven outside by headaches brought on by eye strain from reading, needing to revive myself in the cold air. In the end I put one of the kitchen chairs outside so I didn't have to sit on the tussocky grass. I only needed one inside, after all.

I had always loved cooking but the meals I made in the cottage were nothing compared to my usual productions. To minimise my contact with the outside world I had organised to have groceries delivered weekly, which meant I would be cooking from tins and packets by week's end, looking forward to fresh fruit and vegetables again. My diet lacked variety and I wondered if it would sustain me. It was an intellectual reflection rather than one driven by concern for myself. In truth, I would have been happy not to exist at all but being too much of a coward to kill myself, exile was my sentence.

It wasn't the loneliness that concerned me on my hillside. Being an only child, I had often been lonely. I'd had friends at school, but not many. I was a misfit as a child; my mother had taught me to read and write by the time I started in kindergarten so in class I doodled, sat looking out the window or drew pictures of beetles and ants in my copy book. Insects had always fascinated me. Most other children thought me odd and kept away. No, it wasn't the loneliness I was challenged by but the harshness of the life, the cruelty of the elements and my ineptitude in dealing with them.

A week after my arrival I woke up and realised it was Christmas Day. My body ached from the hard bed and the heavy work I'd been doing. There were no presents to look forward to, no guests to greet. I turned over and faced the wall, pulling the blankets up around my ears and gripping them tight. Later, I made myself get up, light the range and make myself some pot noodles. The whisky bottle had a good outing that day.

Out the door, thick-coated sheep grazed on the coarse grass. Even the birds seemed to have taken to the roost to stay dry and out of the howling wind that had been my constant companion since my arrival.

How different had my previous Christmases been? As a very young child I was always confident in the knowledge that my parents would make a big effort for the day, showering me with presents and attention. As I got older and their marriage crumbled, Christmas was just another day to get through. By the time I left home we'd hardly bothered to celebrate at all for several years.

Christmases as an adult I'd wake in a warm bed, central heating on high, thick rugs on the floor. The day cold and clear, sky the colour of a duck's egg and the branches of the oak I could see from my window brushed with frost. Or grey cloud obscuring a weak sun and snow dusting the branches. Or rain trying relentlessly to dampen my enthusiasm. Nevertheless, I had always leapt from my bed eager to begin the day. I had loved Christmas with the days leading up to it full of the smells of mince pies baking and Christmas pud, the scents of cinnamon and Christmas trees. The day itself I'd spend with my few friends – others who chose not to celebrate the day with family for reasons we didn't discuss.

Of course, even in my chosen exile, it was impossible to avoid people altogether. One day early in the new year, with the weak sun glistening on the frosty ground, I saw two old men walking on the hill above my croft. I call it a hill but in reality, it is more of a swell – the land around here is low-lying moor rather than Alp. But it undulates and because of the lack of trees, the topography is emphasised. The rise behind my cottage is high enough to provide some shelter from the westerly winds.

It wasn't often that people came this way – in the two or three weeks I'd been here I could count on the fingers of one hand how many times I'd had to hide from strangers. I couldn't imagine what would bring people out in the terrible weather we'd been having but supposed there was peat to cut and sheep to tend. As I thought that, one of the men turned his head and saw me. He slowed, stopped and called out to his friend, who also looked my way.

'Just keep going,' I prayed, closing my eyes tight as if not seeing the men would make them vanish.

'A beautiful day, is it not?' A lilting male voice carried on the freezing air. Its owner lifted a hand and waved.

Manners had been drummed into me at home and at school and even though I didn't want to encourage these men, I lifted my hand in response. The second man took a couple of steps down the hill toward me, and I turned and ran, picking my way carelessly through the tussocks. I went over on my ankle and almost fell but managed to right myself and make it to the cottage. Slamming the door, I leant against it and slid to the floor, panting. My ankle was throbbing and I could feel my boot already tightening around it.

Footsteps outside my door a few minutes later preceded a volley of questions.

'Are you all right, missy?'

'Can we be of assistance in any way?'

'You're Jimmy and Aileen's granddaughter, are you no – Morag's girl?'

One of them jiggled the door handle and I gasped and bit down on my knuckles.

There was a murmuring as the two men conferred.

I held my breath.

'Well, we'll be off the noo. If you need anything ask Sheila at the shop for Duncan or Ewan. She knows where to find us.'

My heart started slowing as I heard them walk off. One of them said to the other, 'She's got her granny's red hair, I see. I'd heard she was a recluse, but I think she may have a wee screw loose.'

The other man replied but by then they were too far away for me to make out his response.

So, I was the mad recluse on the hill. Although I deserved the epithet, I was offended by it. If they knew why I could see no one, they would understand. Recluse I may be, but at that moment I was as sane as the next person. Although I knew all about madness. Mania. Obsession. Call it what you will.

The days slowly lengthened after the Solstice. The snow that had fallen intermittently since I'd arrived and had lain around in glistening and then browning drifts, cleared. The island was bathed in pale lemony sunlight although the wind kept the temperatures low. My days were as pale as the sun, as empty as the landscape. I could see the sea from my door and often watched it, a shifting presence sparkling on the horizon. Like a dream. Like hope. At night the moonlight travelled a silver path to the shore.

Once a week a car groaned its way up the track, thumping into potholes, creaking along the ruts, and delivered groceries and other necessities. I tipped the delivery man, the same one who had brought me here, who was middle-aged but with an older man's rasping breath and a pugilist's nose. He eyed me from under bushy eyebrows. I gave him the list for next time, and he nodded, touched his sweat-stained cap as if I was royalty, then manoeuvred himself into the driver's seat and chugged down the hill. We shared no words – he never spoke, and I was happy to stay silent.

I watched until I could see him no more, not because I was lonely but because I wanted to be certain he'd left and the hillside belonged only to me once again. I chose the solitude and guarded it carefully. I had met no one but the shopkeeper and the driver, and no one from my old life knew I was here. Unless... no. No one.

I talked to myself. Sometimes it was a running commentary on my actions but mostly replaying old scenes, giving voice to both sides of the situation. There was no comfort in it, but it was a custom I couldn't break. Like washing my hands before eating or saying my prayers before bed as I had done until I realised that either there was no God, or He had turned his back on me.

By mid-February I had mastered the practicalities of my life, which left me more time to think and made it harder to ignore the painful memories haunting me. I went through my journals, red-faced with shame one minute, outraged the next, and sometimes even heartsore for the woman I was then – the deluded, obsessed person who had invested her whole being, her entire happiness, in one man. Mostly though, I was ashamed. What had I done? Could I have done more to change the ending? Would I ever trust myself to live amongst people again?

The melting snow left soggy ground that sprang under my feet as I walked, water appearing around my footprints before slowly being reabsorbed into the peaty earth. I wrapped myself up against the biting wind and walked, eyes streaming, nose running, lungs hardening against the cold as my breath misted in the air. From a distance, if anyone were around to see, I must have looked like a small steam train puffing around the landscape. I'd had to send a message with the mute asking if the shopkeeper could order me some clothes more suitable for the climate and she'd sent me thick fleece jackets and thermals. Even having lived by the sea in Brighton, where the winds could whip hard enough to roll the pebbles along the beach, I hadn't known how cold a winter could be nor how a wind could enter the smallest of gaps between layers and settle into one's bones. The island may be abundant in peat, but I would single-handedly have burnt it all if I hadn't obtained appropriate clothing.

I longed for my phone, my laptop and a good internet connection but my cottage had no electricity. I had sent a note with the mute asking Sheila if she'd organise getting it reconnected but so far, nothing had happened. My mother now owned the croft, though it had lain empty for many years, and I suspect she ignored everything about it. All I knew was she had left the island as a teenager and had never been back.

I'd found out about it one day when I was about ten. I'd gone into the kitchen, and she was standing at the table, a letter in her hand and a faraway look in her eyes.

'What's up?' I asked. My mother was never still. Agitated was the best word to describe her.

She stuffed the letter into the pocket of her apron and crossed the kitchen to open the fridge. Head deep inside the cool, my mother told me her parents had died.

'Your parents? I thought they were already dead.'

'No.'

'You've never mentioned them. When did they die?'

'Months ago now. The solicitor couldn't find me.'

'Why did he need to?'

'To let me know they'd died within days of each other and been buried together. And to tell me I've been left their croft.'

She sniffed. Her head was still in the fridge.

'Can we go and see it?'

'No.'

'Is there anyone else – do you have brothers and sisters? Have I got cousins?' A new world opened up before me, of adventures shared on holidays with children my own age, of outings, meals where people talked about their day and planned the next. Family. That's what they did, wasn't it, normally?

'There's no one,' she said, pulling her head out of the fridge and slamming its door shut. She turned away and clamped her lips around a Silk Cut, ending my brief fantasy as soon as it had begun. Then she got out the ironing board and worked her way through the washing basket, putting creases in shirts, trousers, tea towels and underpants. Perhaps that day, her hand was a little heavier, the creases sharper.

At the time, I interpreted her behaviour as anger and backed off, afraid I'd become the target of it. Now I believe it was grief.

In my cottage – her cottage – I may have missed technology and blamed its absence on the lack of electricity, but I had made a conscious decision not to bring it anyway. If my exile was to be complete, I couldn't allow myself the temptation of communicating with the outside world. I'd done enough damage for one lifetime.

As spring approached the daylight hours lengthened, yet the nights seemed longer. During the day there were tasks – collecting peat for fires, preparing food, fetching water from the spring, writing, walking the hills to exhaust myself. I would take to the shore, marching along beaches, around headlands, aware of nothing but the scenery and the salt air stinging my eyes. I would return home drenched, exhausted, and drink the whisky the mute delivered each week, falling asleep in the chair only to be visited by unwelcome visitors from my past who filled my dreams with accusations. Often I would rise from my bed and sit outside the front door and let the stars bear witness to my tears and my shame.

Of course, I didn't have enough to occupy me. In spite of living without modern amenities, with only myself to look after, chores were dealt with quickly. I had too much time to think. In my old life, one of my self-help books had suggested keeping a gratitude diary noting five things to be grateful for each day.

Day One
The sun came up.
I wasn't freezing today.
Being alive. I struck that one off.
Being healthy. I didn't care one way or the other.
???

As an exercise, it didn't last long.

Returning from my walk one morning, I saw an old car bumping along the track towards my cottage. It wasn't the mute's. I stopped, crouched down behind a stack of peat cuttings and watched, heart pounding. Surely no one knew where I was, and who would want to see me anyway?

A woman got out and looked about her, holding her hat on her head with one hand and shielding her eyes against the weak sunlight with the other. She knocked on the cottage door and getting no answer, peered in through the window. I was glad I'd tidied up after my breakfast. She got back into her car and closed the door but didn't leave. Minutes later, she got out again, poked something under the front door and finally drove away. I watched until I was sure she'd gone, that it wasn't a trick – her looking in the rear-view mirror to see me coming back so she could turn around and catch me – and then ran to the cottage and threw myself through the door. I couldn't lock myself in because there was no bolt, so I drew a chair across the door and sat on it, shaking.

When it was clear she wasn't coming back, I leant down and retrieved the piece of paper she'd shoved under the door.

Dear Kirstie, it read,

I'm sorry I haven't been before – I was away working on the mainland and came home because my father's been poorly, so I couldn't get away. I just wanted to welcome you to the island. If I'd known you were coming, I would have cleaned the old place up. I'll call again. I'm looking forward to meeting you.
Ishbel.

Ishbel? Who was she and how did she know my name? Why did she want to meet me? I breathed hard to quell the panic roiling like waves of acid in my belly. I had not come here to make friends. I had come to be alone. A naïve idea, of course, to think no one knew I was here – on an island this size, a newcomer, particularly one who made no attempt to engage with the outside world, would be fodder for gossip and speculation.

And I had to admit I was lonely, that after three months of my own company I was going a little mad. It wasn't as if I didn't want to make friends, but I didn't feel I deserved to after what I'd done.

I continued to talk aloud to myself just to hear a voice, words out in the air rather than in my head. I had arguments, discussions. I read out loud and pretended to have an audience, introducing the characters from my books to the mice that still scratched in the roof and left their hard little droppings in the corners. I had ordered mousetraps from the shop but when they came I hadn't the heart to put them out. Those mice were my only companions. Until now. Until this Ishbel.

The next time I went out, I left a note pinned to the door. It had been difficult to write. I thought I wanted to tell Ishbel to leave me alone, to respect my privacy but every time I started, the loneliness welled up in me and my hand would invite her to come at a certain time on a certain day. It said that I was looking forward to meeting her too. I threw those notes away, hurling them into the fire. In the end, I wrote,

Thanks for coming but I'm out. Kirstie.

The note stayed there, fluttering in the wind, for a week. It became tattered and wet, and I replaced it with the same words. Each time I went out, I checked it was there, hoping she'd come, read it and get the message that I wasn't interested. Every time I came home, I was disappointed her car wasn't there, or that she hadn't been and left another note. I decided she wasn't really keen to meet me after all and told myself it was for the best.

To distract myself from this Ishbel, I started the project I'd been putting off since I arrived on Yell – writing down my reason for being here as honestly as I could. I had always thought I would write to get it all straight in my head, to make a coherent whole of all the therapy I had endured over the years, but my journal entries were so often despairing rants and too seldom joyful memories. Now I discovered I was writing a confession.

2

THE CONFESSION

I have done some terrible things. I recognise now that I have an illness but I'm not trying to excuse myself. Or maybe I am. I shudder in horror to remember some of the things I've done, the people I've hurt. I've hurt myself too. Emotionally, physically, mentally. I am writing this in the hope it will help, that the act of remembering and recording the events will help me move beyond this anguish I feel. And the guilt. I've spent thousands of pounds on therapies, from CBT to ACT, Narrative Therapy to Analysis. I've been prescribed medications to slow me down, take away my obsessive thoughts, help me sleep or pep me up. None of them have impacted on my problem, although some of the talking therapies have helped me understand it better. Apparently, I had attachment issues in infancy – a mother who was unpredictable in her care, probably because she was depressed, and a father who was often absent. So, according to one therapist (rather a scary analytic psychotherapist), I'd 'internalised a strong sense of inadequacy and a craving for attention'. I used to blame myself for not being good enough for my parents, then I blamed them for not being good enough for me. Now I'm trying, with mixed success at times, to let go of blame and anger. We all do our best, don't we? But sometimes it's just not good enough.

I will be as honest as I can, lay myself bare. It will not be a pretty sight.

I live constantly with the shame of it all.

My 'problem' – labelled variously as Obsessive Love Disorder, Limerence or Erotomania, depending on who was doing the diagnosing – started when I was thirteen and at high school. I fancied myself in love with Mr Faber, one of the sports teachers, and I had to stop doing games for fear of giving myself away. Each week I would forge my father's signature at the bottom of yet another excuse. Some of my friends had crushes on one boy or another – light-hearted, red-faced dalliances. For me, attraction is not a crush, it's a body blow. I battle with my own expectations, with my desire to be loved completely, to be valued, adored. While other girls would doodle and write a boy's name endlessly in the margins of books, I'd be imagining growing old with Mr Faber, our lives totally entwined, meaningless without each other.

My marks went down and down. Instead of doing my homework I wrote letters and poems to the object of my desire, agonising over every word, every sentiment. Months later when one of the other teachers died suddenly, my mother, then working at the school, dragged me along to the funeral. Mr Faber was there too, standing next to the grave, head bowed, hands wiping ineffectually at the tears running down his cheeks. Perhaps he had been in love with her. I felt nothing for him. I had outgrown my childish attraction as suddenly as it had come on. That night I burned all the letters and poems, getting rid of all traces of my embarrassing infatuation.

It's like that sometimes, this illness – I can fall out of love as quickly as I fell in, as if curtains open and then close with a swooshing finality.

My grades went up again, I made up the work I'd missed, and life got back to normal until I moved on to Danny, the brother of a girl in my class. I started inviting myself to her house after school every day in the hope of seeing him. He was two years older than us, a rugby player and my idea of the perfect man – tall, blond, handsome. I blushed when he looked at me in his offhand way and couldn't look him in the eye. My early forays into masturbation were filled with fantasies of him and what we might get up to if ever I could get him to notice me. Ali eventually got sick of me fawning over him and said I couldn't come round anymore. She also said I was a bad friend, and she was hurt that I only seemed to like her because of her brother. I couldn't deny it – we had nothing in common. Fortunately, at high school I had managed to make some friends, all fringe-dwellers like myself who were clever, hopeless at sport and uninterested in gossip and fashion mags. These friends listened to my indignation at such treatment and to my heartbreak when I discovered the beautiful Danny had a girlfriend.

In between relationships I am normal – by which I mean I work hard, have a social life, enjoy food and good wine. I repair the relationships, both professional and with friends, that were damaged while I was obsessed and unfocused on them. Over the years I built a team around me at work who could manage when I went down the tunnel of obsession. Without them, I would have lost my business, and I am forever grateful to them for keeping things going.

Often I am well for months. But my attractions – I really should not call them relationships – are desperate, suffused with craving, all-consuming; I am engulfed by longing, and I suffocate myself and the other. I am totally absorbed, my every waking moment taken up with thoughts of my love, with memories of the last time we saw each other, with fantasies of our next meeting. I obsess. I plan. I plot.

When I am in it, I believe it is love.

My first 'relationship' as opposed to infatuation, was with a brickie who worked on a building site I passed every day on my way to school. He was blond and tanned and made eyes at me as I walked by. I started taking more care with my appearance, wearing make-up, rolling my uniform skirt a little higher, opening an extra button on my shirt. He came over one Friday morning and started talking. Flirting, I should say. He asked me how old I was, and I told him I was eighteen even though I wasn't, and he asked me out for a drink.

'I'm Jon, by the way. See you at seven in the Carpenter's Arms.'

By the time I got to school, I was married to him, and we were living happily ever after. He adored me, I adored him, nothing would ever come between us. Jon was such an unromantic name; I called him Edward Lewis to myself, easily the most romantic figure I'd come across in my short life. I must have watched *Pretty Woman* a dozen times at least. Jon was going to be everything I had ever wanted in a man and more – he would know what I wanted even before I did and fulfil all my needs.

We met at the pub on the high street. He stood to greet me when I arrived and bought me a gin and tonic, even though I hadn't asked for one. He knew what I wanted to drink even though I'd never tasted gin before. We hardly spoke and after four or five or eight drinks, he suggested we go somewhere else. Totally besotted, I agreed when he suggested his bedsit.

I am biting my lip now, remembering that evening and wishing I could purge it, and others like it over the years, from my memory. But it haunts me. They haunt me.

Enough now.

3

───────

EXILE

I managed to push Ishbel to the back of my mind. There had been no more visits, no notes left, and I began to settle into a lonely routine.

And then one afternoon, as the light was fading to dusk, I was outside emptying the tin bath I washed my clothes in, when I heard an engine and turned to see her car bouncing up the track. She saw me and waved before I had a chance to dart inside. My hand, the same one that had written saying I wanted to see her, waved back and I felt the corners of my mutinous mouth lift into a smile. Then my head took over again and I stood rigid, waiting for her to get out of her damned car and explain herself. Waiting to tell her she wasn't welcome.

'Kirstie – at last!' she said as she got out of her car.

I smiled and said, 'Yes, I'm Kirstie.'

She tried to gather me into a hug which I resisted, so it became an awkward grapple as she held me and I pulled away. Eventually she gave up and stood back, smiling in spite of what she must have perceived as rudeness.

'I'm so sorry not to have been earlier. I've been spending a

21

lot of time on the mainland these past few years, and only been coming back cos a Dad.'

'Yes, how is he?'

'Och, he died a day or two ago.' She wiped a tear from her cheek. 'Not unexpected but a shock nonetheless, if you know what I mean. At least he went peacefully, in his sleep.' More tears flowed and she brushed at them with the back of her hand.

'I'm sorry,' I said.

'No, it was his time. He went out on his fishing boat for the last trip.'

'He went fishing?' I thought she said he'd died in his sleep. I was confused.

'Och, no – only metaphorically. He always said he wanted to die at sea, doing what he loved. It's a shame you didn't get to meet him.' She blew her nose on an old tissue she pulled from her coat pocket.

I agreed, even as I wondered why she would have wanted me to meet an old fisherman.

'He was the last, you know. Unless–'

'The last fisherman?'

Ishbel laughed. 'Och, there's a few more o' them. No, he was the last of his generation.'

I tried to imagine a Shetland with no elderly people. What about the two old men I'd seen walking near the croft – had they also died recently? Surely that's not what she meant? I had imagined it was the young who were leaving, off to find work and more to do than just looking at the weather.

'In our family, anyway,' she added, perhaps seeing my bemused look. 'At least he died knowing you'd come.'

'And that mattered because?' I asked. My question sounded rude. I was well aware of that, and regretted it immediately. I may not have asked for Ishbel to come but she was trying to be welcoming.

She looked at me as if trying to read my face, and then said, 'Oh, my – you dinna ken who I am, do you?'

I shook my head.

'My father was your mother's brother. Did she never mention him?'

I stared at her, trying to understand what she'd just said. I knew, of course, that my mother had come from Yell, this island in the Shetlands that was now my home, but when she'd clamped her lips tight around that Silk Cut all those years ago, she had denied a family or any more talk about her past, and I hadn't pushed. She'd never broken her silence over her parents, let alone a brother. Why hadn't I pressed the one time there was a crack in her silence? Why had I been so timid? Why had she been so reticent? There were people – family – she had run from as a teenager and never seen again.

'No,' I managed.

'We're cousins, Kirstie!'

She seemed excited at the prospect. I was conflicted. I'd always wanted to be part of a larger family with cousins to play with, to share secrets with over the years of our lives. *Be careful what you wish for, Kirstie.* But I had believed my mother when she said there was nobody and I had come to this place to be alone, to reflect, to atone for my past.

'I can see it's all a wee bit to take in,' she said. She was good at smoothing over awkwardness, a trait I have never possessed. I could only nod and hope she would leave me alone soon to consider this news.

'I'll let you get on now. My father's funeral will be on Monday – I hope you'll come?'

I never had any idea what day it was, they all stretched into one. 'Of course,' I said. 'Just let me know where.'

'It's at ten o'clock just doon the road in Mid Yell. Shall I collect you? Sheila says you no have a car.'

'I'll walk,' I said. 'I like walking.'

She nodded, perhaps understanding I had no intention of being there, but she didn't push it. 'Well,' she said, 'it was good to meet you at last.'

After she'd gone, I went over and over the conversation. Her voice had reminded me of my mother's who, despite leaving Yell forever when she was seventeen, hadn't been able to completely shake the accent or the sing-song intonation. Maybe she hadn't tried, allowing this to be her last link with the past, a shared sound, a rounded vowel and a rolled 'r' when all else was gone. I didn't miss her exactly; we'd lived apart too long for that but sometimes the idea of a mother was attractive. Although had I been able to choose, I would have been brought up by a different one. One who wasn't depressed and stuck in a loveless marriage. Or maybe I should've been more understanding, kinder. Less self-absorbed.

Had I been too friendly with Ishbel – would she expect more? What were the rules of engagement for cousins – did we have to see each other again? Would I have to leave this place I had thought was safe, or could I keep her at arm's length? She clearly knew more about me and my mother than I knew about her. I hadn't even asked if there were more of them but suspected there were.

I pulled on my warmest coat and went out. I had to walk the anxiety out of my system. Or was it excitement? Struggling up the hill, fighting for every step against the wind, for a while I could think of nothing except the elements. But a picture of Ishbel outside my house formed in my mind and wouldn't leave – her grey woolly hat pulled low over her ears, reddish-blonde hair escaping in tendrils that danced and whipped in the wind.

Blue eyes with laughter lines fanning out from their edges, pink cheeks on a broad face, an agile mouth – ready to talk, laugh, smile.

The hills were calming in their shades of brown – raw umber to its burnt cousin through chestnut, khaki, russet, taupe and chocolate. I knew my hues and tones. Many an art lesson at school we'd had to mix and name colours. I had little talent for art but the ability to identify colours had stuck.

The snatching wind finally forced me back down to my cottage. All trace of Ishbel erased except for the ruts of her car tyres. My shoulders dropped away from my ears for the first time since I'd seen her, and my breath came more easily. But as I chopped and diced vegetables for my dinner, her face was in front of me, her eyes dancing in the firelight and shake my head as I might, she would not leave. I glanced at the whisky bottle and then away. I would not drink Ishbel out of my life.

That night I tossed and turned. My mother visited me in my fitful sleep, her mouth a thin line of disapproval, her eyes full of disappointment.

Awake as the dawn lifted itself over the rim of the world in a pageant of mauve and pink and orange, I wondered if she and her brother had been alike in any way. Had he been as distant and dismissive as she, at times? Had he found things to do instead of spending time with his family? Had he shunned the company of others? It seemed unlikely in this place. Impossible. And Ishbel had spoken of him with tenderness, had come home to be with him in his last days. I wanted to know why my mother never spoke about her childhood, her family. Had she always been the same or had leaving changed her? I suspected the anger which surrounded her like a cloak had been woven for protection, but from what?

As a child I had thought I was the reason she was sad – I wasn't good enough to make her happy. I tiptoed around doing little things to please her – a vase of flowers picked from a friend's garden, the vase bought with my pocket money from a charity shop. A poem written just for her. A cup of tea when she looked tired. I spent hours trying to work out how to right the wrong I had done, whatever it was, and how to get my mother to smile at me, to look at me as my friends' mothers looked at them. And when nothing worked, I stopped going to the houses of the few friends I had because of the pain I felt, the stab of envy that pierced me when I realised I would never have what they had. I began to hate them all, those girls in their nice clothes with their riding lessons and foreign holidays. With their mothers who smiled and fathers who came home for dinner. Oh, I was well looked after – fed and clothed – but my father was in and out, showering me with affection and attention one minute, distracted or away again the next, and my mother often lived her life as if she wished she was somewhere else. Yell, maybe. Her home.

There were good times too. Sometimes, when my father was away, she'd brighten up, we'd have dinner on our laps in front of the TV and laugh at *George and Mildred* or *Mike Yarwood in Persons*. She'd laugh in a way I never saw except at those times, and we'd have cocoa and stories at bedtime. I began to long for my father's trips.

It wasn't until I was in my twenties and keeping a therapist and several self-help authors in luxury cars and holiday homes that I began to realise I hadn't caused my mother's unhappiness. She'd been depressed all my life. Unhappy in her marriage, unable to leave, perhaps because of me. She certainly sometimes directed her anger at me, perhaps because it was safer than aiming it at my father. It had dawned on me that the bruises my mother bore with martyr-like poise were not the accidents she claimed them to be, and I felt guilty for not realising it before, for not standing with her in feminine solidarity. Sorry enough to go back to Brighton for the day from my home in London to try and talk to her about it.

We sat at the kitchen table. I'd chosen a time when my father was sure to be at work and dropped round unannounced. I made tea for us while she continued vacuuming the already spotless floor.

'Come and sit down, Mum,' I said.

She huffed about wasting time in the middle of the day, but she had nothing else to do. My father had made her give up teaching, complaining that his dinner wasn't on the table as soon as he got home when she had to stay late at school for meetings.

She perched on the edge of a hard kitchen chair, a duster in one hand, her mug of tea in the other. She never once looked at me and I realised she never had, that I had always occupied, at best, her peripheral vision.

'It must be awful, living with Dad and his temper,' I said. As an opening gambit it was probably rather heavy-handed, since she was still living with him and I'd given her no warning about the reason for my visit. She looked as if I'd poured red wine on her beige carpet on purpose – a look I knew, because I had once done that very thing.

'I didn't know what was going on at the time,' I carried on when she said nothing. 'I'm sorry.'

'I think you'd better go now,' she said. 'Your father will be home soon and I must get his dinner ready.'

'It's only eleven thirty in the morning,' I said.

'All the same.' She stood, took my cup from in front of me, poured her tea and mine down the sink, carefully washed and dried the cups and put them back in the cupboard. Then she turned and almost looked at me. 'I'll have no more of your nonsense.'

I put an arm around her, and for a brief moment she allowed herself to be held.

Was that a tear in her eye? I thought it was. I still think it was. I thought she was going to confide in me but instead she pulled away.

By the time I was in the hall putting on my coat, the vacuum cleaner was roaring away, and my mother had her back to me, pushing it angrily into the sitting room.

I had only seen her a few times since. She'd made it abundantly clear my concern was not welcome.

Now I wish I'd persisted but back then I felt rejected. It was all about me. How can I have been so self-centred?

The days passed in their windy, drizzle-filled way. And then the wind died away and a fog descended, dulling the sound of the car bumping up the track so that by the time I heard it, it was too late to hide. Ishbel called a cooee from the door and walked right in. She was wearing the same grey woolly hat as before with a smarter coat and black gloves.

'I know you said you'd walk to the kirk but in this fog, I thought you'd get lost, so I came to get you. The funeral's in half an hour.'

I looked around for an excuse. Damn this woman for forcing my hand.

'I'm expecting groceries to be delivered,' I said.

'Och, dinna worry about that. Dougal's coming to the funeral so he won't be bringing them till this afternoon – or we could pick them up and save him the trouble.'

'Why doesn't he speak?' I asked.

Ishbel raised her eyebrows at the question. It was an odd time to be asking, I supposed, but seemed suddenly important.

'He had his tonsils out as a child and something went wrong. He's been unable to speak since, poor man.'

Well, at least that mystery was explained. Now I had to think of a way to get out of attending the funeral, but nothing came to mind. Short of being rude to her, I wouldn't be getting rid of Ishbel, and although I had quite a reputation for speaking my mind, something stopped me from telling her to bugger off and leave me alone.

'I haven't any decent clothes,' I said.

'Just come as you are – we don't stand on ceremony here.' She put her arm through mine and herded me out the door.

As we drove down the hill, my stomach descended faster than the car. I had spoken to no one except this woman for three months and was about to be thrown into Shetland society feeling naked and unprepared.

***

Ishbel kept up a steady stream of chatter as we drove. I watched the scenery move past our windows, smudged by the wet, grey mist. The same water-swollen land and peat cuttings I saw from my cottage but less windblown as we descended. Not that my hill was high, but it was more exposed to the elements, to the rain that buffeted the island in horizontal squalls.

'You'll meet your relatives,' said Ishbel, catching my attention. 'And most of the people of Mid Yell and the surrounds.'

I stared at her aghast. I'm sure I must have looked mad with my eyes wide and mouth open, trying to suck in air as my chest tightened.

'They're all desperate to meet you.'

My hands went automatically to the door handle. 'I can't do this,' I said, scrabbling at it.

Ishbel looked at me. She had eyes like my mother's, but softer.

'I ken you came here to get away from something, and you don't have to tell me what it is. But this is the land of your forefathers and you canna blame people for wanting to meet you. Surely you've noticed people walking the hills near your croft – why do you think they're out in all weathers instead of home and dry beside the fire? It was to get a peek at you. Sheila told us what you said when you arrived, that you'd been ill and come to recuperate and I made everyone around promise to give you some time, to stay away until you were ready but I canna do it forever.'

I had no idea Ishbel had appointed herself as my gatekeeper. I was grateful and angry simultaneously. She seemed to have assumed the role of protector but was now throwing me to the lions. What right did she have?

'We're all quite nice people, ye ken. No one wants to do you any harm. And you have to realise, we don't get many people moving to Yell. A few tourists in the summer but I canna remember the last time someone came and stayed. You're a wee bit of a celebrity.'

If that was meant to cheer me, it had the opposite effect. 'Please, stop the car. I can't do this,' I repeated more forcefully.

'Of course you can, I'll be right beside you all the way.' Ishbel smiled, and I wanted to punch her crooked teeth down her throat.

We arrived at the church too soon. It was a small building, grey stone and plain, behind a flint wall. People were standing around outside, the men in lumpy suits, baggy at the knees, the women in heavy skirts and thick tights. I took a deep breath and opened the car door. If I could get into the church I could kneel and pretend to pray. That would keep people away. But my plan was scuppered when everyone turned to look at us and Ishbel announced in clear, bright tones that here was Kirstie Henderson at last.

I felt the blood rise to my cheeks as my hands balled into fists in my pockets. Thirty or more people stared at me, and then decided to move all at once. I was enveloped in a maul of hands, arms and eyes, all wanting to welcome me, look at me, declare me the spitting image of my grandmother. My hands went to my face, feeling the broad cheekbones. I'd never known who I looked like but had been aware I didn't resemble either of my parents. It had entrenched my belief that I didn't belong to them, that my real parents would come and find me one day. And now these broad, open-faced folk wanted to claim me as their own.

'Let the poor woman breathe.' Ishbel laughed and drew me out of the melee as the hearse appeared round the corner. All eyes turned to the vehicle and six men walked towards it as it came to a stop.

I took the opportunity to sneak into the church and took a seat at the back, leant forward, head in hands and pretended to be deep in prayer.

I remember nothing about the service except the eulogy which Ishbel and her brother gave, in which they spoke about their father and his love for the Shetlands, the sea, his family and community. He had needed no more and had never left the islands. There was a lot of nose-blowing, but I didn't look up to see whether there were also tears. It was vital that I keep my head down and get away as soon as possible. As the last hymn ended, someone invited everyone to the church hall for refreshments and, heart thudding, I ran from the place as fast as I could, hoping that in the fog I would recognise the way we had come and get home to safety.

Later, by my fire with outer garments steaming on the wooden clothes horse, I sat with my legs tucked under me. I was not proud of my performance, yet I had seen no other course of action. I was angry with Ishbel for orchestrating the whole thing, for manipulating me into something she must have known I didn't want. As the day wore on and my feelings settled, I congratulated myself on not making eye contact with anyone. I had allowed my eyes to slide over the crowd outside the church without focusing on any one person and during the service I had kept my head down, not even lifting it to acknowledge the person who sat next to me even though he was close enough that I could hear his breath and feel it warming the space around us. Let them think me rude, odd or surly. Better that than let them know me.

They didn't even know my name. I was not Kirstie Henderson and never had been. My mother had shed her maiden name and I had not heard it until today. I was Kirstie Bligh, only daughter of William and Morag. There was a certain satisfaction in their ignorance of the fact. Yet underneath that, tugging gently, I had to admit to a yearning to know more about the Hendersons.

Two days later, when I was beginning to think I'd been successful in regaining my solitude, Ishbel came to see me again. She knocked and walked straight in, catching me at my breakfast.

I half rose, unsure whether I was going to greet her or tell her to leave but she started talking first.

'Och, I think my father would've been happy with his send-off. The only thing he'd've been annoyed about was that he couldn't share a dram and a story with everyone there. He was quite the one for a story, was my father.'

I sat again, letting her words drift into the cold air of the croft.

'I'm sorry you had to leave, Kirstie,' she said, standing by the table, making the room appear even smaller. 'No, I'm sorry I made you come. I thought I knew better than you what was good for you, and I surely didn't. And me just meeting you too. I'm known to be a bit bossy. You can always tell me when I'm out of line. I really am sorry.'

Then she looked at me, her eyes begging me to accept her apology. My head said, tell her to leave – I had, after all, tried at least twice to make her stop, had made it clear I didn't want to go to the funeral, wasn't fit to meet the people. But once again, my mouth was mutinous.

'Of course, it's fine.' Having formed those few words, however, my mouth closed firmly.

'Thank you, Kirstie, I'm glad. So – here you are!'

I nodded. It was all I could do. I felt my lips twitch, as if I was going to say something, but nothing came out. On a good day I was capable of some small talk. Now however, the capacity had deserted me. Words rolled around in my head but didn't make it as far as my mouth. Ishbel looked around the room and then went outside to get the second chair and pulled it up to the table, making herself at home.

'You've made the place look nice – homely,' she said, looking around at the stained, lime-washed walls, the rotting wood of the sills, the newly scoured pots and pans hanging from the hooks beside the range.

It was a lie. I had done nothing except clean up a bit and remove the tattered curtains. I had added nothing to the place, not even a flower. It was as our grandparents had left it.

'No one came here after Granny and Grandy died. I always meant to but was too busy and, to tell the truth, it wasn't a priority. They left it to Morag in the hope that she'd come back to it, and anyway, the rest of us were set up in our own houses by then so we didnae need it.'

Still I said nothing but had relaxed in my seat, surrendering to her company.

'I understand you're a very private person, Kirstie. If you don't want to talk about yoursel', how about I tell you a bit about me?' said Ishbel.

I raised my eyebrows which she clearly took as confirmation of my interest, because off she went.

'I was born here in this very croft, in January 1967. My mother had come to see the old folk and a snowstorm had prevented her from leaving. Two days she was stuck here and on the third she was about to leave when her waters broke. Our granny delivered me in the very bed you're sleeping in these days.'

I felt sick at the thought, imagining all the mess of a birth seeping into the mattress, putrefying over the years. I made a mental note to get a new bed as soon as possible.

'Och, but you don't want to hear all that.' She looked out the window for a moment and I wondered if she was going to limit herself to talking about the weather after all, but then she went on, 'I have a brother, Sandy. You saw him at the funeral. Your uncle, Alasdair, didn't make it. He's no been well either. Like your mother, he left the island as a young man, and we rarely see him these days. He worked in a bank until he retired and never married.' She paused. 'He's likely gay and perhaps felt he didn't fit here, although he visited regularly until the old ones passed on. Still, I suppose when you've got used to the city, the islands hold little appeal.' She looked at me, smiled and said, 'Although you've come back.'

If it was meant to be the opening for me to tell her my life story, she was disappointed as I still said nothing, but I did smile in a tight way and say, 'Yes, here I am.'

'Well, I'd better be on my way. I'm away back to the mainland tomorrow and I've got a lot to do.'

'You're going away again?' I asked, before I could stop myself. There was a sinking feeling in my stomach, a disappointment I didn't want to feel. I hadn't asked for her company, nor done much to encourage it but now it was going to be taken away I wanted it. Maybe she could even have helped me make sense of my mother – there must be stories about her and her life before she'd left for England.

'Aye, I have to get back to work but I'll be back and forth, it's no far.'

'I thought you just said you lived in Scotland. That's a fair way,' I said, and I could hear the hostility in my voice, the betrayal.

'Och, no! We call the main island the Mainland here. I work in Lerwick. It's just a short ferry ride away. You'll have been through there on your way here. I'll be back some weekends. My son, Tavis, and his wife, Catriona, are expecting their first child soon and they still live here on Yell – one of the few young couples who do, I might add. And I've decided to move back very soon so I can help with the bairn. I just have to clear out my father's cottage and move my stuff in. My other son, Graeme, went to university in Aberdeen and still lives there. They were all at the funeral. You'd 'a' seen them.'

I might have done if I'd lifted my head.

'And your husband?' I had to ask and was relieved when she said she was divorced. A man would have complicated things. In fact, if there had been a man in her life, I could not have continued to see her.

I looked around for something to moor her to me for a few moments more.

'Who played the violin?' I asked, pointing to it. I'd cleaned it, polished the wood and wiped the strings. It now hung on the wall next to the hearth.

'Our grandy – oh, he was a fine one for a tune. He knew all the folk songs and played at weddings and funerals, christenings and wakes. He'd close his eyes and play for hours. Do you play yourself?'

'No.' I took the instrument from the wall and held it out to her. 'Do you?'

She shook her head. 'Never had the inclination,' she said.

The conversation faltered again and I could think of nothing else to keep her there.

'May I come and see you when I'm back?' she asked.

I was surprised and glad I hadn't put her off.

'Yes,' I said, but when she tried to take my hand in a gesture of friendship, my first impulse was to draw away, my automatic response to physical contact. I let her pull me in for the briefest of hugs.

I went back to my solitary routine, preparing food for my lonely meals, walking along the beach and the windswept cliffs, hands jammed into my pockets, head down as I battled the wind. A voice in my head whispered I was missing Ishbel, that our brief contact had been more important than I wanted to admit.

'I will not let myself miss her,' I said aloud to the grey North Sea. I picked up a stone and chucked it as hard as I could to punctuate my statement. 'I was alone before I met her and I was fine.'

But another voice answered, 'It's different now.'

And it was. I had warmed to Ishbel more than I had to anyone for a long time, and allowed myself to start enjoying the companionship. I had believed we could become friends and then she'd left. The loneliness I now felt was the deeper for the loss of her company.

'Damn you, Ishbel,' I shouted, and threw another, heavier stone.

A new part of my routine was taking the violin down every day and twanging the strings. Holding it beneath my chin, I imagined the bristles of my grandfather's jaw, the tilt of his head, the quiet of the moment before he played the first note. Most of the hairs of the bow were torn and hung from one end in useless tresses.

My other focus was my confession, which I now realised I was addressing to Ishbel.

4

THE CONFESSION

Is it rape when a fifteen-year-old is too ashamed of being a virgin and too infatuated to say no? Jon was on me like an octopus as soon as we were through his door. His hands were everywhere and his tongue down my throat. I heard my new top ripping and felt the cold air on my breasts. But I didn't fight him off as he sank with me onto his bed because this was love, wasn't it? He sucked on my nipples, and I ran my hands up and down his back as he lay half on top of me, grinding his erection into my hip. I wanted him to look longingly into my eyes, but he had his shut, so in the end I closed mine too and felt him climb on top of me and push his way into my dry vagina. I gasped and tried to move away but he put his hands under my buttocks and lifted me to him and pumped away until his sweat made my hands slip across his shoulders and then he groaned, shuddered and lay on top of me, panting slightly.

All I could think was that this wasn't the way I had thought I would lose my virginity. I had imagined silk sheets, a light breeze wafting the smell of roses through the room, sunshine, champagne. A lover who gazed into my eyes as he eased himself gently into me and whispered that he loved me. And yet when I felt the weight of Jon on top of me none of that mattered anymore. I felt myself a fool for entertaining such childish fantasies. This was more real. And next time I'd be more relaxed so it wouldn't hurt as much.

When his breath had settled, he left, saying he was going to the bathroom. He hadn't used a condom and now there was semen mixing with drops of blood running down my thighs. I was sore. I lay in the bed with its rumpled sheets, holding myself, and looked around his room. It was dirty and shabby, nothing like the romantic boudoir that was my fantasy setting for my deflowering. But Jon had made love to me, proof of his adoration, his commitment, and I had given myself to him, body and soul.

When he came back he turned on the TV and flicked through the channels. He didn't look at me as he sat on the end of the bed engrossed, finally, in a game of football. I wanted him to touch me again, to curl around me and talk of love and our future but when the game was over and I was still lying there watching him, he pulled the sheet off me, handed me my clothes and told me where the bathroom was. Of course, I told myself, he's being a gentleman and allowing me time to lie in the afterglow and then bathe at my leisure. A novice in the ways of love, I had been naïve to expect more intimacy immediately.

I ran a shallow bath, but it was tepid – Jon must have used all the hot water. Washing hastily, I used the only towel I could find, which was already damp from his body, feeling close to him because he had used this very towel only a while before.

When I entered the bedroom again, hair groomed with my fingers, lip gloss reapplied, he stood, took my hand and said, 'I'll show you out. Are you okay to get home?'

'Of course,' I said, wanting him to admire how independent I was. 'When will I see you again?' I couldn't help adding, hope in my voice.

He looked at me sideways, his eyes narrowed. 'Probably Monday,' he said.

I wrote my phone number down for him and he put it on top of the TV but didn't offer his.

I floated home, in love, loved. I wrote in my diary that I was finally in a relationship, had given myself to Mr Right who was charming, handsome and very sexy. I phoned my friend, Lucy, as early as was decently possible in the morning and told her all about Jon and our romantic evening. She made all the right noises and asked enough questions to satisfy me she was

1. Happy for me
2. A bit jealous and
3. Excited I'd lost my virginity, although I knew she wasn't really because she'd always thought she'd lose hers first.

That Saturday was the longest of my entire life. He didn't call and the building site was closed. I spent my time reliving the evening – every look, every gesture, every touch. I wondered what Jon was doing, what he was eating, where he was and who he was with. By Sunday morning I couldn't stand it any longer, I had to see him, so I took the bus to his house and rang the doorbell. Another bloke answered and said he thought Jon was away for the weekend, but I must have looked so disappointed that he went to check for me.

'Yep, he's away.'

I felt tears gather and turned away so this bloke didn't see them. I walked all the way home, blind to everything around me, thinking only of my disappointment.

I had a major assignment due on Monday and had a fair

amount of work to do on it but I couldn't concentrate. Jon consumed my mind and my heart and there was no room for anything else. I veered between joy at the memory of him and despair at his absence. Even my mother noticed that something was going on.

'Are you coming down with something, Kirsten?'

Can you come down with love?

I hardly slept on Sunday night. Instead, I counted the minutes until I would see Jon again. I was up too early and spent longer than usual in the bathroom getting ready. How should I wear my hair – up or down? My make-up took ages. I wanted to look natural but highlight my best feature, my eyes. We weren't meant to wear make-up for school, but I didn't care. I hated the fact I had to wear my ugly school uniform but cheered myself with the knowledge that he'd seen me in it every day for weeks and still asked me out, still loved me. There were men, I knew, who had a thing for girls in school uniform. I knew Jon wasn't one of those shallow people, he still found me attractive whatever I wore. As for him, I loved him in his work clothes, in no clothes, in the tux I'd imagined him wearing for our wedding, in jeans and a T-shirt as we strolled arm in arm through the sunny days of our lives.

I had to leave the house at the same time as usual to make sure I saw him, even though I knew he'd be looking out for me. Fussing with my shirt – should I undo one more button or would it look slutty? – I forced myself not to run to the building site. Slowing as I approached, I searched for him, but he was nowhere to be seen. I stopped and looked but the only workers were older men with paunches bulging over their trousers. My stomach lurched with disappointment. Was he ill? Had his bastard of a boss moved him to another area of the site? I shielded my eyes with my hands and looked up to the higher floors and still didn't see him.

Athena, a girl in my year, came up and asked what I was doing. I couldn't answer her. I was too dejected to speak, my heart was breaking. Eventually she pulled me away from there and made me go to school. All day, I could only think of Jon and wonder where he had been, when I would see him. I made a poor excuse for my assignment being late and was given an extension.

By the time I left school the building site was closed for the day, but I walked slowly past, searching the wire fencing for a note, some sign that Jon had missed me too. There was nothing.

That night I cut myself. I couldn't stand the pain of not seeing him, of not knowing when I would see him. I took the Stanley knife out of my father's toolbox and drew it across the soft skin of my inner forearm. Blood oozed and dripped in claret drops and for a few moments my attention was diverted.

***

I read this back and know it sounds as if I'm exaggerating everything. I know, Ishbel, (it is you I see in my mind's eye as I write this, you to whom I am confessing my shame) you will find it hard to believe I could have felt that way after one night, but it's true. I became obsessed with Jon. Over the next few days, if I saw him in the morning, my day was made, even if he didn't look at me. I would tell myself he hadn't seen me, that if he had, he would have rushed over to talk to me, to kiss me and demand we see each other again. If he did see me, I made excuses for why he didn't smile or even acknowledge me – he was tired, his boss was around and he couldn't stop what he was doing.

The days I saw him, I walked around on a cloud, joyful, elated.

The days I didn't see him, I hated the world, hated whatever it was that kept us apart. I wrote him letters and left them on the fence. I went to his house and asked for him, but he was always out.

What had happened to my friends, you may ask? They soon became sick of hearing about Jon and the ups and downs of my life. Changing for PE one day, Lucy saw the scar on my arm.

'Jeez, Kirstie – what happened?'

'Nothing,' I mumbled, pulling my sleeves down quickly.

'Did you do that to yourself? What the fuck?' she asked, eyebrows shooting up her forehead.

'It's nothing, really.'

'He's not worth it, Kirstie. No bloke is. Get over him. Come out with me this weekend, we'll have a blast.'

She didn't understand. I saw it then. She'd never been in love.

'Nah,' I said. 'But thanks.'

She turned away and didn't ask again.

Lauren was less subtle.

'You're fooling yourself, you know. If he really wanted you, he'd find you, even if his boss was around, even if the other blokes laughed at him for mooning over you. But the fact is, he doesn't give a shit. All he wanted was to fuck a schoolgirl.'

I listened to her and half of me wanted to laugh, because what did she know, and the other half – well, the other half won.

I punched her in the face and almost broke her nose.

I am not a violent person. I do not punch people. My sickness does that, not me. And I am not my sickness, but I am overtaken by it at times. I know this now.

Lauren didn't understand – neither did I at the time, so I can't blame her. She didn't speak to me ever again, but I used to hear her telling other people what a fruit loop I was. That's a moniker that's often been applied to me since.

Lucy and Lauren weren't the only ones. Slowly all my friends fell away, unable to compete with the obsession that was

Jon. I don't blame them; I would probably have done the same in their shoes. It must be hard to see a friend delude herself into believing she'd met the love of her life.

One good thing came of their reactions though. I made a promise to myself I wouldn't resort to cutting myself again. It was too obvious, and I didn't want my lover to notice the scars and feel guilty that he was the cause of my pain. Instead, I would suffer through it.

The building was finished, the site gone. People moved into the flats and still I walked past hoping to see Jon.

Eventually I had to admit he'd gone without saying goodbye. My days were empty of everything but despair. I didn't bother getting out of bed, I didn't eat.

I was filled with rage and grief and self-loathing. It was bottomless and topless and sideless. It was black and grey and brown, the colours of swamp and bog, stretching endlessly. I almost drowned in it.

I only spoke to my parents to fight with them, and when my father tried to haul me out of bed to go to school, I wrestled him off and screamed until he left.

And then, one morning, I woke up and realised I hadn't dreamed about Jon. And over the next few days I caught myself thinking about other things, normal things. I got up one afternoon and watched some television. And the day after that realised I felt okay, I wasn't thinking about Jon, and I was hungry. I got up, had a bath, soaking for a long time and washing my greasy hair. Then I made myself a huge breakfast and sat at the kitchen table until I had finished it an hour later. My stomach had shrunk and I vomited most of it up again, but I was back. I was over Jon. I was better.

Ishbel, I can tell you I am so ashamed of my behaviour when I think back over it. I'd been mad. I thought Jon had somehow put a spell on me, or a curse. It had lasted months, I'm not sure how many. I'd failed all my exams at school and had no hope of catching up all the work I'd been too distracted to do, so I dropped out and went to work in a café. I started as a waitress and kitchen hand, but I was interested in learning about food and the cook was happy to let me help – it meant he had less to do. Within six months when he left, I was offered his job. I took over a mediocre café with a dull menu and introduced new ideas. I'd stay back in the evenings, partly to avoid going home to my parents' house but mostly to experiment with new recipes, playing with aromatic spices and herbs my mother had never used. I badgered the owner into letting me try them out on the customers. I doubled her turnover within a few months and had to employ another cook to help me. After a year I moved to a bigger café in a better location and not long after that, I was offered a job in London. I was eighteen, single, had hardly anything to do with my parents although I was still living at home, had very few friends left and no time to make new ones. There was nothing holding me back.

I stepped onto the train to London with a suitcase and a backpack. I had nowhere to live but I did have some money saved, a job to go to and a new life ahead of me.

Oh, Ishbel, I wonder if you'll ever talk to me again if you read this. I so want someone to understand, to stand by me, to be there when my life turns to shit again. I have exiled myself from my old life, from other people, and yet, I can't believe I will never become obsessed again. I am exhausted by it, disgusted by it. But when I'm living it, at least I know I'm alive. That's the paradox, you see. When I'm not 'in love', I'm only half alive.

When I am 'in love', some of the time I am full of joy and life is wonderful. Most of the time though, I am filled with despair. Maybe I am addicted to the drama of it, but I do crave my old life sometimes.

Mostly I just want 'normal' love.

Kahlil Gibran wrote about what I want:

'Let there be spaces in your togetherness,

And let the winds of the heavens dance between you.

Love one another, but make not a bond of love.'

If only I knew how to do that.

That's all for now.

5

———

EXILE

After Ishbel had gone back to Lerwick I used to pull out a chair for her and imagine her sitting there. We'd talk at my kitchen table. I would sit facing the window, one eye out for unwanted visitors, and we would chat. I asked her questions about the family, and she would answer in her lilting brogue, head tilted to one side. A tilting, lilting informer. Not a reliable one however.

'Why did my mother leave?' I asked one evening as the sun set behind my imaginary friend.

'Och, she was always a wild one. My father said that from a wee bairn, she was wanting to be off. Yell was no big enough for her. She had great imaginings of cities and travels in far-off lands.'

That didn't fit with my knowledge of my mother, so I thanked her, and she nodded and smiled. Eating my dinner later – my imaginary Ishbel never stayed for a meal – I pulled her answer to the front of my mind and turned it over.

The most exciting thing my mother had ever done apart from leaving Yell, if even that had been exciting to her, was buying a lottery ticket. From the time it started in the nineties,

47

she went to the newsagent every Friday and filled in her numbers, crossing her fingers for the big win.

Another night, I pulled up the chair for my imaginary Ishbel again. 'Why did my mother leave?'

'Well, there was a rumour she was having a baby and her father – our grandfather – drummed her out of the house.'

I considered that at length. Had my mother been pregnant to someone on the island, and if so who, and what happened to the baby? It certainly wasn't me – it was many years after she left Yell that I came along. She was already in her thirties when I was born, and had reconciled herself to not having children. In fact, she had reconciled herself to it so well that she often seemed to forget she had one and resented it when she was reminded.

And what of the supposed father? Who was he? A local, a visitor – perhaps a birdwatcher or naturalist come to see the otters and the puffins? Did she love him and follow him to England to marry him only to discover he had a wife and family and wanted no other?

'Why did my mother leave?' I tried a third time. By now I was losing faith in the suggestions of my imaginary Ishbel, but in the absence of the real one I had no option.

'She had a huge fight with her parents – our grandparents – about marrying one of the local boys and ran away on the eve of their wedding. They had been promised to each other at birth, but your mother was intent on marrying her own choice of husband.'

Was there something in that? The part about being promised to someone at birth was far-fetched. I knew my mother could be stubborn, but had she once had a temper? She was a husk of a woman by the time I was old enough to form an opinion of her. I wished she would stand up for something, feel strongly enough about anything to make a judgement. She seemed to me to be a person who had an outline but no internal workings and no courage. Now I realise it took guts just to stay in her marriage and to look after me.

I didn't see the real Ishbel for nearly three weeks after her departure to Lerwick but one Sunday morning, her car came bouncing up the track making a clanking noise as it did so.

'I think the exhaust's about to drop off,' she said by way of greeting, and smiled as if exhausts dropping off were a source of amusement.

'Oh,' I said and turned to go back inside. The sun was shining after a night of rain and high winds and a rainbow lurked over the sea. I was pleased to see her, grateful she had come. But part of me also resented the intrusion, her assumption that I would want her there.

'Let's sit out here, shall we?' said Ishbel.

'I'll get tea,' I said, tight-lipped.

When we were sitting on a blanket she'd found in the boot of her car we looked at the rainbow and were silent for a while. My question was pressing on my lips, but it seemed too soon to ask. There were other things that needed to come first. Small talk. Informal chit-chat. Getting-to-know-you questions.

'Where have you been for the last three weeks?' I asked. It wasn't what I had intended to ask and the tone of aggression which accompanied the question was also inadvertent.

Ishbel didn't seem to think it a strange or unwelcome question. 'Catriona had the baby ten days ago, so I've been caught up with that. My first grandchild and, if Catriona has any say in it, the last or so she says now!'

'Congratulations.'

'Thank you. She's a pretty wee thing. They've called her

Lorna, which seems a mite old-fashioned, but all these names are coming back in, aren't they?'

'I don't know.' I knew more was required of me. 'It's a nice name.'

'Aye, it is, I suppose. Anyway, it's not up to me. At least they didn't call her one of these awful newfangled names like Ebony or Beyoncé. Och, listen to me going on, you must think I'm a terrible old sulk.'

'No.'

We lapsed into silence again, but Ishbel wasn't very good at it.

'So, Kirstie, what have you been doing with yourself these past few days?'

I couldn't tell her about my confession, she might want to read it and although it was addressed to her, it was still mine.

'Cooking.'

'Cooking?' Her eyebrows almost disappeared into her hair.

'I like cooking.' Did I sound defensive?

'Sooner you than me then.' She laughed.

'I had a catering business,' I said. The first piece of information about my previous life I had offered up to her.

'Well then, you must be good at it. A catering business, eh?'

'Yes. Weddings and corporate functions mostly. I sold it before I came here.' I pulled my knees into my chest and hugged them. Talking about myself had made me feel exposed. 'What about you?'

'I'm a teacher. Geography mainly, but these days it's so difficult to get teachers up here that I've been known to teach English and history as well. Sometimes even maths. I pity the poor kids who have me for that – I'm only one step ahead of them. Still, I have to say they all seem to do okay in their exams. And then they leave to go to university or off to work in Scotland and we rarely see them again. There's not enough for them to do here. It's sad to see so few young people stay, or return once they've left.'

We chatted for a while longer. I let her do most of the talking. When she left, I let the quiet settle over me again, a comfortable mantle. The air was heavy with more rain. The rainbow had gone and left grey clouds in its place.

I didn't want to like her. I didn't want to need her company. One day she would read my confession and I would never see her again.

The next time she came, she brought the baby with her. 'I'm giving them a break, some time for each other without the wee one,' she said. 'That's what I told them anyway. Really, I just wanted the bairn to myself.'

Lorna was bundled up in a hat, mittens and blanket, her tiny face soft in sleep. Long eyelashes quivered on her cheeks as her eyes moved behind almost translucent eyelids, and I wondered what one so young could possibly dream about.

'You've no children yourself?' asked Ishbel.

'No.'

There's usually an awkward silence after such an emphatic negative. But not this time.

'Why not?' she asked.

I'd never had to answer that question before. No one else had been so blunt. Or interested enough to ask.

'Never met the right man,' I said. Which was shorthand for, 'I'm totally fucked up and can't have a normal relationship. I don't usually get to the conversation about dating, let alone whether we'll have children together.' And the thought of having a child on my own was beyond me. Children were meant to be the natural extension of a loving relationship.

'Sorry to hear that,' she said. 'Children are the best and the hardest thing that has ever happened to me. So much time spent worrying about them but such joy too.' She looked at me. 'That was insensitive of me. Sorry.'

'Don't apologise. I'm fine the way I am. Really.' I felt my jaw clenching in the reflexive way it did when I was stirred up.

Lorna started crying as soon as Ishbel handed her to me for a hold, and I passed her straight back. They left soon after; the baby needed feeding and I needed to be alone.

I looked out over the harsh landscape. I had desperately wanted children in my twenties and thirties. I still felt a yearning each month when I bled, a reminder of what might have been but could never have been. Not in my life.

I took the empty teacups in to wash and managed not to throw them at the wall.

I still hadn't asked Ishbel about my mother. It now occurred to me to ask the woman herself, to write and ask her what had happened to make her leave and never talk about the place or the people again. Or not to me anyway.

But maybe I could do it. Perhaps the physical distance between us now would make communication easier. I only hoped the tattered shreds of our relationship would survive the intrusion. I took out a piece of paper and chewed the end of my pen as I thought, then started writing.

Dear Mother,

I hope you are well. I am feeling quite settled here on the island, although it took a while to get used to the slower rhythm and quieter life. Winter was hard – I don't think I've ever been so cold, and the days were so short the sun hardly brushed the land

with colour before it was plunging below the horizon again. But spring is upon us now, and I am getting out for long walks. When I'm battling the wind on the headlands and beaches, I often wonder if you trod the same paths when you were a girl, and what you thought of the place; to me it is all new and fresh, but you grew up here and maybe took it all for granted, as I did Brighton when I was young. I also wonder what made you leave this place. I've made up a few stories to explain it to myself, all probably more fanciful than the real reason. Do you think you could tell me now?
I look forward to hearing from you,
Kirstie.

As I wrote the address on the envelope, I wondered if I should send it. What if my mother replied? What if she didn't? I put it with my shopping list for Dougal and thrust it at him without letting myself think too hard about it when next he came.

April announced itself with milder temperatures, softer wind and longer days. Often, I would be able to sit outside until after nine, reading in the natural light. The short tourist season started at Easter, with strangers tramping across the landscape in their shorts and hiking boots, Gortex jackets attached to their day packs, ready for the weather to change.

I waited for a response from my mother but as the days went by, realised there wasn't going to be one. It seemed my letter had been an intrusion into a past she wanted to forget, and while I found it frustrating, it was in keeping with the rules of our relationship – ask little, tell less.

My only visitor was Ishbel; she had taken to visiting with

the baby every Sunday afternoon before leaving again for Lerwick on the evening ferry. Lorna was changing fast, week by week getting a little chubbier, a bit more hair, then less again as the baby down fell out, and for a while she was as bald as the newborn mice I'd spied the week before, but a hundred times prettier. She was a quiet little thing with watchful eyes. An old soul, François would have said, in his sexy French accent.

6

THE CONFESSION

I found a place to live in a shared house just off Finchley Road. The other residents were all students, and I don't think they knew quite what to make of me, a woman the same age as them with no interest in studying. All I wanted to do was prove myself in my new job.

The trouble began in the first week. François was from Rouen and was doing an intensive English language course before starting at London University. He was six foot two with dark-blond hair, brown eyes and a sexy accent. There was also no girlfriend which made things less complicated. I felt my attraction to him hit me like a tsunami. I was powerless to stop it even if I had wanted to. In those days I hadn't realised I had an illness, or the way I went about relationships wasn't the way other people approached them. I had written Jon off as a case of nice guy, wrong time. He hadn't been ready for the kind of commitment I wanted.

I'd started work at a café in the centre of London and was expected from day one to be creating new dishes, experimenting with the menu – doing what I had done in Brighton. But I could think of nothing but François. The conversation we'd had over breakfast in which he had smiled at me for a fraction of a second longer than necessary, meant he was interested in me too. That one thought could take over my whole mind for hours at a time leaving no space for creativity. My boss spoke to me at the end of the first week and asked if I was okay – homesick?

'No, not at all,' I said. 'Glad to be away from the place.'

'Well, what's up then? I hired you because you were innovative, your dishes were inspired, sensational.'

'I'm just settling in,' I said, avoiding his gaze, hating him for finding fault.

'Well, settle and then get onto it, okay? I can't afford to have you here if you're not going to come up with the goods. Capiche?'

Capiche was his favourite word. Yes, I fucking capiche.

François was often around in the evenings, not having made many friends yet, and we'd hang out at the house. I made dinner – the creative dishes I'd been hired to come up with but seemed only able to make for him. He bought bottles of wine and we ate and drank together. I lost myself in his eyes, imagined making a life with him so that I'd be blushing as we ate. He never commented on it. Perhaps he didn't have the words in a language I would understand. Or maybe he was too much of a gentleman, too considerate of my feelings.

At work I would make what I had cooked for François the night before and in that way I kept my job and started to build my reputation. It was the only way I could channel my obsession with him constructively. I would be cooking and fantasising about him at the same time, or remember him taking the first mouthful of the meal, his lips closing around the food I'd prepared for him. I would see his eyes shut, the better to savour the flavours, and then his look of delight. I spent hours in the kitchen so lost in the romance of our affair I could hardly stir a sauce but somehow, I managed to recreate the dishes he loved, and my job was secure.

When we slept together, François and I, it felt like the culmination of weeks of sexual tension and longing, at least on my part, and also the true beginning of our life together. I had only had the one sexual experience before, the night with Jon, and was little prepared for the lingering gentle lovemaking that I shared with my Frenchman. He was sensitive and attentive. He was as experienced in the bedroom as I was in the kitchen, and we spent hours in bed finding new ways to bring each other pleasure. When I had to go to work, I longed to be at home. When I was at home, I counted the seconds until he was there too, and we could be together. Every touch, every look, I recorded in my mind and played it over and over. This was love.

Oh, Ishbel, I know I make it sound like a real relationship that lasted months. In reality, his part in it was over in twenty-seven days. He became bored of me. He said he couldn't take my neediness, my desire to be with him and only him all our waking moments. When he said he thought we should end whatever it was we had, I cried, I begged, I implored. He unhooked my fingers from his arm and walked out of the room. He turned down my offers of food and stayed out as much as he could. And still I waited for him to come home. Of course he needed to make other friends, but it didn't mean he didn't love me, I told myself. He was only refusing my food because he was worried I was spending all my money on him – he was being thoughtful. Such was my tortuous thinking.

When he moved out he told me he had come to hate me and my fanatical behaviour. He thought I needed to see a psychologist (he pronounced the P in his sexy French way) and get sorted out. I knew that all I needed was him. If only he would love me, everything would be all right.

I saw him one day outside the café. I was just leaving, and I almost called out but thought better of it. Instead, I followed him. He turned off the busy main road and into a residential street. Hanging back, I watched as he took out a key and let himself into number twenty-two. It was a run-down house, typical student accommodation.

For the next few weeks, every day after work I'd go and hang out in his street, hoping for a glimpse of him. There was a house opposite with an overgrown hedge I hid in. Eventually my patience paid off – I saw him. He was talking on his phone, laughing at something the other person had said. I left my hiding place. As I was walking across the road he turned and saw me. His smile faded and he ended the call, put his phone in his pocket.

'François,' I said.

'Do not come near me, Kirstie. I told you to leave me alone.'

I took a deep breath. He didn't mean it. He couldn't.

'How about a drink for old times' sake,' I said, working hard to keep my voice level.

'I'm sorry, but no.'

My stomach clenched. 'Just one little drink?'

'No. You need help. You were obsessed with me and now you turn up here and I think you were waiting for me, watching me. It is stalking, yes?'

'Stalking? No, of course not. I just wanted to see you.'

'Leave me alone!'

He turned and jogged off down the road.

I stood staring after him. Stalking? What an absurd idea. It wasn't like that. Lunatics stalk people, not normal people like me. He'd got it all wrong. How dare he accuse me of being mad?

I never saw him again but for months I kept searching, punished myself with memories of our time together, fantasised about him coming back, admitting he'd made a mistake, that he loved me totally and couldn't live without me.

I think I knew deep down it wouldn't happen. I dragged myself through days at work hardly able to poach an egg let alone create new dishes. I lost my job and spent days in bed, the duvet pulled over my head.

I didn't snap out of my obsession with François as I had with Jon. Instead, I slowly came to realise what had happened and talked myself back to normality. One of the other girls in the house, Tessa, whom I had little to do with up until then, turned out to be a great support. She had just come out of a relationship. One night we shared a couple of bottles of wine.

'Men are all the same.' She slurred her words slightly.

'I know. Bastards, the lot of them,' I agreed.

'We're better off without them.'

'We are. We're strong, independent women.'

'We have each other. We don't need men to complete our lives.'

I thought for a moment. 'What about sex?'

'Ah, there is that. We need friends with benefits, not relationships. Use them like they use us.'

'It's quite nice being wined and dined, though, isn't it?'

She groaned. 'So nice.' She started crying. 'I like being in love.'

'Me too.'

Within a month she had a new boyfriend and I was alone again. I felt betrayed but I understood. What was life without love? And what was life with it?

My housemates moved out at the end of the academic year and a new lot moved in, fresh out of suburbia and mothers who did everything for them. They forgot to shop for themselves and ate my food out of the fridge. They were unacquainted with a vacuum cleaner and bathroom cleansers. My savings were running out and it was time to find another job. Fortunately, my old boss was kind enough to give me a reasonable reference and within a week I was in a kitchen again, doing what I loved best and turning down all invitations to socialise. I couldn't afford to slip up again and falling for someone was the major slip-up I had to avoid.

The house had become unworkable for me. These new students were a rowdy lot who preferred partying to studying, so I moved out. My new home was a small bedsit in a large old Victorian house in Acton. It was furnished in what can only be described as seventies' tat but I loved it. The walls were purple, a large pink flamingo had been painted on one of them, standing forever on one leg. The lightshade was a pink tasselled monstrosity, the sofa covered in crocheted blankets to hide the fact that the springs were coming through, and the fabric was torn and threadbare. It was the first place that was mine and mine alone. I could shut the front door and not expect to be interrupted by anyone else's demands. I could trust that the food I put in the fridge would still be there when I wanted it and I could keep the tiny bathroom as clean or as dirty as I wanted.

One of the waiters at work asked me out. I had no particular interest in him but said yes because I was bored of being a hermit, scuttling from home to work and back again, keeping my eyes on the ground and making myself invisible. Ahmed was kind, funny, well read and pigeon-chested. Not at all my type physically. I liked him, I was even fond of him, but I never fell in love with him, which was probably what made it possible for us to go out together for over a year. We went walking on our days off, or to the movies. I cooked for him, he massaged my shoulders when they were sore. We cared for each other but there was no passion. Our lovemaking was infrequent but gentle, respectful. Looking back, this was the relationship I had always thought I wanted, the Kahlil Gibran kind of love,

'Fill each other's cup but drink not from one cup.

Give one another of your bread but eat not from the same loaf.

Sing and dance together and be joyous, but let each one of you be alone.

Even as the strings of a lute are alone though they quiver with the same music.'

Kahlil Gibran has a lot to answer for, if you ask me, with his romantic ideas. Where was the roller coaster, the heart-stopping joy of feeling cherished and the crushing misery of uncertainty? What was love without these highs and lows?

I broke Ahmed's heart. One day we were eating in a café in Covent Garden and at the next table was a Greek Adonis – tall, swarthy, unselfconscious. I felt the body-blow of infatuation. My eyes followed him. Everything Ahmed did and said annoyed me all of a sudden.

He looked at me with his limpid eyes – the very eyes I had looked into that morning when we made love and wondered if maybe I was falling for him. Now those same eyes seemed needy rather than loving, trying to suck me in to some pale facsimile of passion. I looked away and he put his hand over mine, a gesture he had made so often before, and which had made me feel cherished and safe. I pulled my hand away and made a fist in my lap, turned from him slightly and lifted my chin. I was not his property. He was the only thing preventing me from being with my new love.

When Adonis (I never learnt his real name, never saw him again, although not for want of trying) had left, Ahmed pulled me away from the café and led me toward home. I couldn't even look at him, all I could talk about, even though I knew it was hurting him, was this other man – what he might do, where he might live, what he might enjoy.

Ahmed left me at my front door, and I hardly registered the tears in his eyes, the pain etched into his features. I had felt passion, and nothing else mattered. Sitting on my bed, I thought about my Adonis, imagined his hands on my body, his eyes locked onto mine as he declared his desire for me. I ignored Ahmed and spent every moment I wasn't at work searching Covent Garden for my love, drinking endless coffees in the café where I had seen him, hoping for his return. I left my job and started working in that very café, peering out of the kitchen at the customers so often I almost got fired.

I am not proud of myself. I didn't mean to hurt Ahmed. He was collateral damage in this illness called obsession. This curse. When finally the fantasy of Adonis burnt itself out several months later, I wrote to Ahmed apologising, trying to explain. The letter was returned unopened, '*Not known at this address*' written across the top of the envelope but it was his handwriting. I feel guilty still and can only hope Ahmed found someone who deserved his quiet attention, his respect, his care.

All that was half a lifetime ago, Ishbel, yet I remember it as if it was yesterday. If only I had recognised the pattern, had hauled myself out of my denial, my fantasy that I was doing fine and just needed to find Mr Right for my life to be perfect. Do we all think what we are experiencing is normal? Do we march forward without regard for our personal history, without attending to the lessons we could be learning? I certainly did. My life for the next twenty years was one long string of unreciprocated 'loves'. I never found another Ahmed to love me tenderly, softly. I veered from joy to despair, self-esteem to self-loathing and nothing in between. Life was brilliant or it was terrible. When it was bad – when the object of my desire was out of reach, was unaware of me, or had outright rejected me – I took to my bed with whisky and Valium, looking for oblivion.

One day, coming out of yet another failed 'affair', I realised I needed help. I joined a Sex and Love Addicts group and listened to other people's stories, but these people's stories were not mine. They just wanted sex, and much as I enjoyed the physical side of relationships, I wanted the whole shebang. Love, romance, marriage, forevers. I stopped attending the group when one of the men told me he had a crush on me and had started fantasising about having sex with me while he masturbated.

Of course, they weren't all like that really, but I was still in denial then, still thought I was better than them, more in control. In fact, I was ten times more naïve and stupid than any of them who were trying to face their truth through all the pain and humiliation it brought them.

It was another year before I went to the first of a string of psychiatrists, therapists and counsellors, all lovely people, some more helpful than others.

I am a coward, Ishbel, unfit for human contact. A sad, pathetic failure who deserved all I got. And you haven't heard the worst of it yet, not by a long shot. I cannot write it now. The shame is too recent, the misery too raw. If it's of any consequence in your estimation of me, I am crushed by remorse, I disgust myself. If I could undo my life, unravel it all the way back to the moment of my conception, I would make sure my mother was wearing a chastity belt. Even better, my parents never would have met.

The story goes that my father was drunk as a fart, ricocheting along the street after a lads' night out. My mother, damn her, had missed the last bus and was having to walk home. My father, William Bligh, but certainly no relation to the honourable captain of the same name, lurched towards her and unceremoniously vomited in the gutter.

If only my mother had a bit of the pirate about her. Instead of looking after him and making sure he got home safely she should have set him adrift and never thought of him again. Instead, she gave him her number and he phoned and asked if he could take her out to thank her for her trouble. She should have recognised that he *was* the trouble and was unwilling to change his ways to accommodate a woman in his life long-term, let alone a child. Was that when my mother became depressed and angry? I still haven't asked you about her, have I, Ishbel? Maybe it's time.

7

———

EXILE

I didn't get around to asking if Ishbel knew anything about my mother immediately. When she had Lorna with her, the baby was our focus, and I was happy to let her be. I realised I wasn't ready to hear anything that might dent my anger towards my mother. Despite my years of therapy, it had been with me for so long, I wasn't sure what I would do without it, or what might take its place. I might have to take charge of my life without someone else to blame, and even though I was an adult, I'm not sure I knew how.

The weeks went by, each one the same, stretching towards summer. The only change was the weather, mild and wet, which turned the colours of the landscape to emerald and pink, yellow and mauve. Not being a botanist, I had no idea what all these wildflowers were, but I enjoyed them all the same. The island seemed more welcoming in its summer mantle and, although strong winds still occasionally blew into the corners of my cottage and flattened the coarse grass in the fields, I spent more and more time outdoors walking and watching the sea in all its moods.

Ishbel had moved into her father's cottage in the village and still came most Sundays, bringing the lovely Lorna with her.

'Tell me about our family,' I said one time. It was safer than starting with Mother. My heart was in my throat. I had never called the people around me my family before and had not shown any interest in them. Ishbel was still somehow keeping them away – either that or word had got round that I really was mad, and they were too scared to come.

Ishbel looked at me long and hard. 'Where do I start?'

'It doesn't matter,' I said, but Ishbel was staring off beyond the horizon, back into the history of the Hendersons on Yell.

'I remember our great grandparents, both sets actually. As a child I thought they were ancient, but the Hendersons have always tended to have children quite young, so they were probably only in their fifties when I came along. Our grandparents, Jimmy and Aileen, were married at eighteen and my father born the year after. They lived here, in the croft but Jimmy went to sea – he and his brother owned a trawler and off they'd go for days at a time. He smelled of fish and salt and wind. Granny was a wee bird of a woman, tiny compared to Grandy, who was a bear of a man, and although they were poor as church mice, they were kind and loving. Although Granny did have a temper on her at times, and my father said she was the disciplinarian when the children were young. A wooden spoon to the backside or a slap on the hand.'

She paused and shifted Lorna on her lap. The baby was playing with the colourful beads Ishbel had round her neck, gumming them and covering them in spittle. I was itching to wipe them, but Ishbel didn't seem to mind, and Lorna was quiet.

'There were several miscarriages after my father was born. Granny never said much about them but my father told me once that when your mother came along eleven years after him, there was a great celebration. He said it was like the whole island breathed a sigh of relief. And then two years later came Alasdair. And Granny still only thirty-two. Old then, for having children but quite normal now.'

Lorna had grown bored of the beads and was fussing, trying to get off Ishbel's lap. I cleared the teacups off the table and suggested a walk, offering to take Lorna on my hip. We had become used to each other over the weeks and she was often quite happy to be in my arms for a while. I enjoyed the weight and warmth of her, the smell of her hair and the feeling of her little fingers holding on to my jumper as she snuggled in. She was a lesson in living in the moment, her feelings expressed as they arose – her fascination, curiosity, her boredom and her frustration. I was mesmerised by her, enthralled, enchanted. It was only later, when she'd gone that I would weep for the child I never had.

Walking along the beach, Ishbel carried on with the family history.

'Your mother was a bonnie wee lass by all accounts, and very bright. She could wind her daddy round her little finger, although Granny was stricter. And my father adored her. He taught her to ride their pony, Ned, although it was meant to be a working animal, not for riding. By the time she started at the wee school, he'd already had enough of an education and was helping out on the croft and on the trawler but whenever he could he walked her to school and went back again to walk her home. I say walked, but usually he gave her a piggyback or took Ned so she could ride home. When I was little I was always hearing stories of his wee Morag.'

I couldn't reconcile the 'wee Morag' of the story with my mother. I had little memory of laughter in our house, except those times when Father was away. And the idea of her doing something as unhygienic as riding a pony was preposterous. She was almost as obsessive about cleanliness as I could be about men.

'Did she have friends?' I asked.

'Och, all the children used to go around together. She'd 'a' had to help with chores, of course, like everyone else but she and Alasdair would've been all over the hills and the beaches. If it was anything like my childhood, and I suspect little had changed, there was a lot of freedom and older kids looking after the younger ones out and about.'

My mother, running about this landscape. I imagined her now, hunched by disappointment, chiselled into points and angles.

'Do you know why she left?' There, it was out, the question that had been on my mind since the day I found out she came from this place. She hadn't responded to my letter, so I was still in the dark.

'I dinnae ken, to be honest. There are stories, of course, but I've no idea what's true and what's rumour. I believe the person you need to talk to is Duncan – he was a great friend of your mother's and apparently once let slip he knew the reason for her going but when he realised what he'd said he clammed up again and hasn't said a word about it since. I think you've met him – he and his brother, Ewan, are often about up here.'

Lorna must have felt me stiffen, because she had been dropping off to sleep on my shoulder but now started crying. Ishbel took her and murmured soothing words to her while I tried to still my breath and keep calm. The idea of talking to someone else after all this time was scary.

'I have... I mean... I don't know,' I said, clenching my fists in my pockets.

Ishbel swayed gently with Lorna in her arms, the baby quietening as she did so.

'Can you no tell me what it is you're hiding from up here?

Have we not known each other long enough for that? You can surely trust me not to tell a soul but do you no need to talk about it? I sometimes see such sadness in your eyes, Kirstie, it fair makes my heart heavy. 'Tis not natural for a person to live so alone. Surely whatever it is you think you have done doesn't require such a dire punishment?'

Biting my lip, I turned away from her. I did want to confess, and it was true I had cast her in the role of confessor. But I found her company comforting and wasn't ready to lose it, as I was sure I would once she knew the real me. And yet she deserved something.

'I behaved badly at the end of an affair with a married man and people got hurt – emotionally, I mean. I am here to prevent myself from ever doing the same thing again.' It was true, in essence, and she didn't need to know the detail. Although it haunted me, kept me from sleep or filled my dreams, I wasn't ready to confess to the full extent of my recent conduct.

Ishbel pursed her lips and leant her head against Lorna's. 'I'm sure no one would judge you as harshly as you judge yourself, Kirstie,' she said. 'And while I'm not saying I approve of affairs with married men – having been the wronged wife – many relationships end badly with hurt all round. I cannot believe you are so much worse than anyone else.'

I nodded because in that moment it was all I could think to do. 'I'm sorry your husband cheated on you,' I said. 'And thank you for your faith in me.' Even though it was misguided.

She smiled. 'We're family, Kirstie, we have to stand together. And as to Angus and the divorce, it's water under the bridge now. We have come to the point where we can be civil, and I actually like his new wife. In fact, I like her better than I like him!'

Would Vanessa, the wife I had wronged, ever say the same thing? I very much doubted it.

'Maybe I could speak to Duncan if you were there too,' I said.

'Of course, if that's what you want, although there's nothing to fear with old Duncan, he's a gentle soul if ever I met one. Shall I bring him with me next time I come?'

I let the idea I was now in some way scared of men slip past like the almost truth it was, because I was scared: not of men, but of myself around them, and that wasn't the same thing, and it was the same thing.

Letting Ishbel bring him meant waiting a week. Seven days of getting worked up over meeting him, what to say, how to be. Time to change my mind a hundred times and torture myself with uncertainty. 'Yes, fine,' I said, and swallowed all the other words that crowded my mouth.

I watched Ishbel's car bump down the track and heard Lorna giggling in the baby seat as if she was having the ride of her life. The space they left behind felt larger than usual, and the days until their return empty. I got my journal out and sat outside in the low afternoon sun and wrote to try and work out what I felt.

There is a loneliness in not being able to tell anyone anything about myself, but I do value Ishbel's undemanding friendship. I also find myself thinking of Ahmed, my one true relationship, and missing him. For a year, our love was enough. Is it possible I'll find someone else like him? And if I do, will I appreciate it or crave the drama of obsession?

I took my book and sat on the beach wrapped in a blanket. Summer was approaching in name only, the temperatures still well below my expectations of the season. My book sat in my lap unopened as I was entranced by an otter creeping under a flank of kelp and then tossing it into the air and watching it fall. It was so unselfconscious in its play that I felt like an intruder, yet I couldn't tear myself away from such obvious pleasure. Some may say animals don't play and all their activity is directed towards survival, but they haven't seen an otter and a clump of seaweed.

Long after the otter had taken to the water and swum away, I sat looking at the wavelets breaking on the shore, small bubbles rising from the sand in their wake as the cockles buried there exhaled. And as the tide ebbed, I started digging, filling my pockets with the small bivalves until they bulged.

I washed my bounty in the spring and took them to my table. I sautéed an onion, threw in some sliced courgette and a slug of whisky and a little of the vegetable stock I'd made the day before. In went the cockles, and as they heated, they opened, presenting themselves in their pale fawn blush. I cooked some spaghetti and tossed everything together when it was ready, with a dash of cream and a generous handful of parsley as the final ingredients. My first new dish – strictly speaking a new take on an old recipe – in well over a year. I called it Shetland Cockle Pasta and decided to make it for Ishbel and Duncan's visit. It would provide a focal point other than my mother, should I need one.

They arrived without Lorna which made a shiver run down my spine, as if her absence was a portent of what was to come. The food was ready, the whisky and glasses on the table. Ishbel was her usual, easy self, commenting on the smell of the cockles which filled the room, the crockery with its age-cracked glaze she had eaten from all through her childhood. I felt the outsider

I was, distant, dislocated as Ishbel claimed her history, this home more hers than mine.

Duncan held his hat in his hands, hovering at the door. I turned to him and smiled, feeling awkward. Would he expect an explanation for my isolation? The moment passed. As Ishbel had said, there was nothing to fear with Duncan. His cheeks retained the years of the sun, and he regarded me out of eyes that held the colours of the sea. Then he nodded and hung his hat on the peg by the door in the way that frequent visitors know the habits of a place, and sat at the table. I had dragged the wooden crate out from the alcove and made it the third chair, sitting on it myself, slightly lower than the other two, a child at my own table.

Ishbel talked about Lerwick and the preparations for the midsummer party the children at her school were organising. Duncan listened, chopped his spaghetti into inch-long pieces, chewing each mouthful of his food carefully. I watched them both as they slotted easily into their roles – the talker and the listener, sitting at my table, eating my food, holding my history between them.

'A delicious meal, Kirstie, thank you. I can understand how you were successful in your catering business if all your meals were like that. I have not eaten so well for a long time,' said Ishbel.

Duncan nodded, hands on his stomach.

We took our drinks and our chairs outside – whisky for Duncan, tea for Ishbel and me – and sat watching the birds soar and swoop as they rode the thermals. The sun was low, the evenings long at this time of year.

'Skuas and kittywakes the day,' said Duncan in his first utterance since, 'pleased te finally meet you,' and 'yes please,' to food and drink.

I looked up and followed the birds with eyes watering in the cold that Ishbel and Duncan seemed impervious to.

'So, Duncan, Kirstie here wants to know why her mother left the island and I believe you're the one to tell her.'

He turned to look at me and the sea colours of his eyes had darkened to grey under his thick white brows. 'I havenae told a soul these last many years, and she may not thank me for telling it now. 'Tis her story to tell, not mine.' He looked up at the birds again, and I bit the inside of my cheek and wanted to shake him.

Ishbel, obviously as keen as I was to hear the story, said, 'Aye, that may be, but she has not told, and young Kirstie here also has a right to know why she didnae have the comfort of growing up here with her family around her, so maybe it's time to say what you know. Morag wouldnae hate you for it – she may even thank you, for a secret is always better shared, and easier to talk about once the first words are spoken.'

'It may be true, what you say, Ishbel,' said Duncan. 'Will she no be coming back then, now you're here?' He turned to look at me, his eyes narrowed, trying, perhaps to see Morag in me.

'I very much doubt it. We're not close,' I said, and saw his face crease briefly in sadness.

Duncan sighed and nodded, eyes averted.

I looked at Ishbel, who smiled, leant back in her chair and took a sip of her tea. I could only wait. As puffy white clouds drifted across the sun, bringing shade and a further drop in temperature, Duncan, lifting his eyes to the sky, started talking, as if this was the sign he'd been waiting for.

'Ever since you came here, I've wondered what you knew of your maether. I suspected she had told no one of her past wherever it was she went, just as she could not tell anyone here the reason she left, nor imagine a future on the island. I do believe you have the right to know, and I dinnae ken whether I have the right but since you're here and she'll no be coming back, I've reconciled mysel' to being the one to tell it.' He took a deep breath, grief etched into his features.

'Your maether, Morag, was a wee slip of a thing, always running about and laughing. She was a cure for a bad mood or a sore heart, that's the truth. When she was a teenager, she was a beauty and we all loved her, although I was afraid her heart belonged to Andrew from over yonder.' He tilted his head towards the hill.

'Andrew Tulloch would that be?' said Ishbel.

'Aye, he's the one, God rest his soul. He died a few years back from some sort of wasting disease.'

I couldn't tally this young woman who made people love her with the mother I had grown up with, but I tucked the information away to examine later, not wanting to interrupt Duncan's tale.

'It was the autumn of 1957. 'Twas a warm one and one of the first years I can remember strangers coming to look at the birds. Not too many, mind, but they came with their binoculars and their enthusiasm and walked all over, eyes to the sky. They wanted locals to show them the best places to see puffins and guillemots, skuas and terns.' He looked towards the sea and the cliffs in the distance before continuing.

'The tourists were also hoping to catch a glimpse of the rarer birds, but they didn't even know what might be here, so couldn't ask for them by name. Morag was one of the first to offer to be a guide and she would tell stories at the end of the day about their strange accents and the way they wrote down everything she said in their notebooks along with a description of the birds they sighted. She thought it was all a nonsense, grown men interested in the birds we saw every day of our lives, but they were paying her, and I think she liked the money and the sense of importance it gave her.'

That was more like the woman I knew – my mother loved

money, even though she had a strange relationship with it – on the one hand it gave her a sense of security, and perhaps a private feeling of superiority over people who had less. But she used to tut and shake her head at ostentatious displays of wealth, said it made people look cheap when they wanted to look the opposite.

'One day, she took a man out to look for a sea eagle even though we all knew there'd not been any around these parts for years. He was a wealthy man from down south, waving his money around and expecting us to do what he wanted. Morag was happy to take his money, laughing behind his back that he wasn't a very good birdwatcher if he didn't even know there weren't any sea eagles here. They went off a'right but some of us got to talking and didnae feel comfortable with her going off with him – there was something about him I didnae like and the others felt the same. So we decided to go after them and bring her back. They'd not been gone so very long, so they wouldn't be far away.' Duncan paused to wipe a tear from his cheek and then looked at me.

'Are you sure you want to hear this, lassie?'

I nodded. Ishbel put a hand on my shoulder and I let it rest there.

'Well, we split up and I headed towards the headland, the Ness of Vatsetter.' He looked out over the scenery as if looking for her all over again, his gaze sweeping the surrounds as his hands gripped his thighs.

'Go on,' I said, thinking I knew what he was going to say – she and this man had fallen in love and were planning their elopement. She'd left all she knew for him and then he'd dumped her. Surely that was the story.

He took a deep breath. 'I never told a living soul. I promised Morag I never would but I canna go to the grave with such a secret.' He was whispering, as if saying the words softly would lessen their impact. 'I saw them. He was on top of her, and she was struggling. I called out but the wind took my words and they didnae hear.'

I gasped. My mother was raped?

Ishbel held me close. 'You don't have to hear this, Kirstie, really you don't.'

'I need to know,' I said. I looked at Duncan, who had paused, head down. 'Please go on.'

He glanced up at Ishbel, then at me. I nodded encouragement but held Ishbel's hand when she offered it.

'I ran towards them, shouting,' Duncan continued softly, 'but they didnae look my way. He stood up, did up his breeks and pulled her to her feet. He put his arm around her but she shook him off and walked a few paces away. I was still calling to her, but the wind was too loud for her to hear, even then. I ran to her and touched her shoulder. She flinched, spun round, eyes wide with fear.'

Ishbel and I both gasped and looked at each other. I felt sick. Duncan closed his eyes and nodded slowly. ''Tis all true. She was crying and her clothes were all askew, one shoe on and the other lying in the heather. There was a smear of blood on her skirt.

"Duncan," she said, and then she threw herself on the ground and wept. I sat with her until she was quiet and then lifted her to her feet. The man had gone by then. We never saw him again.'

The sun had come out again, casting its mellow light on the three of us – the one who had kept my mother's secret all these years and the two who were hearing it for the first time. Ishbel got up quietly and brought out the whisky, poured some into our teacups and refilled Duncan's glass. I sat waiting, a queer sensation sitting lumpen in my stomach. Pity, anger, disbelief.

'What happened?' I asked.

Duncan sighed. 'We agreed not to tell anyone. She made me promise. She never told a soul about it, but I knew she would never pick a husband from amongst us after that. I often wondered what would have happened if I hadn't seen it all – would she have been able to stay if no one else had known? Was it because there was a witness to her shame that she had to go? All I know is that she started staying away from me and then from everyone else. Her once bonnie face grew haggard and her eyes watchful.

'One day she finally agreed to see me. She told me she was leaving. She couldnae stand the sight of the place anymore, said she felt haunted by the man and he would give her no peace. I tried to persuade her to change her mind. I offered to marry her, and not just out of pity – I'd always loved her. But she'd have none of it. She made me promise again, on my mother's life, I'd not speak a word, and she went. That's the last I saw of her and the truth of it as far as I know.' The old man leant his elbows on his knees and let his head drop into his hands. From time to time he let out a deep sigh as if he'd finally eased himself of his burden.

Ishbel, for once in her life, was speechless, and I looked towards the sea, watching the sun shimmer across its surface, unable to form a thought.

When I could think straight again, days later, I knew what I had to do.

Dear Mother,

I met Duncan a few days ago. He is well and sends his best wishes. He remembers you with such fondness and I must tell you that he has been the reliable custodian of your secret for sixty years. He only agreed to tell me after I'd sworn not to talk about it to anyone else, but I think, in sharing it, an enormous weight was lifted from his shoulders. Being such a small community, your

departure caused a huge jolt. I had a number of theories about why you left the islands as you did but nothing could have prepared me for the truth.
I was shocked by what I heard, of course. It was a terrible thing that happened to you, but can you finally put it behind you now after all these years?
That's it really; I just wanted you to know that I know, and that it changes nothing, and it changes everything.
Yours,
Kirstie

I regretted sending it the moment I handed the letter over. This was more of an intrusion than the first (still unanswered) letter. I almost ran after Dougal's car as he bumped down the track, carrying it to the post office, the ferry, the train, the sorting office, my mother's house, the kitchen table where she would sit to open it, read it. How would she receive such news, out of the blue – the secret she'd held for so many years being suddenly shared? She had left this place and never allowed herself to return. I saw the irony of our positions. Faced with impossible situations, we had exiled ourselves in mirror.

But after my initial misgivings I allowed myself to hope that it would feel like an unburdening for her, as it clearly had for Duncan – that she might permit herself a moment's respite from her fear and anger and take the hand I had clumsily offered.

With my next delivery of food, Dougal handed me a letter. I held it in my hand, feeling the thinness of it but still hoping it contained answers, that she would finally have unburdened herself.

Kirsten,
I don't know what that old man's been telling you but bear in mind he always was one for stretching the truth for the sake of a

*story. Please pay him and his tales no heed. I want to hear no
more of it.
I trust you are well,
Mother*

So that was it.

I had, of course, approached it all wrong. She had ignored
my first letter, so we'd had no contact for several months, since I
had asked her about the cottage and whether I could stay there.
It had been a tense conversation, as they always were, but this
one with an added edge because my mother held the power. She
was the one who could agree or not, who could bestow the
favour or withhold it. It wasn't a position she occupied very
often, and she felt her way into it tentatively but once there,
inhabited it fully.

We'd been in her kitchen.

'I was wondering what happened to the croft?' I had said.

My mother stopped her wiping for a moment and half
turned to me. 'What croft would you be talking about?'

For God's sake, how many crofts did we have in the family?
'The one that belonged to your parents,' I said as evenly as I
could.

'I expect it's fallen down.'

'Really?'

'Why are you asking – what do you want with it?'

'I was thinking about going away for a while so I thought I
might go up to the islands.'

'Why there?'

'Because I'd like to see the place where you grew up.'

My mother twisted the cloth in her hands but otherwise was
completely still, hardly even breathing. Her gaze rested on the
wall a few inches to my right. I considered moving into her line
of sight, but it would only have annoyed her.

'I had to put it all behind me.' She spoke quietly, gazing out the window.

'All these years – why?'

'I have my reasons,' she added, still not moving, still not looking at me. I wondered how much effort it took to deny so many memories, to suppress every hint of emotion connected to her past.

'Well, maybe I could stay in the cottage for a while anyway?'

'No.'

Such an effective wall when I was a child, my mother's No was the end point of too many of our interactions. It was one of these Noes that had resulted in the red wine incident, my frustration guiding my actions. There had to be a way around her No this time.

'Maybe I could do it up a bit – paint it, clean it up.'

'There's no point in doing anything to a ruin.'

'But what if it's not a ruin, why let it just sit there unused?'

The conversation – if me wheedling and begging, and her saying No could be construed as a conversation – went on and on. I would not give up. I needed somewhere to go and Yell was the perfect location. I'd done my homework – population 966 in an area of 82 square miles. It meant I could easily avoid people.

In the end, my mother resorted to her other wall. 'Because. I mean it, Kirsten–' My parents were the only people ever to call me by my proper name.

'Stop this now.'

She moved then, turning away and busying herself with the dishes on the draining board. She'd wanted a dishwasher for years and my father was too mean to buy one.

And that's what gave me the idea.

'What if I do it up and you can rent it out to tourists and earn a bit of your own money?'

Her wiping stopped and her head turned ever so slightly

towards me. Since my father's selfishness had forced her to give up work, she'd complained often about the lack of her own money. And now they were on a pension which he controlled. Would she take the bait? I dropped my eyes to the floor in case she looked at me and took the glint in my eye for triumph.

She didn't agree immediately, she was too entrenched by then in denying me my request, but she lifted her head and looked out to the bird feeder and I knew it was only a matter of time, that if I stayed quiet, she would talk herself into my proposal.

I made a pot of tea, set the cups in the saucers, put the milk into a jug, invited her to sit. She hadn't said a word, but she sat, allowed me to pour and pass her a cup of tea. She sipped it quietly and asked for a top-up.

'I haven't any money to pay for repairs,' she said when I'd all but given up hope of her ever saying a word again.

'I'll pay,' I said. 'In return for staying there while I do it.'

'And how much could it be rented for?'

I had no idea, and no intention of renting it out anyway. I was desperate to get away and stay away. 'A couple of hundred a week in summer, I suspect. Tourists have discovered the Shetlands these days, so I've read.'

My mother smiled briefly, although I don't know if it was at the thought of the money or at my attempt at levity.

'Two hundred pounds, you say?' A gleam in her eye.

She sat looking at the teapot on the table and then suddenly got up, went out of the room and returned with a piece of paper. 'This is how to get there,' she said.

I put it in my pocket and didn't look at it until I was at home later. It was old and worn, small tears appearing along the creases. In my mother's writing were the directions to get to the croft from the ferry and a hand-drawn map of the surroundings with buildings marked, the houses with people's names next to them. My heart faltered as I realised this had been her way of remembering her childhood home and she must, over the years, have got it out to look at every so often, before folding it away and hiding it again in a drawer.

I rang her to say thank you, but my father answered and didn't call her to the phone and when, a few days later I dropped in to say goodbye, she couldn't get me out of there fast enough.

I'd said in my letter to my mother that knowing what had happened changed nothing and everything. Now I knew some of her story, I felt sorry for her. How could anyone carry a secret like that through their life without it festering, causing a once happy, carefree character to become so confined and depressed.

Yet for all my efforts, I could still fall into anger over her treatment of me. She had let her own wounds get in the way of being able to express her love for her only child. That was the conflict I lived with in the days after Duncan's visit.

Long days they were, too, with not enough to fill them or take my mind off Duncan's story. I pitied my mother and was angry with her. I raged at the man who had defiled her. I felt angry that he hadn't faced the consequences of his actions. Perhaps if he'd had to stand trial and been convicted of rape my mother would have been able to stay in Shetland. When my head hurt from all the confused thoughts, I went for long walks on the beach trying to exhaust myself so I would fall into a sleep so deep dreams would not find me.

I asked Duncan to take me to the place my mother had been raped. My reasoning for it wasn't clear but a part of me felt I needed to see it in order to fully empathise with her, to understand the horror she went through. He was reluctant at first, but I kept asking and, in the end, he took me. We walked over the Hill of Lussetter across the narrow land bridge between the Wick and the Loch of Vatsetter and up onto the Ness of Vatsetter, a windblown heath with cliffs dropping to an unsettled sea. We didn't talk much as we went and when we got there, Duncan pointed out a place on the edge of the land.

'That's the spot,' he said, and started walking back the way we'd come, stopping to wait a hundred metres or so away from me.

I stood with the wind clawing at my clothes, the sound of the waves crashing below and thought of my seventeen-year-old mother being held down on the rough heather, a stranger grunting away on top of her. I turned and joined Duncan and pretended to trip as I reached him so I could hold on to him for comfort. He was the first man I'd touched since Ed.

8

———————

THE CONFESSION

I'm taking a deep breath, Ishbel. Several, in fact. I have a glass of whisky beside me too. Three fingers' worth. It's time to tell you about Ed. There were others – a fair few in my twenties and thirties. My life lurched from one doomed relationship to another. But Ed was the one who finished me. Ed's was the family I destroyed.

By the time I met him, I'd had my own catering company for ten years and in that regard, was doing very nicely, thank you. I ran my business out of a converted warehouse in Camden Town and lived above the commercial kitchen in a large, airy loft. He worked near Tottenham Court Road, a few stops away on the Tube.

So, what can I say about Edward Harvey Bannerman? Actually, not a lot. I realise now I never really knew him as a person; he was merely the recipient of my obsessive fantasies which left no room to discover the real person.

What I do know is that he was the marketing director of a large company, it doesn't matter which one, and was overseeing the organisation of a big conference. Hundreds of businessmen and women who would need feeding several times a day and a silver service dinner at the end of the three days. It wasn't his job to find the caterer, nor to agree to the menus but he did hold the budget and he was one of those people who found it hard to delegate, so when his team decided my catering company was the one to nourish them through rounds of meetings, presentations and speeches, he wanted to meet me to go through the menus and ensure I kept to the budget.

It was love at first sight, for me, anyway. He was in his fifties but fit, hard-muscled, tanned. I was forty-two, single, lonely. I was always lonely between men, in the way women can be when they feel incomplete, invisible without a man around.

He signed off on the menus and we went out for a drink which became dinner which became sex back at my place. His sensitivity as a lover bound me to him. Only someone who loved me could fulfil my needs so delicately. His breath smelled of the brandy we'd shared after dinner, his skin of an expensive cologne I hadn't come across before. He had a scar on his left knee – a reconstruction after a rugby injury – a mole on his ribs just below his heart. After that one night I could have drawn every line of him, coloured in his greying hair, his brown eyes, the exact tone of his skin.

He didn't stay the night. I should have known why but I didn't want to. I lay after he'd gone, with my hand between my legs, resting softly on the place he'd kissed me, feeling his lips still.

You see, Ishbel, there I was again, in love with someone I'd just met, didn't know, but had already planned a future with, encompassing family and overseas holidays, romantic dinners and quiet evenings reading. So attuned to each other there was no need for words. I mistook our lovemaking for the prelude to a life together, but for him it was never anything more than sex.

You don't need all these details, I know, and may prefer not to read them but I want you to build the picture of our relationship fully, to understand my affliction. I was totally in love from that moment on and believed he was too.

It sounds so ridiculous now and seeing the words written on the page makes it seem even more so. Which makes the rest of the story harder to tell. I hardly need to warn you that there was no happy ending. This was a tragedy not a comedy, and one perhaps even the Bard himself could not have imagined, although he was pretty good at death, doom and destruction. No one dies in my tale, but lives were destroyed.

But I'm getting ahead of myself. I want you to hear the whole tragic story of my delusion and shameful actions.

I was right, we did continue to see each other. Two or three times a week. He'd text, I'd respond. We'd meet at my place. Sometimes in the evening, more often during the day. We never went out together after that first evening, were not seen in public. I spent hundreds of pounds on linen sheets, silk lingerie, crotchless underwear. Sometimes we didn't even have enough time to undress each other, other times we lingered, tracing the contours of each other's body, talking about nothing but I believed, understanding everything.

God, how I hate myself. I put myself back in that place, that bed, that mind, and all I want to do is die of shame.

He never loved me. He *never* loved me. HE NEVER LOVED ME.

I loved him to distraction. Literally. I could do nothing else but think of him. I allowed my chefs to plan menus, my PA to tender for work. I walked through my life, playing a role I was not part of. Every thought, every deed, every breath was for Ed. I planned what to wear in case I bumped into him, burned fragrant candles to appeal to his senses in case he dropped by. He mentioned a particular perfume he liked, and I bought it. Of course, I later discovered it was the one his wife used, and it would make it less likely that she would detect another woman's fragrance if we used the same one.

I now also realise he was a sex addict. I'm not excusing my behaviour, but he had issues too.

How stupid was I? How blind?

I cannot write more now. I am too ashamed.

9
___

EXILE

'I'd like you to cater for Lorna's christening,' said Ishbel as she came and sat herself down at the table.

'Good morning to you too,' I said, closing my journal and leaning my forearms on it.

Ishbel smiled. She always smiled. I'd never met anyone like her for smiling. 'I've been telling everyone who'll listen about the lunch you made for Duncan and me. Tavis and Catriona said that if you were really that good they wanted you to do the food for the wee bairn's baptism.'

I gazed out the window. A christening meant people, lots of people. But it also meant I had a good excuse not to go to the service, could stay in the kitchen and not meet any of them.

'I couldn't prepare food for an event like that in this kitchen,' I said. 'Sorry.'

I thought that would be the end of it, but I hadn't banked on Ishbel's persistence.

'You could use mine,' she said. 'Or Duncan and Ewan's – it's closer to the kirk.'

I closed my eyes and took a deep breath.

'How many people?' I asked.

'Och, I'd say about forty maybe. All family and friends.' She took my hand. 'It's time, now, isn't it?'

'You're still convinced I have to meet all these people, aren't you?'

'You can't avoid it forever. If you're going to stay, you can't live like a hermit. For one thing, it's not natural, and for another, everybody wants to welcome you. It's a small town and the folk can be annoying at times but they're good at heart, and they're your people.'

I shook my head, not because I disagreed but because I couldn't fight her any longer. She was right. I couldn't live like I had been in spite of the idea that meeting people these days terrified me. I sighed.

'When and what time of day?'

'Three weeks on Sunday – July 14th. The service is at half past ten, so they're thinking a buffet lunch at twelve. So you'll do it?'

I was already planning a menu and wondering about who could help – Ishbel would have to organise that, of course. Frittatas, salads, dressed salmon, maybe a dish using local lamb, and huge bowlfuls of local berries and cream. There'd also be a christening cake to make and decorate.

'So?' asked Ishbel again.

'I'll do it,' I said, taking a deep breath and clasping my hands together in what may have looked like prayer. 'Do they have a budget?'

When Ishbel had had her cup of tea and driven away I sat down to plan properly. She had said she could find some local girls to help with preparation and that Tavis and Catriona were decorating the village hall where the lunch was to be held. Duncan and Ewan would let me use their kitchen, and they'd be at the service so I would have the place to myself. The budget was tiny. If I was to stay within their allowance, it would be sandwiches and cake for forty. But I loved little Lorna and decided my gift to her would be a feast for her christening. Not that she'd get to enjoy it – she'd just started on solids and was only eating mushed-up fruit and vegetables.

A couple of days later, Duncan appeared at my door. His hair was so thin I could see the liver spots on his scalp, and as he entered, he reached up and smoothed his hair down as if he'd read my thoughts. I offered him a cup of tea but he declined.

'I came to ask a favour.'

What a surprise – what did I have that he could want? 'Yes?' I said, inclining my head.

'I'd like to get old Jimmy's violin repaired and have Ewan play it at the bairn's christening. He's a great one for a tune and I've a mind it would be a nice thing to have the old fiddle played again, welcoming in a new generation.'

'What a lovely idea. Of course you can take it. I'll pay for whatever needs to be done. I'd love to hear it played properly.'

Duncan smiled and nodded. 'Well, I might have that tea after all,' he said, as if the relief of getting the positive response he had hoped for had made him thirsty. He settled into the chair with a sigh and rested his hands in his lap. The silence lengthened into the dusty corners and glinted off the windows. Eventually, he lifted his chin, sucked in some air and said, 'I have to thank you for coming back, young Kirstie, and for asking me to tell you Morag's story. It's been a stone in my heart for a long time, and now it's gone, and I feel like myself again after all these years. 'Tis a cruel thing to ask a person to hold such a secret, and yet Morag didnae mean it that way, I'm sure. But it eats away at ye, ye ken? You canna ever truly relax around your friends in case you spill the words ye've vowed to keep. I've lived with my brother, Ewan, all my life and for the first time in fifty and more years, we can sip a wee dram of an evening and I'm no afraid of saying the wrong thing. Don't get me wrong, lassie, I'm no going to tell – the secret is buried deep in my bones and, if you hadnae come, it would ha' died with me, but I'm not afeared of it anymore, that's the difference. It's your secret now, not mine.' He let his head fall forward and his mouth moved but no sound came out of it. Perhaps he was thanking God.

He left with the violin cradled in his arms like a baby. Like the treasure it was, with the respect it was due.

I watched him go, walking with the gait of a man thirty years younger than the almost eighty he'd clocked up. He traversed the rutted track with easy familiarity, and I couldn't help but admire him, this man who had kept my mother's secret, who had been her best and truest friend down through the years and her not even aware of it. When I could see him no more, I sat outside for a while with paper and pen and wrote again to my mother. I told her Duncan did love a story but seldom embellished the truth, that he was a kind man, a man of his word. I told her he'd never married, lived with his brother and they took walking groups out still. I said he'd made a life out of the birds and animals of the Shetland he so loved. And I told her about Ishbel, my cousin and friend, and Lorna, the baby who brought joy to my life with her uncomplicated love and her unfettered laughter.

I had found happiness where I had expected none.

There were questions I wanted to ask her, but I knew I had to bide my time, that if I pressed her too hard or too soon she would dig her heels in even deeper and never give me what I wanted – her story. It should have been such a simple thing for a daughter to ask of her mother but given the history of our relationship and the little I now knew of her life in Shetland, there was no such thing as simple. Over the years, through misunderstandings and our separate struggles, ours had developed into a complex, embittered affiliation and not one to be easily repaired.

So my plan was to write chatty letters about my life on the island and see whether she evinced any interest. It might be a slow process, but I had time. I only hoped that at her age, she did too.

Ishbel invited me to Lerwick for the midsummer celebrations. I declined, of course. Instead, I crouched in the dunes a few yards back from the beach, watching as the locals from Mid Yell celebrated with a bonfire and music provided by various people playing guitars, fiddles and spoons. One young man added more percussion by thumping away on an oil drum. An older woman sang folk songs in a rich alto, others joining in the chorus. A few people sat, passing bottles around and filling up their glasses, others Stripped the Willow and jigged the jigs. I found my feet tapping along in a solitary dance. The sea was calm, wavelets gently lapping the shore. The sun barely set – at midnight, when the party was in full swing, there was still a glimmer of light on the horizon and as I walked back up to the croft I had no need for a torch. I felt a sense of connection with the place, a warm satisfaction that this was my land, I had a right to be there and I was safe.

Duncan started dropping in for tea most days and I began to look forward to his visits. Often we'd sit quietly together, looking out at the broad expanse of green that the spring rains had given us and the pale summer sun hadn't yet had the energy or the heat to sear to brown. Sometimes he'd point at the sky to indicate birds – guillemot, arctic skua, storm petrel. The names rolling off his tongue with an intimacy that made them into old friends.

One day he brought Ewan with him, a year or two younger but with the same piercing eyes and upright stature. He had the violin with him and offered it to me with a bow.

'Like new but better,' he said. 'It sounds bright.' He nodded his head towards me as if expecting me to play. I shook my head and handed it back to him.

'I'd love to hear it, and maybe you'd teach me to play it one day?'

He smiled, needing no further encouragement, and placing it under his chin, drew the bow across the strings, tweaked the tuning and started playing. Duncan closed his eyes and tapped his fingers lightly on the table in time with the tune. I sat caught in the embrace of the music, a capering, happy tune leaping from note to note and then a slower, sadder piece that carried me to the edge of tears. When he'd finished, the silence seemed deeper than usual, as if even the air around us craved more and the walls of the croft had drawn all sound into themselves and wouldn't let it go.

I received a letter from my mother.

Dear Kirsten,
I don't know how to tell you this, so I'll just say it. Your father died suddenly from a heart attack. The funeral was this morning – so by the time you get this, he'll be gone. There was no time to

*tell you, what with all the arrangements, and at least this way you
don't have to spend any energy wondering if you should come.
There wasn't much of a turnout. My friend, Molly, came, and the
neighbours, June and Harry. A woman we didn't know wailed as
the coffin disappeared. His latest and his last, no doubt. She had
bright red nail polish and wore high heels she could hardly walk
in, and she couldn't have been a day under seventy.
He left me the house and contents, which was the least he could
do, and most of the money but there's something for you too.
When it's all sorted, I'll transfer it into your account. I presume
you're not working and will need funds, though what you're still
doing up in that place, I can't imagine.
I must go to my bridge club now.
Mother.
PS. I hope you're well.*

I held the letter in my hand long after I had finished
reading. Its weightlessness belied the news it held but matched
my feelings: nothingness. I could find no sadness in me, no grief.
I had an image of my father as I had last seen him; thin, bent,
with beak-like nose and close-set eyes and wispy white hair that
needed a cut. He'd asked me to leave his house over some minor
infraction, his voice shrill, finger pointing shakily to the door.
Perhaps I had asked about his latest trip. They had not stopped
when he retired, they just became 'walking holidays' or
'personal development workshops'. I might have laughed,
wondering when he was going to find a personality to develop,
or whose path he was walking up these days. My life certainly
wouldn't change with him gone and I doubted my mother's
would either, except now she wouldn't have to wonder where he
was and who he was with.

He had taken me out when I was little, had played games
with me. But he'd tired of family life quickly and needed more

than my mother and me. As an adult I realised he wasn't the cocksure man he tried so hard to be but a fragile person who had a narcissist's need for the admiration of others. Lots of others. Mother and I weren't enough, so he had to look elsewhere. Maybe I would have been less angry with him if I'd realised it all sooner, and now it was too late. Oh, the wisdom of hindsight and years of therapy. The initial nothingness morphed into regret.

The unexpected consequence of hearing about his death was that I immediately felt more Scottish. Specifically, more Shetlandish. It was as if, with him gone, my English heritage had no further claim on me. There were no relatives left on his side of the family, nothing to lure me back to England. And with that realisation came a growing sense of contentment.

A week before the christening I asked Dougal for a lift down to the shop after he'd delivered my weeks' groceries. I needed to know what was available and what might have to be ordered from Lerwick. He showed no surprise at my request, just opened the passenger door and then got into the driver's seat. The suspension had gone in his car and by the time we got down the hill my back was crying out for a chiropractor.

Sheila at the shop looked up from sticking price tags on toilet rolls as I walked in, and raised an eyebrow.

'Well, if it isn't the lady herself,' she said, and got back to her pricing, pressing hard with the sticker gun. 'What brings you off your hill?' she asked, without looking up again.

She had dyed red hair, greying at the roots, and a large, round face. The arms of her glasses cut into the flesh beside her eyes.

'I needed to talk to you, face to face,' I said.

She raised her head and smiled but underneath it was a current of resentment. Anger even. As if she thought I'd been avoiding her in particular, although I had told her when I arrived and discussed my needs that I was staying in my grandparent's croft to recuperate and get away from everyone.

'I have to thank you for your great service these last few months,' I continued. 'But I've discovered even a hermit needs to see people once in a while.' I gave a little laugh to melt the ice. She looked interested but didn't return my smile.

'You've probably heard that Ishbel asked me to do a bit of cooking for the christening?'

She nodded. 'Aye, there's not a one who hasnae heard.'

'Right. Well, I thought if anyone can get what I need, it's you, so I've come to discuss the menu and the ingredients I'll be needing.'

Old and crusty she may be, but I knew how to butter her up. She smiled then, safe in the knowledge that I respected her position.

'So, what is it you're needing?'

I showed her the menu I'd planned, and she raised her eyebrows and shook her head as she read it.

'Fancy,' she said. 'I'll have to order this spelt thing you want from the mainland. The rest I can get locally. Young Jock will supply the fruit from his greenhouses. You'll get all you need.'

'Thank you,' I said. 'I knew I could count on you. You'll be at the lunch, I expect?'

'Aye – I've known your family all my life.' There was a note of reproof in her voice that I chose to ignore.

When I turned to go, I noticed the three other shoppers had stopped, half-filled baskets over their arms, and were staring at me. I smiled, nodded to them, and made a hasty retreat, heart beating hard against my ribs. Well, what had I expected – that no one would be out shopping? That I could creep into the village unnoticed and get away again without being seen? I leant against the church wall taking calming breaths, eyes closed, concentrating on nothing but the sensation of the cold, uneven stones pressing into my back.

'I was beginning to think you must have two heads or a hunchback,' said a soft voice.

Opening my eyes, I saw an elderly woman standing in front of me, studying my face with her piercing blue eyes. 'I dinna see Morag in you but I can see your grandfather. I'm Una, Duncan and Ewan's cousin. You've met them, I know.'

'Kirstie,' I said, introducing myself unnecessarily.

'I was only ten when your mother left but I remember her. She was a kindly soul, always had time for the young ones. Did she have a big family? She always said she wanted a football team!'

A strange tingling spread through my body and then was gone. I felt a deep sadness – I wasn't sure whether it was for me or my mother. I had always wondered what it would be like to have siblings, what I was missing out on by being an only child, but it had never crossed my mind my mother might also have wanted more children. She had struggled so with the one she had.

'Only me,' I said, and shrugged.

'Well, that's a shame,' said Una. 'We were hoping there might be more of you coming back.'

'Sorry.'

'Anyway, it's good to meet you finally. You've been the talk of the town, but Ishbel said you needed time.'

'Thanks,' I said. 'Maybe I've had enough time on my own now.' The words were out before I could stop them but once said, I felt the truth of them. I was ready to be around people. I wanted to be part of this community that could fill in the blanks for me. And yet I also felt fear and knew my entrée back into a social world would need careful planning and a watchful eye.

Una nodded and limped off, the string shopping bag over her arm misshapen by the vegetables it contained. I ran to catch her up and offered to carry her bag. She smiled and gave it to me and led me along the street to her house.

Behind the cheery yellow door it was neat and sparsely furnished. Una told me to put the shopping in the kitchen and followed me in to put the kettle on. There were blue gingham curtains at the window and a geranium in a pot on the sill, flowering in a profusion of pink.

I decided there and then to buy some fabric and make curtains for the croft instead of using the rotting wooden shutters. I had told my mother I would do the place up, and apart from cleaning it thoroughly and shifting a few shingles back into place on the roof, I had done nothing. I still didn't plan for it to be rented out but I would make it into a home.

My home.

Later, I wrote another letter.

Dear Mother,

I don't know what to say about Father's death. I haven't been close to him for so long, but I still feel an emptiness where he should be. If you are grieving, you have my condolences.

As to the money, you didn't say how much it was, but I would like to buy the croft from you, or at least rent it long term, so keep it against either of those options.

I met Una today. She told me you'd wanted a big family. How disappointing for you to only have me. When did your dreams change?

The locals are out in T-shirts these days but I am still in long sleeves and a jacket. I don't know if I'll ever get used to the weather here, but I have fallen in love with the landscape. Who

would have thought that someone born and bred in a big town could take so easily to the wilds of Yell? Maybe it's because it's already in my blood. I feel it coursing, telling me I am where I am meant to be. I am meeting family and have been asked to cater for a christening – Lorna is your great-great-niece, and a pretty, happy little thing.
I hope you are well,
Kirstie.

I spent too much time thinking about my mother. She was with me in the cottage, and when I walked on the beach. I would never tell her she occupied so much of my time. The distance between us was so much more than the miles separating us.

To distract myself I cut the cloth for my curtains, bright yellow backgrounding huge red poppies. Happy fabric which now felt like it didn't belong at my windows after all. I watered the geranium cutting Una had given me and sat looking at it, trying to summon the energy to eat and wash and move through my day. With the christening only a few days away, I actually had things to do for a change.

After a brief summer shower which left behind a magnificent rainbow, I made my way down to the village, to Duncan and Ewan's house. I had to assess the kitchen and decide how I was going to manage to cook everything. In my mind's eye I saw myself moving between fridge, stove, sink and counter, washing, chopping, slicing, whipping, basting, excited to be in a real kitchen again. It was well-designed but smaller than I was used to. But for one person, even cooking for forty people, it would work.

I was glad, however, that Ishbel was making the christening cake. She'd made it the same week she had asked me to do the catering and been injecting it with whisky every other day since.

Duncan and Ewan stood in the doorway, arms folded, while I appraised their kitchen.

'Will it do, lassie?'

'It'll be fine. Perfect in fact.' It was clean and orderly with no clutter on the surfaces. A man's kitchen.

The calendar hanging on the wall showed the date: 11th July. Two years ago to the day I had met up with Ed in Paris.

10

THE CONFESSION

We went away together. Ed had to attend a conference in Paris and he invited me to meet him there afterwards for a long weekend.

Paris, the city of lovers. I knew he was telling me he loved me and only me. This was his way of saying he wanted us to be together, that he'd leave his wife and make a new life with me. I was ecstatic. Shopping for the trip, I spent extravagantly. Expensive dresses for dinners along the Seine in the evenings, new trousers and tops for our daytime sightseeing. I had practically my whole body waxed, my hair cut, eyebrows shaped and nails done.

Ed didn't meet me at the Gare du Nord, so I got a taxi to the hotel. He was waiting for me in our room, naked under the sheets. He appreciated the waxing, tousled my new hair, enjoyed my nails trailing lightly down his back. Our lovemaking was energetic, as if he was sloughing off the tedium of the previous days of meetings and presentations.

Afterwards we lay entwined, and I suggested all the places I wanted to see in our few days. He had been to them all already.

He and his wife, Vanessa, had honeymooned in Paris. He said all he wanted to do was stay in bed and bonk all weekend.

I thought of all the money I'd spent on clothes, the time I'd spent researching things to see and do. Out were the romantic walks we'd take along the Seine, the dinners we'd eat in cosy bistros. I told myself none of it mattered, because he wanted me. Me. And nothing and no one else.

We ordered room service, giggled when it came and we were in the bath together, bubbled up and splashing water over the floor. We slept little and made love a lot. I had never known love like it – my skin ached for him when we were only inches apart, my fingers itched to touch him constantly. We were like junkies with a new and exciting drug.

We still didn't talk of a future. We didn't talk much at all. I imagined weekends in a country house, perhaps his children coming to stay once in a while, me becoming their confidante when their hearts got broken or things weren't going well at school. Ed would say I understood them better than his wife, and I'd smile and kiss him full on the lips.

Or we'd go skiing, swooshing down the slopes of Austria or Switzerland, evenings would be spent drinking Glühwein and eating fondues. People would wonder about who this attractive couple was, who so obviously adored each other.

In London there'd be nights at the theatre, dinners, functions to attend. We'd catch each other's eyes across rooms and make our excuses to leave, needing to be alone together, just us, away from the world.

None of this came to pass. I had built a fantasy out of nothing. I realised later the reason Ed didn't want to go out was because he couldn't run the risk of being seen with me – some of his colleagues had also stayed after the conference, their wives or partners joining them. Perhaps I had sat next to one of them on the train, although I doubted it – Ed had probably bought me a Eurostar ticket because he knew they'd all be flying.

Of course, as was the pattern with the men I fell for, Ed tired of me after a while. He called less and less and when we did meet up the sex was perfunctory, leaving both of us dissatisfied. The more he pulled away, the more I chased after him.

After a quickie one day at my flat, I told him I was pregnant to try and get him to stay but he laughed in my face and told me there was no chance of that, he'd had the snip.

'Those things can fail,' I said.

'It'd be a miracle – I've been tested. Zero little swimmers these days.'

'I'm sorry,' I said, sinking to my knees and taking his hand. 'I didn't mean to trick you. I just don't want you to leave me. I love you.'

His lip curled in horror. 'I didn't ask you to.'

He left then. No long goodbye. No 'I'll always remember you'. Nothing. Just silence where minutes before, he'd inhabited the space in my flat.

I didn't believe it was the last time I'd see him. We never arranged when we'd see each other but he always got in contact eventually. Usually when I was going out of my mind with desperation and desire.

I tried to take my mind off him by throwing myself into work, tendering for bigger and bigger jobs and then having to rely on my staff to handle everything when my concentration flagged, as thoughts of Ed filled my mind.

I relived our time together, the smiles, the laughter, the conversations, the sex. He loved me, I was sure of it. He must still, otherwise what was the point of going on?

I texted him, rang his office, left messages. He ignored them all. I made excuses for him – he was snowed under at work, his wife was being unusually demanding, one of the kids was sick and needed him.

I can hardly bear to write what I did next, but I must tell the whole story.

I found his address.

Actually, I followed him home one evening, having loitered outside his office for hours waiting for him to leave. He walked down to Tottenham Court Road station and got on a train. I stepped into the next carriage, watching him through the window in the door separating us. Seven stops later, at Holland Park, he got off, left the station and walked quickly towards the park itself, turning off just before he got there into a street full of tall, elegant, cream-and-white double-fronted houses. He disappeared into one of them and closed the navy-blue door behind him. I hid behind a tree on the opposite side of the road and watched. Lights came on upstairs and I saw the silhouette of him passing the window. I imagined him taking off his clothes, stepping into the en suite for a quick shower, towelling himself dry. I had seen him do it so often I knew his routine. He dried his hair first, then his arms, shoulders, neck, chest. Slipped the towel behind him to dry his back, and then lingered over his penis and balls, making sure to leave no moisture there. Then his legs and feet. He'd wrap the towel around his waist and walk back into the bedroom, where I'd be waiting for him on the bed, watching for the first stirring of his cock before he ripped the towel off and came to me.

All this I thought as I stood beneath the tree. He'd told me he sometimes still had sex with his wife so she didn't get suspicious. Knowing it was her he would be making love to instead of me was unbearable. I rushed home and drank half a bottle of whisky but even that didn't stop me from imagining them together.

You see, Ishbel, I am a fuck-up. A fantasist. A bloody lunatic. I will forgive you if you never want to see me again.

11

EXILE

The day of the christening was cool and bright. The wind had dropped too, and as I drank my first cup of tea just after the July dawn, the sea was calm and the horizon sharp. I was less worried about the food preparation than I was the people aspect of the day. Ishbel and Una had promised to look after me – Una believed the story that I was recovering from an illness and needed quiet.

The food had been delivered to Duncan's and was waiting for my creative magic. Ishbel collected me just after six and the work began. She had offered to help but I wanted to enjoy a real kitchen on my own. I had been cooking on a hearth for so many months that the idea of an electric oven and gas hob excited me. Duncan and Ewan had given the kitchen an extra clean and invited themselves to Una's for breakfast, so there was no distraction.

I lay all the ingredients out on the table and started sorting them according to what dish they were needed for. I hoped my choices weren't too unusual for the locals. I had no idea what they were used to. There was a diner in the village serving pizzas and such, but that was all I'd noticed in my brief visits to

Mid Yell. Lerwick might have restaurants but how often did people from Yell go to the mainland to eat out?

I realised how little I knew about my neighbours.

But it was too late to change the menu:

The dips – hummus and baba ganoush, served with crudités and breadsticks
Mains –
Salmon with fresh herbs and lemon
Souvlaki wraps with tzatziki
Salads –
Spelt, sweet potato and fennel
Greek salad to go with the souvlaki
Rocket, pear and feta
Sides –
Boiled black Shetland potatoes with burnt sage butter
Bread rolls from the local baker
Dessert –
Christening cake with berries and cream

I turned the radio on while I cooked but it was tuned to a local station and I couldn't understand a word of what was being said so I found a music station instead. This was my element – a decent kitchen, the raw ingredients for a meal and time to prepare it. I hadn't felt so happy for a long time.

As I was pushing the lamb onto the skewers with onion and green pepper in between chunks, Ishbel looked in.

'How's it all going?'

'Fine. On schedule.'

'And you're sure I can't do anything to help?'

'No, really – a job this size I prefer to do myself. I have a method.'

Once she'd gone, I got into the zone, the state of mind where everything had a rhythm to it, the sequence of tasks familiar, soothing. I heard a noise and realised I was humming. I hadn't sung since... I couldn't remember when.

I heard the bells ringing, announcing the service, calling one and all to come and witness the naming and entry into the church of this new soul. From the window I saw people gathering outside the kirk, chatting, laughing, looking to the sky, no doubt to comment on the fact that the rain had stayed away for this auspicious day. Then slowly they turned and entered through the tall wooden doors and were lost to sight. Opening the window, I could hear the strains of the organ playing the first hymn and I turned the radio off and sang along, surprised I remembered the words.

All things bright and beautiful,
All creatures great and small,
All things wise and wonderful,
The Lord God made them all.

The hymn reminded me of my father. We weren't a churchgoing family, but Dad was always whistling, and hymns seemed to be his favourites.

'Catchy tunes,' he'd say, and wink at me like we were sharing a big secret. He'd taught me to whistle and sometimes when I was little we'd go on walks together and have competitions to see who could whistle the loudest. He always won, of course, but he judged me the more tuneful. I'd swell with pride and imagine myself a nightingale.

At half past eleven there was a knock at the door and two girls walked in.

'I'm Bridie and this is Ann,' said the taller of the two. 'We're here to help.' They stared at me with undisguised curiosity. The hermit lady from the hill. Did she have two heads, a forked tongue, a scaly tail?

I wiped my forehead with my arm and smiled, repressing the urge to do a twirl for them so they could see for themselves that I was untailed and normal. 'Sit down for a minute – I'm not quite ready.'

They sat, now trying not to look at me too obviously. And I snuck a look at them. Sisters, perhaps even twins, they were dark-haired and pale-skinned, freckles dusting the bridges of their noses and upper cheeks. I poured two cups of tea from the pot I'd made and pushed them across. They raised their heads and smiled at me.

'It's nice to meet you. I just need to roll the wraps and dress the salads then you can start getting the food to the hall. How's it looking over there?'

'It's lovely – flowers and balloons everywhere and pink cloths on the tables.'

As Bridie and Ann left with the last of the food I sank into a chair and breathed a sigh of relief. I had done my part and would have a quick bite before clearing up and returning Duncan and Ewan's kitchen to its former state.

Ishbel, of course, had other ideas. She came in as I was taking my first mouthful of salad.

'You'll no be eating here on your own, Kirstie. Everyone is saying what a marvellous spread you've put on and they want you to come and eat with us.'

My heart sank. I should have known I wouldn't get away

with hiding in the kitchen. Taking some deep breaths, I nodded. 'I'll be over shortly.'

Ishbel looked at me as if to say, 'I've heard that one before,' so I reassured her that, for Lorna, I would make an appearance. I may not stay very long but I would say hello and congratulate Tavis and Catriona.

The drink had been flowing by the time I got there, and the adults were sitting back with full stomachs watching the children run around between the tables. Everyone turned to the door as I entered and Ishbel stood and invited me to her table where several other people sat, including Tavis and Catriona, with Lorna on her lap.

Trying not to look closely at anyone, especially the men, I made my way over and took a seat with my back to the room. Ishbel introduced me to her family – Tavis was the image of his mother, red-haired and round-faced, and Graeme must have taken after his father. He was taller and leaner, his hair darker. Lorna was staring up at her mother out of big blue eyes and crushing a strawberry in her hands, the red juice staining her dress and her mouth.

'Thanks for doing all this,' said Tavis, gesturing round the room at the food table and the empty plates. 'It was truly clinkin'.'

I looked at him, then at Ishbel. She laughed. 'He means it was splendid. And it was.'

'Aye,' said Catriona, taking Lorna's hand away from her mouth where the baby was trying to post the squished-up strawberry. 'The food was delicious, and it is so good to finally meet you. I was beginning to think Ishbel had made you up just so she could steal Lorna every Sunday and have her to herself!'

At our table, all eyes were on me, and I shifted in my seat. 'No, I'm real.' I felt myself redden. And then I realised I needed to say more. 'It's good to meet you too.'

Una came over to congratulate me on the food and then I heard a knife tapping a glass and Duncan cleared his throat.

'Kirstie, you're a very private person and we all respect that but today we welcome you into our wee community and thank you for the tasty food you made. So everyone, if you'll raise a glass, we'll drink to both our new lassies, Lorna and Kirstie.'

My heart thudded in my chest and I felt too hot. This was Lorna's day, and I didn't want to take any attention away from her, but Ishbel and Tavis were smiling and encouraged me to respond. I stood on shaky legs, turned to the assembly and looked over their heads so not a single face came into focus.

'Thank you for your welcome and for your patience with me living away on the hill. I'm glad you liked the menu, and it was my pleasure to make it for you all to share.'

Heart hammering in my chest, I sat down and took a gulp of champagne.

'There, that wasnae so bad, was it?' said Ishbel, giving my hand a squeeze. 'And I've already heard Duncan telling Sheila he's going to ask you to do the catering for his eightieth birthday party. You may find yourself in demand after today.'

I sat back and thought about what she'd said. I would gladly cater for Duncan, he had been so kind and welcoming, but did I want to go into business again, in however small a way? Could I do it and avoid having to deal with strangers – male strangers specifically? I decided not to think about it. Chances were, no one would ask, and if they did, I'd consider it then. Today was Lorna's day and when she put her arms out to me for a cuddle, I drew her in close and buried my nose in the sweet warmth of her neck as she chuckled.

That night I reflected on my success. Not the catering but the fact I had attended a social gathering and my obsession hadn't been triggered. Granted, I had not actually looked directly at any men apart from Tavis and Graeme, who were family, and Duncan and Ewan with whom I already felt safe, but perhaps it meant I could go out a bit more and keep myself and my 'illness' in check.

I also wrote another letter.

Dear Mother,
Lorna's christening went well. I couldn't be at the service because I was preparing the lunch, but I heard she smiled and laughed her way through it. She's a dear wee thing, so loving. I wonder if I was like her as a baby? My earliest memory is of falling off the swing at the park – do you remember? I hit my tooth on the seat as it swung back towards me, and it went grey and eventually fell out leaving me with a gap for years until the new tooth grew in. I still usually smile with my mouth shut.

I stopped for a moment, realising I'd been smiling more of late, that my life, while hardly busy, was richer than it had been for a long time and the anxiety I lived with so much of the time was dissipating. I put my chin in my hand and looked out through the open door, across the heathland to the sea. The sun was lowering, the sky showing the first signs of mauve, the water ruffled by a breeze. Taking a deep breath, drawing it into me, I filled myself with its gentle comfort.

I don't think I told you that Ewan took Grandy's violin and had it repaired. He played at the lunch in the hall after the christening. It has a lovely tone and the men pushed the tables back and everyone got up and danced to the old tunes.

I hadn't danced, of course. I didn't know the steps and couldn't trust myself to be too close to any strangers. But I tapped my feet and drummed out the beat on the table with a spoon.

So, Mother, here I am in the bosom of our family. They are good people. They look after each other and look out for each other. I suppose that's what communities are all about really. I thought it would be annoying, everyone knowing your business, so kept myself apart. But it's actually been okay.

I thought how little of my business anyone here actually knew and how liberating it was. I could make up any past I wanted, delete the bits I didn't want to own, add in details to make me sound interesting and engaging. And yet I knew that in reality I would tell as little as possible and my new neighbours could fill in the gaps as they chose. If they chose.

It's light here until almost eleven at night. You must remember the long summer evenings, the softness of the sun as it fades towards the long twilight and finally deepens into the brief night. But do you remember the night sky? The trillions of stars sending their brilliance through space and across thousands of years, so they may not even exist any more when we finally see them – they may have imploded and become black holes. They make me feel small. They make me realise that whatever we do in our lifetime, it is insignificant in comparison. I find it a comforting thought.
I hope you are well,
Kirstie x

My hand had hovered above the page for several moments, as I wondered whether I should add the 'x' at the end of the letter. In the end it seemed to act on its own, as I turned to look at a bird flying across the shore. I smiled when I saw it. My hand with a will of its own, sending an olive branch to my mother.

Almost by return of post, I received a letter from my mother. It was longer than any I'd received until then but although she must have got mine before she sent hers, she made no response to anything I'd said.

Dear Kirsten,
I thought you should know I have decided to go away for a while. Your father left rather a lot more money than I had thought, and I've decided to enjoy some of it. I always thought he financed his 'business trips' but it looks like he was as stingy with his other 'associates' as he was with me – they must have paid for their little weekend mini-breaks and holidays to who knows where. When I thought he was spending money like it was going out of fashion and I was scrimping and saving to make ends meet, he was stashing thousands away, who knows who or what for? I'm going on a cruise. I haven't had a proper holiday since that terrible one in Italy when you were young. And before that the only other one was to Cornwall with your father when I was pregnant with you, and it rained every day so we came home three days early, not having anything to do and nothing to say to each other that couldn't be said at home.
I'll send a postcard.
Mother.

I read the letter several times. I couldn't imagine my mother on a cruise, lying on a sunlounger, cocktail in hand. Would she talk to any of the other passengers? She only really had one friend, Molly, whom she'd known since before I was born. And the neighbours, Harry and June, who had moved in next door when I was about eight and were at least ten years older than my parents. I hoped she'd enjoy herself.

Interesting that my father turned out to have been a bit of a squirrel. He'd had a well-paying job, and over the years I'd seen letters on the hall table from pension companies – presumably he had extra money coming in after retirement. He never spent a penny on the house or his family, so he'd probably left a nice pot for my mother.

I was surprised she had known about my father's affairs all along. But then I realised that if I knew, she must have too. He didn't try that hard to hide them, coming back from his 'business trips' all tanned and smiling. I'd known since I was in my early teens they were no such thing when I'd seen my father and a flashy woman in a red coat out together. They got out of a taxi, crossed the road and entered a posh pub, his hand resting on the small of her back in a way it never rested on my mother's. And they were both smiling, which gave the game away.

It was the beginning of the end for us. I couldn't move past this betrayal. I was meant to be his special girl. Our interactions became hostile, and in the end, minimal. I couldn't forgive him, and he hated the fact that I made it clear I knew what was going on. I don't think he felt guilty though. It was more that he'd been discovered doing something he thought he'd managed to keep secret. His pride was hurt more than his morals.

When he came home, I asked him about his trip. It was then I realised how long his lies had been going on. He answered every question without hesitation, without looking away, without embarrassment. Not a blush, not a sheen of sweat broke out on his forehead. He didn't change the subject or make an excuse and leave the room. He lied as easily as he told the truth. Maybe he didn't know the difference anymore.

I read the letter from my mother once more. I wanted her to

have a good time, but I was surprised to find myself feeling disappointed she'd chosen to go on a cruise rather than come to see me.

The next morning I ventured into town. I say town, but of course I mean Mid Yell, population not very many. Some teenagers loitered around the shop and two women clutched the hands of their young children, dragging the reluctant youngsters towards the school.

I knocked on Duncan's door, leaning into the alcove to escape the wind.

'Kirstie, what a surprise. Come away in,' said Ewan, stepping back to allow me to enter.

Duncan was sitting at the kitchen table, a cup of tea the colour of tanned leather and a plate of oatcakes and something that looked like blood sausage in front of him.

He turned and smiled as if my visit was an everyday occurrence and offered me some black pudding.

'Not for me, thanks,' I said, 'but a cup of tea would go down well.'

'I'll make a fresh pot and then I'm away out,' said Ewan, and busied himself at the sink. I wondered what he thought of my relationship with Duncan – did he think there was something going on between us? The idea almost made me laugh.

'Don't go on my account,' I said.

'I'm not. I've an appointment to keep.'

When he'd gone, Duncan and I settled at the table. He showed no curiosity as to the reason for my visit. In fact, he said nothing at all, and we sat in a comfortable silence for a few minutes, sipping our tea in the warm kitchen.

'I had a letter from my mother,' I said at last. 'She's going on a holiday – a cruise.'

'Aye,' said Duncan, nodding and looking into the distance.

'Oh – did you know?'

'Nay, but she'd like a cruise.'

I thought about that. How would he know what she'd like or dislike, he hadn't seen her for so long he could probably pass her on the street and not know it was her.

'I was hoping she might come here to see me but apparently I'm not worth the time.' I was surprised at my own words. By the anger in my voice.

Duncan focused on me with his sea-grey eyes. 'Mebbe it's no you she's staying away from, lass.' He looked away again and continued, 'It's no an easy thing to return to your past, to come back to the people you left behind and find it all changed.' His face held such sadness and as he lifted his cup to his lips his hand shook.

'Nothing's changed here, surely?'

'Perhaps not, but we're all older and mebbe not the wiser.' He shrugged.

'You still miss her, after all these years?'

'Aye, lass, I do.'

'But she left so long ago.'

'Love doesnae obey the rules of time,' he said, shaking his head.

I wondered what he would have thought of my mother had he met her again years after she left. He held on to an idealised memory of her that I couldn't reconcile to the real thing.

'Duncan, she changed. Maybe it was the rape–'

The old man sucked in a deep breath and closed his eyes. 'A terrible thing, a terrible, terrible thing,' he whispered.

'Yes, it was. Maybe it was that, or perhaps it was homesickness and then being married to my father that made her what she was, but she became a – different – woman.' I stopped myself from adding that she was bitter, worn down by life. 'I have very few memories of her ever being happy or taking delight in anything. I don't think she's deserved your love all these years.'

'Love doesnae have to be deserved, it just is. It pains me to hear her life was so unhappy and that you have such an impression of her. If she'd no gone away, things would ha' been different.'

'You might have been my father – you'd surely have made a better one than the one I got.'

Duncan smiled. 'You, my daughter. I'd ha' been so proud.'

I put my hand over his. 'Me too,' I said and then we both took deep breaths and wiped our eyes.

'I'm sorry I said what I did about my mother. I should have let you keep your memory of her unsullied. It's just that we know different versions of her. I wish I'd known her before – you know.'

Duncan sat up straighter, his fingers drumming on the table and the faraway look in his eyes again that I'd come to recognise as him trying to make a decision. I sat waiting. The tap dripped and the fridge hummed.

We both jumped when there was a knock on the window and Una walked in, red-cheeked from the wind. She untied her scarf and greeted us with her cheery smile.

'Not interrupting anything, am I?' she asked.

'Nay, not a thing,' said Duncan. 'Kirstie just came by for a cup o' tea.'

I pasted a neutral expression over my disappointment. I had been sure Duncan was about to tell me something more about my mother.

I had nothing else to do all day, but I didn't feel up to any more socialising, so as soon as I could without appearing rude, I left and made my way back to the croft, head down, hands in pockets, dejected. As I walked, I went over the conversation with Duncan and became certain he knew more about my mother than he was letting on. Something he had considered telling me until Una spoiled the moment.

As I made my dinner, I planned to go and see Duncan again the following day but woke the next morning with a sore throat and glands the size of golf balls in my neck. I could hardly swallow a cup of tea and certainly didn't have the energy to walk down to the village and share my germs with anyone. For the next few days I kept myself warm and drank gallons of tea and hot lemon with whisky in it, and tried not to spend too much time trying to guess what Duncan had been going to tell me. If anything.

In the end, to stop myself from idle thoughts, and to make the days go faster, I got back to my confession.

12

THE CONFESSION

I continued watching the house as often as I could. I'd go when I didn't have any work on in the evening and sometimes even when I did but couldn't make myself stay away. I'd leave someone else in charge and run to the Tube, trembling with anticipation. Once or twice I saw Ed's wife entering or leaving. A tall, attractive blonde who favoured jeans and fitted jackets. I had imagined her in twinsets and pearls, a dowdy, drab woman who couldn't keep her man. I hated her.

Although I watched from behind the same tree each time, I was always careful to wear different clothes so as not to be recognised by any nosy locals. The nights I was rewarded with a glimpse of Ed, I would go home in a haze of joy, imagining the two of us together. I would lie in bed reliving every moment of my observation, interpreting his movements and gestures. When, at the window, he paused before drawing the curtains, I was certain he knew I was watching and was letting me feast my eyes on him before he reluctantly turned away. If the upstairs lights didn't go on while I was there, I took it as a sign he had to be careful, that he mustn't let his wife know about us. I convinced myself he wanted to be with me, and he'd only drawn away because his wife had become suspicious. He was, after all, a kind man who didn't want to upset anyone.

Thinking of it now I am so ashamed. How could I have thought these things? But at the time, how could I not? I was gripped by something more powerful than logic.

One evening, when I'd been watching his house for some weeks, I was exiting Holland Park station, head down, slipping my Oyster card back into its case when I bumped into someone. Looking up, an apology already on my lips, I found myself staring into Ed's eyes. My words died where they were as my throat tightened and adrenaline shot through my body.

'Kirstie,' he said. 'What are you doing in this neck of the woods?'

He'd spoken to me! The words may not have been the most romantic, but his voice was soft and his eyes, as they peered into mine, were loving, weren't they?

What could I say? A lie? The truth?

There was a thin streak of rationality in me that knew the truth would be my undoing, and I let it guide my words. 'I have a friend near here – we're...'

'How have you been?'

He wasn't interested in my friend, my excuses. I saw lust in his eyes and my body strained to be closer to his, my breath coming in snatches, mingling with his as we stood inches apart.

'My wife's out tonight.'

I shut my eyes and took a deep breath. He loved me.

We went back to his house. He ushered me up the front steps looking around for any prying eyes but there were none. I don't remember the house from that night. He was so horny he was on me almost before we even got to the stairs, but I insisted we make it to the bedroom and he wasn't in a state to refuse. We fucked like rabbits in the marital bed, on the Egyptian cotton sheets he slept between with his wife.

Afterwards, I wrote my name in the sweat on his chest and he took my hand and kissed it.

'You'd better have a shower before you go,' he said. 'You wouldn't want to turn up at your friend's house looking like that.' He gestured towards my hair, my glistening body.

'I don't have to go yet,' I said. 'We could have a shower together.'

He rolled off the bed and started picking up his clothes. 'No can do – Vanessa will be home soon. Off you go, be a good girl.'

The words stung. Not, as you're no doubt thinking, the patronising 'good girl', but the idea of Vanessa coming home, of her being there with him after I'd been banished. But even in my madness, in my obsession with him, I realised I had to play the game. For now, at least, I was the 'other woman'.

At home I wrote in my diary that I had never been happier, I had proof that Ed loved me and couldn't live without me. No, he hadn't suggested we see each other again but I knew that he expected me to turn up at the station so that we could see each other, and if Vanessa was at home, we'd snatch whatever brief moments we could, and if she was out, we'd have the evening together making plans, working out how we could spend our lives together. It was only a matter of time.

<hr>

I said there was a rational part to me but in reality it was tiny and easily overridden. I spent hours, days reliving our time together, planning our future, naming our children, dreaming about holidays in exotic places, sex in hot tubs, in lifts, on silken sheets, in the sea – wherever we could be alone.

My staff pulled together to take up the slack, appease disgruntled clients whom I had forgotten to call back or hadn't sent information to when I'd said I would. My business was a well-oiled machine by then, my staff hand-picked and able to work without me looking over their shoulders all the time. Until I forgot to turn up to a job. Between making the agreement and saying goodbye to the client and turning to write the job in my calendar, it slipped out of my mind altogether, there being little space for anything but Ed.

'Kirstie, this has to stop – you have to focus on the business. We can't afford to make another mistake like this one, it'll ruin our reputation,' said Svetlana. She'd just got off the phone having had her ear blasted off by the company whose convention we had failed to supply with dinner.

Svetlana had been with me for several years by then and knew of my roller-coaster love life. She was one of the group who commiserated with each other at regular intervals when our relationships were going down the tubes or partners were straying, or we wished they were, but they were hanging around instead.

'You're right,' I said. 'Thank you for talking to–' I didn't even know who I'd let down so badly. I had refused to answer the call when it was put through because I was too full of having seen Ed the night before. We'd spent an evening together again the week after that first time but since then I hadn't seen him for weeks and I'd been distraught and distracted. What did it mean? I was sure his wife was behind it, was preventing us from seeing each other. I had to work out a way to take her out of the picture, it was the only way. And then, the night before, I had seen him at the station and tried to talk to him, but he was talking to another man and didn't even acknowledge me as he swept past. I had gone home, hurt then angry and finally forlorn, and spent the evening with my whisky bottle yet again.

I did manage to heave my mind back to work. The offer of a free event for the company I had failed so badly prevented them from telling the world about my mistake. By the time I'd taken the MD out for lunch and apologised for the tenth time, she was laughing at the whole episode.

'You should have seen the faces of all those people when we realised it was going to be pizza or nothing! Thank God we didn't get the drink through you – at least we could all get drunk on Pimms and champagne. I heard one of the managers telling his wife that it was all the rage to eat low and drink high!'

I smiled with her, my reputation saved this time, but I knew I couldn't afford to fuck up again. I put Svetlana in charge of tendering for work and took a week off to try and pull myself together. That was the official reason anyway. In reality, of course, I spent the week with Ed – in my head, if not in body.

I know you can't imagine the level of obsession, Ishbel, and you may well think I'm exaggerating it in order to get your sympathy, or to dodge responsibility for my actions. I would think the same if I hadn't been through it and someone told me this story. But the truth is, I was totally unable to see what I was doing at the time. It felt normal. No – not even that, I didn't give it any consideration at all. It was just what it was – my life. I was on the path to destruction.

13

EXILE

Duncan came the following Sunday afternoon just as Ishbel and Lorna were getting ready to leave. He ambled up the track, hands behind his back, watching the sky rather than where he was placing his feet. I looked up, too, and saw a flock of birds wheeling around above us, knowing he would tell me what they were and where they nested while I made him a cup of tea.

'Sorry I've no been to see you,' he said. 'Caught masel' a fine dose of something. Didnae want to share it with you.'

I smiled. 'I think we shared it with each other. I've been a bit off colour too. Better now?'

He nodded. Then he turned to Ishbel and asked how she'd been and how work was. Then he gently placed his old, work-worn hand on Lorna's head. But she was tired and fractious, and Ishbel took her home soon after Duncan's arrival. He sat at my table, having hung his cap on the hook by the door, and I could feel his eyes on me as I filled the kettle and put it on the range. Then I sat opposite him and waited.

Glancing out the window, he said, 'Arctic terns. They'll be heading south soon enough.'

I nodded. 'They're not rare, are they?'

'Och, no, but they migrate all the way to the Antarctic for their summer doon there, and then all the way back here again next year. They have the longest migration of any bird on the planet.'

'Is there anything you don't know about birds, Duncan?'

'Aye, plenty, but I do ken a bit about the ones around here. We see a few rare ones too, but not so often, of course. There was a wee purple sandpiper doon on the shore t'other day, and what I believe was a Siberian rubythroat, though I didnae get close enough for certainty.'

I poured the tea and offered him a biscuit which he dunked in his drink. Gazing past me out the window, his eyes took on a faraway look. His biscuit, too long in the hot liquid, fell apart but he didn't seem to notice.

'I been thinking about what you said about your maether, and it fair breaks my heart that you have such a poor impression of her. I think it's time I telt you more, if you've a mind to listen.'

I leant forward, my pulse quickening. This was what he had been going to say when Una interrupted us, I was sure of it. Duncan felt the need to paint me a positive portrait of my mother to balance out my own.

'Go on,' I said, expecting him to tell me more about her life growing up on the island.

'I havenae told you the whole truth about your maether. She swore me to secrecy – so many secrets she made me keep – but it seems to me mebbe it's time to speak out, for 'tis not right you dinnae know her story and I think it will help if you do. She didnae want her maether to know what she was doing, and although it went against what I thought was right, I kept the letters from her–'

'Letters? She wrote to you after she left?' I sat up straighter, stopped fiddling with my teaspoon.

'Aye, she did for a while.' He nodded and took a long drink of his tea. I thought he was swallowing all his feelings with it but still he looked sad.

'Go on,' I prompted gently.

'At the time, it seemed like the only thing to do – I worried that if I didnae hide the letters she would stop writing, but when I look back, she had no idea if I was keeping her secret, for she never let me know her address so I couldnae write back.' Duncan shook his head sadly and shrugged.

'But surely in a community this size the postmaster would have known who the letters were from and told my grandmother?'

'Aye, true enough. That's why in the first one, which she sent from Aberdeen as soon as she got there, she told me she'd write to the post office in Lerwick, and they'd hold the letters for me until I fetched them. She knew I used to go there regularly for work on the boats.'

She'd been so cunning, desperate to maintain some connection with her old life. I wondered why she never allowed Duncan to write to her – was it because she couldn't bear to hear if nobody was missing her, or she couldn't bear it if they were?

Duncan continued.

'Sometimes, I would see Aileen or Jimmy, her parents, and I would be so near to telling them that I had to run in the other direction. You see, Aileen came to regret sending her off, and took to praying for her return, and Jimmy was never the same again after she went – she'd been the apple of his eye.'

'Wait – did you say her mother sent her away?'

Duncan nodded. 'Aye.'

I felt angry. Not *with* my mother, for a change, but *for* her. Had her mother known about the rape and sent her off anyway? Or perhaps because of it? Whatever had happened, it seemed such a waste. All these people torn apart, never to see each other again. What was wrong with the women in this family – the lack of empathy, the distance between them all?

Us all.

And then it hit me. My mother had been in the same position with her mother – we had both been cast adrift at an early age. I had made the move away from my parents out of choice, it was true, but neither of them had wasted their breath trying to stop me, and they hadn't made any attempt to contact me after I left – any visits or calls were initiated by me, either because I needed something or from a sense of guilt. I had been expecting – hoping – that my move to Yell would have made my mother more interested in me somehow but it was never going to happen. Her life was one of endings.

And yet, with the anger at my grandmother came a quiet stirring of empathy for my mother.

Duncan carried on. 'The letters were long and telt of her life in England, almost as if she needed a witness to it. I was not surprised when the first one arrived. After all, I thought she was in Aberdeen and had no reason to keep it a secret. But the next one was a great shock to me. A great shock.' He wiped a hand over his eyes and laid it, shaking slightly, back on the table. 'She was not in Aberdeen at all, and didnae know where she might end up. I was mighty worried for her but there was nothing I could do.'

'You never told anyone about the letters?'

He shook his head. 'Never. I thought it was my duty to Morag to do as she asked, hard though it was. When Aileen lay dying, she wanted to ask her daughter for forgiveness. I couldnae say anything.'

'Because you'd promised not to?'

'Nay, lass. Because in her letters, Morag never gave it.'

Once again, Duncan stopped talking. He sat with his eyes

shut, his breath quiet but for the occasional sniff. I put a hand on his arm, and we sat in silence as the setting sun spangled the sea, the light fracturing into a million shards, each one a diamond on the water.

When the light began to fade I got up to light the lamp. We hadn't said anything for a long time, lost in our thoughts. 'I'll make us some tea,' I said.

It was as if he hadn't heard me.

'You know nothing of your maether's life at all?' He looked at me then with such tenderness I got a lump in my throat.

'She never talked about it. It wasn't until she was tracked down by the solicitors when her parents died that I even knew she had any family.'

Duncan rubbed his eyes and shook his head. 'She needed to put it all out of her head I 'spect.'

I nodded and shrugged. I had no idea why she'd never said anything.

He started talking, closing his eyes again as if replaying the images in his mind as the words came out of his mouth.

'Before she left, Morag telt me it was her decision to go, but in her letter she said her maether had sent her away when she found out what had happened. She didn't say how her maether knew but Aileen had said if she could find out, anyone could, and she couldn't live with the shame of it, her daughter a mockit wee hussy. Her maether was a God-fearing soul, that's the truth.

'So, Morag left. She never stayed in Aberdeen. She telt me she was going for the secretarial, and her maether thought she did but she didnae. Morag had other ideas. A wee bit of money, a few clothes in her satchel and she was off. She said she was so angry with her maether for sending her away she was going as far as she could, where Aileen would never find her, even if she wanted to.'

I tried to imagine my mother leaving. The anger towards her

own mother for sending her away, the fear of not knowing what was to come. I knew my mother was able to hold on to anger for long periods of time. There had been days during my childhood when she barely spoke to me because I'd done something to annoy or offend her. When I was young, I'd tried to make it up to her, to right whatever wrong I had committed, but as a teenager, I'd fanned the flames, taunting her and increasing her rage. I wasn't going to let her know how hurt I was, how rejected I felt. I didn't really understand my feelings myself at the time, and certainly couldn't have articulated them. Now I knew what had happened, her behaviour began to make more sense.

Duncan carried on.

'She wrote that she was helped by a kind lady when she got off the ferry in Aberdeen, and went to Edinburgh with her, thinking the lady, Mrs McCready, might take her in or help her find work. But when they got to the city, Mrs McCready was met by her husband and said goodbye to Morag, leaving her alone again, and afeared in an unfamiliar place.'

I thought of my journey to the island, the reverse of my mother's trip. I had thought Edinburgh an attractive city, one that in other circumstances I might have stayed in for a while and explored. But I was used to London and a city's hustle and bustle. It must have been terrifying for my mother, whose experience until then had been a few trips into Lerwick, which even now is hardly a throbbing metropolis.

'She said she felt so far away in Edinburgh but not far enough. I didnae understand how she could feel that way, but it wasnae for me to know. She just wanted to get as far away as possible, out of Scotland even. And yet, she telt me she missed her da and her brothers, Robbie in particular. And she said she missed me–' Duncan reddened and his voice faltered. I laid a hand on his but said nothing. Anything I could have said would have sounded trite.

He took a breath and started again. 'She wrote about the places she passed through. Her second night away was spent in Newcastle. She was in England – the land of the Sassenachs she called it, where she couldn't understand what people were saying and there was grime on all the buildings. And she carried on. South. She got to London and knew she couldn't stay there because it was too big and noisy and no one looked at her, no one smiled, everyone rushed along the streets looking miserable. Then she took another train.'

'And ended up in Brighton,' I said. 'That's where I was born and raised. As far away from here as she could get.' I sighed, and Duncan nodded slowly.

'She never telt me the name of the town she lived in. I think she thought I might hae gone to look for her, and I might've too. But she didnae want to be found, not then, not ever.'

He lifted his eyes from his hands and gazed out the window as if looking for her out on the hill.

It was dark out. 'I'll make us some dinner,' I said and got up to add some peat to the hearth.

'Not for me, lass, I'm away home, but thank you.' He stood and took my hand in both of his. 'I'm glad you've come back, Kirstie.' Then he let out a sigh, took his cap from the hook and walked out the door with a backward wave.

After he'd gone, I sat thinking about what he'd told me, filling in details for myself – her feelings, the scenery she'd passed that I knew from my own journey. And I imagined Duncan receiving her letters, the envelopes battered and worn from the mailbags, the postmarks smudged. And I thought of him taking them out in private and reading and rereading them until he knew them by heart, as I'm sure he did.

I poured myself a large whisky and sat until the sun started coming up.

I was left with mixed emotions. Sadness, admiration,

outrage and curiosity. I could hardly equate this frightened young woman with the later version of her that I knew. I realised how naïve she must have been when she left. I had been the same age when I left home and was also full of anger but hope as well. She seemed to have none of the latter, just a desperate need to get as far away from her birthplace as possible.

For days after Duncan's visit and his revelations, I couldn't stop thinking about my mother and her departure from the island. She'd been so afraid but so determined. I had no idea if she ever regretted leaving or staying away. And then I remembered the map she'd given me of the village and the way to the croft and realised she had missed her home all her life. I wondered if she'd ever told anyone in her new life about what had happened, but I doubted it. If I knew her at all, she would have secured her memories and her feelings in a deep part of her mind and kept them there where they couldn't escape and take her unawares. From carefree girl roaming the hills with her friends to bitter, isolated woman in – how long had it taken – minutes, months, years? Was there an instant in which she realised she would never go back? Was that the moment she hardened into the depressed, caustic woman I knew, or had it been a longer process with disappointments and loneliness slowly taking their toll?

I also thought about how Duncan had loved my mother in such an uncomplicated way and how he still loved her, or his memory of her, after all these years. I was envious of her for that. Not because I wanted Duncan for myself, but because of his feelings for her.

14

THE CONFESSION

For several months, Ed and I would meet at his house when his wife was out. It wasn't enough but it was better than nothing.

I was happy, most of the time.

One time, after we'd made love, Ed went to have a shower and I went down to get a glass of water. It was a beautiful new granite and steel kitchen, every surface gleaming and top of the range appliances fitting perfectly into their allotted spaces. I stood at the breakfast bar sipping my water and noticed the calendar had been taken off the wall and was sitting next to the fruit bowl. A date had been circled about eight weeks hence with 'Hugo's 21st' written inside it, and a note to remind the writer (Ed's wife I presumed) to call some caterers for quotes.

As I re-entered the bedroom Ed came out of the shower drying his hair. I was still in the nude and he started getting hard again when he saw me, but his wife was due home soon and it was time for me to leave.

The next day, I wrote a short note to the wife mentioning that a mutual friend, whose name I failed to produce, had mentioned she was looking for a caterer for her son's birthday party. I included my card and a brochure and waited for her call, certain in the knowledge I would be the caterer for her, even if it meant making a loss on the job.

Sure enough, a couple of days later, I got the call. Vanessa Bannerman did indeed need a caterer and liked the look of my brochure. I offered to go round and talk to her about her plans and how best I could help her fulfil them.

I took great care with my appearance for our first meeting, choosing a pair of trousers and a fitted jacket, little make-up and neat hair. I dabbed some of the perfume Ed had given me behind each ear and on my wrists. Looking at myself in the mirror I saw a confident, well-groomed woman, which belied the butterflies cavorting in my stomach.

Half an hour later, I stood on Ed's front doorstep taking deep breaths as I heard footsteps approach. The door opened and there she was: the wife. A little taller than me, and thinner, she had the indefinable something that alerts others to the fact she came from money. The velvet hairband holding back her blonde bob, the narrow feet in their patent leather flats and delicate ankles showing beneath her capri pants. And more than any of these signs was her bearing, the confident manner in which she inhabited her space. Every gesture, every movement, quietly and without fuss, declared her sovereignty over this territory. Her absolute right to live the life she lived with all the trappings of wealth. I had a nose for these things, having never had them myself.

She smiled and invited me in, taking the hand I thrust out and shaking it warmly.

'Let's talk in here,' she said, leading the way into the lounge with its tall windows and expensive furniture. She gestured for me to take a seat on the navy brocade sofa on one side of the fireplace and sat opposite me on the other side of the Javanese coffee table, on a matching armchair, knees and delicate ankles together, shins slightly angled, like the queen.

'Thank you for coming all this way,' she said.

'No trouble at all,' I said. 'All part of the service. Now, what did you have in mind?'

I had to take control of the conversation so she would forget to ask which of her friends had recommended me.

She shrugged. 'Well, what I want and what Hugo wants are two different things.' She laughed. 'He wants a bit of finger food and as much booze as we can fit in the marquee, and I prefer a sit-down meal so at least I know he and his friends are lining their stomachs. They'll be going out clubbing after the formal part of the evening, you see.'

I nodded and smiled a smile that said, 'Youngsters these days, eh?'

'I see you understand,' said Vanessa.

'Of course,' I said. 'But in my experience, the young people will enjoy whatever you organise for them as long as they have their friends around, and I think your idea of filling them up is a good one.'

I had drawn up several sample menus after her call, from finger food to six-course banquet. The one I pushed over to her was a three-course sit-down meal, with alternatives for vegetarians, vegans and gluten-free options.

'Was this the sort of thing you were thinking of?' I asked as she glanced at it.

'Or perhaps this?' I passed another piece of paper over. This one offered several options for finger food to be passed around with pre-dinner drinks, then two sit-down courses and birthday cake.

'Oh, this looks good,' she said. 'Hugo gets his finger food and I get my sit-down dinner.'

'How many people will there be?' I asked.

'About a hundred, I think. We're having it in a marquee in the garden.'

I'd never seen the garden, having only been to the house at night, and having other things on my mind when I was there.

We spent some time talking menus and other arrangements – waiting staff, logistics and use of the kitchen for last-minute preparation, and then Vanessa showed me the garden. It was large for London, certainly bigger than the postage-stamp-sized piece of concrete outside my flat. Carefully tended flower beds were bursting with dahlias and roses, lupins and hollyhocks. A shock of bougainvillea trailed over one wall and wisteria over the other. There was enough space for the main marquee and a smaller one for the food and drink to be served from.

'Perfect,' I said. 'I'll prepare the quote and get it to you as soon as possible. I'm sure you're talking to other caterers and want this finalised as soon as possible?'

'Other caterers – yes, of course.' She pursed her lips. 'Actually, no. I haven't got round to it yet. I thought I'd meet you first and see what you had to offer since you came so highly recommended by...'

'Well, thank you,' I said. 'I hope you like what you've seen?'

'Yes, very much. Really, I'm happy to go with you. I've got a lot on in the next few weeks, and it would be marvellous if you could just take care of everything.'

'You don't want to discuss it with your husband?' I asked, heart pounding.

'Oh, no. Ed won't want to be bothered with any of this, he's too busy at work. He'll be happy whatever we do.'

'Consider it done then,' I said, and let my shoulders subside.

I liked her. I didn't want to, but I couldn't help it. She was one of those people who was in charge one minute, and in the next was happy to let others take over. In my experience, they were the best people to work for, as long as I let them think they were the ones coming up with the ideas and I was only the hired help.

Along with the quote I sent, I offered to organise the whole event, from hiring the marquees to the decorations and security staff if they were required. Vanessa rang almost as soon as I had emailed her.

'Do you really mean it? That would be fantastic. I told you I'd be busy over the next few weeks, didn't I?'

'Yes. That's why I thought you might prefer someone to take on the party for you. Shall we meet again to discuss your thoughts?'

And so it was that the next day I was at Ed's house again, sitting with his wife drinking wine and planning his son's 21st birthday party.

'I can't believe you're doing all this – my mother's ill and I have to go and see to her every day. Daddy can't cope, and Janet, their help, has broken her hip. It couldn't have come at a worse time.' She shook her head and looked at me. 'That sounds awful, doesn't it? I am sorry for poor Janet, of course I am, but...'

I smiled and put a hand over hers. 'I know what you mean. You poor thing. It must be awful for you. I can't tell you how happy it makes me that I can relieve you of the burden of Hugo's party.'

'I'm so glad I found you.' She poured us another glass of wine and raised hers. 'Cheers.'

Over the next couple of weeks I organised everything Vanessa wanted down to the last detail. I emailed her with all the arrangements, and she invited me round to go over it all face to face. I was beginning to think she was rather lonely, and she was certainly feeling overwhelmed by her filial duties.

'Do you not have brothers or sisters who can help?' I asked.

'No. My brothers think looking after parents is the

daughter's duty. Anyway, one lives in Edinburgh and the other is in Chicago, so they're not much help.'

'Perhaps I could make up a few meals for your parents so you don't have to do it all?'

Vanessa looked like she'd won the lottery. 'Would you? That would be marvellous. Nothing too fancy, just plain home cooking.'

'A couple of casseroles and a chicken-and-vegetable tagine, short on the spices?'

'Brilliant. You're an angel.'

She hugged me when I left. We'd hardly spoken about the party.

Interestingly, when I saw Ed during that time, I managed to put Vanessa out of my mind completely. I thought of her, if I thought of her at all, as 'the wife', not the charming, rather overwhelmed woman I was getting to know.

One evening, after Ed and I had made love, I sat at her dressing table and ran my hands over her possessions – silver-handled hairbrush, earrings strewn about, necklaces hanging over the mirror. I dipped a finger into her moisturiser and smoothed it over my cheeks, lifted her perfume to squirt some in my décolletage.

'Don't do that!' said Ed, coming up behind me. 'She'll smell it when she comes in if you spray that bloody stuff everywhere.'

I smiled. He was protecting our affair from the wife. I noticed he never referred to her by name when we were together either. Turning, I stood and pressed against him, felt him harden again. He pushed me against the wall and had me there, hard, fast, sweaty.

15
___

EXILE

I wanted to ask Duncan what else Mother had written to him – he had said a couple of things about her life in England and I knew he had more letters. I would have liked to have read them for myself, to know all the details, but they were his and he seemed to want to guard them for a bit longer. He had, after all, kept them to himself for so long, I think he was still in two minds about sharing them at all.

I continued to see him most days. He'd stroll up the path for a cup of tea, or we'd go out walking together and he'd give me nature lessons. Sometimes he'd tell me more about my mother's childhood. She had roamed over heathland with a tribe of children, broken her wrist falling into an old peat-cutting trench and been top of the class in English. She had loved writing poetry and told her classmates she was going to be a famous poet when she grew up. While I envied her happy, people-filled childhood, it had done nothing to prepare her for life beyond Yell.

I was struck by the difference in our childhoods, and the differences the thirty or so years between her departure and mine had made to our experiences of leaving home. By 1990 when I left Brighton, it was quite acceptable for women to live on their own and have a career. In 1957, I doubted that was the case.

One day, Duncan made his way up the path faster than usual and was puffing by the time he reached my door.

'What on earth's the matter?' I asked.

He was bent over, hands on his knees, trying to regain his breath. 'It's Ishbel,' he said, 'she's been in an accident. She's in the hospital in Lerwick.'

I felt the colour drain from my face. 'Is she okay – no, silly question, she's in hospital, of course she's not. What happened?'

'A car hit her. She is going to be all right – but she's concussed and has a broken leg and some bruised ribs.'

'Oh, thank God it's not worse.'

'Aye. I was wondering if you'd drive me over to see her. I said I'd take some things to her in the hospital since Tavis and Catriona are away in Edinburgh for a few days but neither Ewan nor I have driven for many a year the noo, and I'm not sure I want to drive in all the traffic of Lerwick.'

His idea and mine about the traffic in Lerwick were clearly different. My concern wasn't for the driving but for the people I might meet. But this wasn't the time to think of me. Ishbel needed us, and I would deal with the consequences.

I grabbed my bag and my Goretex jacket and we set off. Ewan was waiting for us at Ishbel's house.

I hadn't been there before – she always came to see me. It was a small stone cottage on the outskirts of the village, with a neat garden of hardy flowers – no doubt Duncan could have told me what they were had we the time to talk. Inside, it was sparsely furnished and very tidy. A pile of children's books on the coffee table and a basket of toys in one corner was proof that Lorna spent time there with her.

'You'll find what she wants in her room,' said Ewan,

nodding his head to indicate the stairs. 'She wants a nightgown, some under-drawers and toiletries as well as an outfit to come home in when they let her out.' He had reddened at the mention of the personal items and turned away from me as he spoke. He and Duncan were such innocents in some ways, and so worldly in others.

I found what she needed in the neat bedroom and tiny bathroom, an overnight bag to put them all in and joined the brothers downstairs again.

'Well, we'd better get going I suppose,' said Ewan. He looked like he was being led to the gallows.

'Aye,' said Duncan, who didn't look much better.

'Do you go to the mainland much?' I asked.

They looked at each other. 'Last time was about ten years ago, for the Up-Helly-Aa festival in January – we used to go every year, but it got too much for us – too many tourists and the streets all crowded. 'Twas no the place for the likes of us anymore.'

'Ten years?'

'Aye. We've no need of the place the noo.'

'You mean you literally haven't been there in all that time?'

'What would we need there that we canna get here?'

'Well, I'm happy to go on my own if you'd rather stay here?'

They looked so relieved I smiled.

'Are you sure, lassie – will you find your way?'

'I'm from London, which is a hell of a lot bigger than Lerwick. I'm sure I'll manage.'

Their car was an ancient Volvo Estate which they had kept in pristine condition, but which lacked power steering and so felt like driving a tank. There was no satnav either, of course. They gave me detailed directions about how to get to the ferry and then to Lerwick, which were redundant as there was only the one main road. Once in Lerwick, I was to ask the way to the Gilbert Bain Hospital. What could go wrong?

As it happened, nothing, except I was exhausted by the time I got to the hospital and thought my arms would never feel the same again. I found a parking space easily and made my way to the main door, head down looking at my feet, as had become my habit when others were around.

Ishbel had just woken up and was still in recovery, having had surgery to screw several bits of metal into her leg. She looked small and drawn on the bed, covered by a tented hospital blanket. There were bruises and cuts along her jawline and left arm. I thought, too late, that I should have bought her some flowers, but she saw me and smiled and I knew gifts didn't matter to her.

'Kirstie!' she said, her speech still slurred from the drugs they'd given her, although she seemed quite alert. 'You, in Lerwick. I am honoured.'

I laughed despite my uneasiness. 'Yes, well, you should have seen Ewan and Duncan grappling with the idea of coming to the big city. They were terrified. They decided that cooking a few meals for you was better use of their time. So – how are you feeling?'

'A wee bit like I've been trampled by a raging bull, but I'll be fine.'

'What happened?'

'A van came out of a side street without looking and went straight into me. The driver's in surgery now. He went through the windscreen apparently. I don't remember much.'

'Wow – sounds like you're lucky to have got off with just a broken leg.'

Ishbel grimaced. 'I could have done without it at all! I won't be able to work until I can get around and I won't be driving for a while.'

'Sorry – that was a bit insensitive.'

'Och, don't apologise. I'm just annoyed to be here and about all the inconvenience, 'tis all.'

'Well, it's school holidays now, isn't it? You don't have to work for a few weeks. And I can drive you around if you need to go anywhere – I've nothing else that can't be put off and my social life isn't exactly hectic.'

'You'd do that for me?'

'Of course. Anyway, who else is going to do it? Tavis works, Catriona is busy with Lorna, Duncan and Ewan would rather pole dance naked in the moonlight than drive to Lerwick – and anyway, I want to do it.'

Before Ishbel could respond, a nurse arrived at her side. 'We're ready to transfer you to the ward. This is Mikey – he's going to take you up there now.'

She moved aside to make room for a small man with carrot-red hair and a straggly beard to take the foot of the gurney. I looked away quickly but was pretty sure I was okay – he wasn't my type at all, but then again, I'd rarely been so long between 'relationships' so I was worried I might not have a type at all anymore, that any man might trigger my obsession.

Picking up Ishbel's handbag from the chair beside her, and hitching her overnight bag onto my shoulder, I kept my head down and followed them into a lift, along a corridor and into a ward.

Once she was settled in a bed near the window, the porter left, and I breathed fully again.

I stayed for a while but Ishbel was tired, so I told her I'd be back in the morning and left. In the car on the way home I allowed myself to feel proud for being out in the big wide world again and keeping myself safe. It was a relief to know that perhaps I could broaden my horizons a bit without panicking about activating my illness. Such are life's little rewards.

But *Pride goeth before a fall*, as they say.

I was sitting on the deck of the ferry on the way home, eyes closed, holding my hair down as it blew annoyingly around my face. The weak sun was doing little to warm me, but I had long ago given up expecting it to.

I felt someone sit down next to me and without thinking, opened my eyes.

Brown eyes looked at me, a well-trimmed beard covered the lower half of an olive-skinned face. I gasped and turned my head away. Heart racing, I dug my nails into my palms and screwed my eyes shut.

'Are you okay?'

A soft voice, concern in the tone. I wanted to put my hands over my ears and fold myself into a little ball, rocking in a corner.

Nononononononono! I shouted in my head. I am stronger than this. I am happy on my own. I don't need a man to complete me. I'm happy. I *am* happy. I am *happy*.

My heart rate slowed a little. I took a breath.

I didn't look at him again but managed to say, 'Seasick.'

'Aye. There is a swell. I'll fetch you some water.' And he left.

So did I, although it was a battle. I wanted to stay and see him again. I needed to go in order to save myself.

Self-preservation, for the first time in my life, won out. I wrenched myself off the bench and found a toilet, staying there until we docked and then scurried to the car, keeping my eyes front and forward as I waited to drive off the ferry and home to safety.

On the road home I thought about the man. Those dark eyes, the gentle voice. The kindness. I tried to think of other things, but he kept coming back. I wondered what his skin would feel like under my hands, what he was like as a lover, whether he was thinking of me as I was about him.

When I dropped the car back to Duncan and Ewan's I had to force myself to focus on them, to answer all their questions, to assure them Ishbel would be fine. It was all I could do not to tell them to shut up so I could leave. Eventually they were satisfied I had told them everything and let me go.

As I walked back to the croft I imagined the man beside me, reaching for my hand. And when I opened the front door, I was almost surprised he wasn't there, kissing me, unbuttoning my shirt, pulling down my jeans as I pushed him onto the bed and sat on top of him feeling him harden under me.

Instead, I poured myself a tumbler of whisky, pulled my journal out and wrote over and over again:

this is not happening. I will not allow my happiness to be ripped away from me. I don't need a man in my life. I have people here who love me, and who I love. That is enough. ENOUGH.

Time and time again I had to pull myself away from my imaginings and force the words onto the page, pressing harder and harder until the paper tore and I threw the pen across the room.

I didn't dare go to bed, where I knew my fantasies would run riot, so I stayed at the table and drank whisky.

I must have fallen into a drunken sleep, because I woke, still in the kitchen chair, stiff, sore and hung-over. Out the window, a flock of terns wheeled and banked in the sky. Running my hand through my hair, I thought about getting it cut next time I was in Lerwick visiting Ishbel. I splashed cold water on my face and stood in my doorway breathing in the tranquillity of my view.

It was only as I ate my porridge that I realised I wasn't thinking about the man on the ferry. Tears of relief washed my cheeks, and I laughed as I danced round the kitchen, enjoying even the thudding headache accompanying every step.

A little later, with a Berocca and a cup of tea beside me, I read what I had written in my journal the night before. I had written it out of a desperate longing but now, in the clear light of day, I realised I had been right: I was loved here, in a normal, uncomplicated way, and I loved Ishbel and Duncan in return. It was a great comfort but was it enough?

My challenge began the minute I set out to see Ishbel again that day. As I walked down to fetch the car from Duncan, my heart began to beat faster. My mind, however hard I tried to keep it focused on my surroundings, on what Ishbel might need or on counting backwards by sevens from three hundred, set off on journeys of its own in which the man on the ferry was waiting for me, had been dreaming of me, wanted me.

I should have realised my 'cure' had been all too easy and quick and couldn't last. How naïve I had been to think that being loved by Ishbel and Duncan was enough, when what I craved was infatuation, total absorption in another. There was no joy in platonic love. I needed the high of obsession.

No. I didn't. The highs were too short-lived, the despair when I felt my love wasn't reciprocated too profound.

Alone on the track, with fingernails breaking the skin on my palms, I screamed into the wind, 'Stop this shit!' until I was hoarse but calmer and could continue.

· · ·

My mouth was dry as I drove onto the ferry. My eyes, which I had been determined to keep focused in front of me swept the deck and the other cars for a sign of the man. A glimpse of brown jacket set my stomach alight with butterflies of anticipation and I was about to approach when the man turned, and I felt the crushing let-down of staring into an old, wrinkled face.

I forced my steps to the back of the boat and watched the island recede, gulls swooping over the choppy wake, in the hope that a shoal of fish had been disturbed and would provide rich pickings. Smiling, I thought about telling Duncan later, to illustrate how his lessons on birdlife were affecting me, making me notice things I wouldn't have otherwise. And in thinking of all that, I wasn't thinking about the man, and my smile widened with the realisation.

Thoughts of That Man might try and capture me, and perhaps I would stumble and allow them in for a while, but I would not fall. I would not fall.

Ishbel was kept in hospital for three days until the swelling went down and her leg could be put in a brace. Three days in which she fretted and fussed, telling anyone who would listen and those who wouldn't, that she was fine to go home and didn't need to take the bed from someone who might need it more than her. When I walked in the nurses sighed with relief, happy to let me be the one to listen to her liturgy for a while.

When I went in on the fourth morning she was dressed and ready to go. The doctor had already seen her and pronounced her fit enough to go home as long as she had help. I think Ishbel would have said anything to get out of the place, so she'd assured him she had a relative staying who would run around after her.

'You don't have to really though,' she said, as we left the ward, her in a wheelchair being pushed by a nurse.

'Oh, yes I do,' I said. 'I'm not going to make a liar of you.'

She had to be lifted into the back of the Volvo with her leg along the seat. We drove back to Yell chatting about what was happening in the world instead of focusing on Ishbel; the protests in Hong Kong, Boris Johnson becoming Prime Minister, which made me shudder, and a suicide bomber killing people at a wedding in Afghanistan. I had hardly listened to any news in the months I'd been on the island, but Ishbel had spent the nights in hospital awake, watching TV and felt it her duty to enlighten me. I hadn't missed tuning in to the rest of the world; there was too much misery out there and I didn't need it.

Back at her house, I made the sofa bed in the sitting room up for Ishbel and prepared some lunch. She was a terrible patient, trying to get up and help, refusing just to rest with her leg up as she'd been ordered by the long-suffering nursing staff. She wasn't meant to bear any weight on her leg until she'd been seen at the fracture clinic the following week, but she wouldn't stay off it. In the end I told her if she didn't follow orders, she'd end up back in hospital with another broken leg from me kicking it out from under her. After that, she settled a bit.

I also told her about my friend who had broken his ankle and made it worse by ignoring it and ended up needing to have it pinned and plated.

Ed.

16

———————————

THE CONFESSION

Yes, Ed had broken his ankle. He did it playing football one weekend. He wasn't a regular player but jogged and worked out, so was certainly fit. It was a corporate football match, one of these things that charities organise, and big companies volunteer their upper management to play in. A recipe for disaster, in other words.

The first I heard about it was when Vanessa rang me in a tizz about something to do with Hugo's party – whether the marquee I'd ordered would be big enough if it rained or some such nonsense – and added that her husband's injury was all she needed, three weeks out from the event.

'Oh,' I said, heart pounding. I started imagining Ed in a wheelchair or on life support in hospital. 'Is he okay?'

'He'll be fine – he broke his ankle trying to recapture his childhood.' She sounded pissed off. I was desperate to see him, to confirm with my own eyes that he was all right.

'I'll drop a couple of meals off so you don't have the added stress of cooking while you look after him.'

'Oh, you're an angel, Kirstie. I have no idea how I managed before I met you.'

'No problem. I'll bring them this evening.'

'Oh, I'll be out tonight – a friend's product launch – but Ed will be in, of course. You are a real gem. Thanks.'

Ed opened the door in his bathrobe. When he saw it was me, he instinctively glanced up and down the street before pulling me in.

'Kirstie – what are you doing here?'

That was good – it meant either Vanessa hadn't mentioned there was food being dropped off, or she hadn't said who was doing the dropping. I still didn't want him to know I was the caterer for his son's party and had worried all afternoon about how to manage the situation if he'd found out. I wasn't sure how he'd feel about his wife and his lover meeting. I'd left the food bag on the doorstep and he hadn't noticed it.

'It's Wednesday and I know your wife is usually out, so I came on the off-chance. If she'd answered the door I would have said I'd got the wrong house. I'm not stupid. But here you are, and here I am, and it looks like you could do with some TLC.' I let my eyes travel down to the Moon Boot on his foot. 'What happened?' I asked.

As he told me, I directed him into the lounge and sat him on the sofa. Listening with one ear, I pushed him gently back, so he was propped up against the cushions and started massaging his shoulders. He soon stopped talking.

Ed hopped into the hall to see me off later, and I 'noticed' the food bag on the doorstep.

'Oh, yeah, Vanessa said someone was dropping something off tonight. Some do-gooder she's adopted. Put it in the kitchen, would you?'

I was less than pleased at being described as a do-gooder but it was better than being found out, so swallowed my retort.

A week later Ed tripped at the Tube station on his way to work and ended up back in hospital, this time having his ankle, which he had been walking on against advice, pinned and plated. He was in hospital for a couple of days and on crutches for weeks and needed an awful lot of my particular style of pain management. Whenever he knew Vanessa was going to be out he called, and I went over to take his mind off things. I was never happier. He needed me to look after him. He wanted me to be there.

The day of the party, I was at the house bright and early to supervise the set-up. The marquee had been put up the day before, the tables and chairs delivered. Vanessa, without make-up and frazzled-looking, greeted me at the door, pulled me inside and started listing all the problems before we'd got to the kitchen. The marquee was too small, there weren't enough chairs for all the guests, the flowers weren't there yet, the balloons weren't inflated – the list went on. I had arranged for two of my staff to do the grunt work during the day and there was plenty of time to get everything done. I tried to reassure her, but she was intent on panicking.

'And to cap it all,' she said, 'Hugo crashed in at four this morning so won't get out of bed until mid-afternoon, Julia didn't come home at all last night and I sent Ed off with a friend for the day to get him out the way – he's useless at things like this. Thinks he's helping but just gets in the way all the time.'

Thank the Lord, I thought. I wouldn't have to see him until the evening. What a surprise he'd have.

I was looking forward to meeting Ed's children. Hugo, I knew, was at a second-rate university somewhere doing a degree in drinking and partying, and Julia, the daughter, was at boarding school with her pony.

'Kirstie – are you listening?' asked Vanessa.

I spun round to look at her. 'Of course, sorry. Good thing you've got me instead of that husband of yours, eh? Let's get going, shall we?'

By lunchtime I had everything under control. We'd counted the chairs again and discovered there were enough, and Gavin and Tracy had set the tables and blown up the helium balloons, the flowers had arrived and looked stunning in their tall vases in each corner of the marquee, the table decorations were in place – all that was needed was the food, the drink and the guests. I left Vanessa having her hair and nails done and got back to my kitchen, where all was well in hand. My well-oiled machine. I helped with the finishing touches to the cake decoration and then went upstairs to my flat to shower and change. By the time I was ready, the food was being loaded into the van and we were off.

I started getting anxious on the drive to Holland Park. I wanted Ed to be surprised but I was afraid he'd be angry. Not so much for the fact I was doing the catering but that I hadn't told him. But I kept telling myself he loved me and wanted to be with me and so would see it, as I did, as a way of us getting closer. I would be at a family event, sharing it with him.

I was in the kitchen when he came in. I heard him before I saw him – the tap-tap of his crutches on the polished wood floor.

'My wife says to ask you if we're on schedule?' he said.

I turned and looked him in the eye. I'll never forget the look of shock on his face – his eyebrows nearly hit his hairline and his mouth formed a perfect O. He stumbled back into a chair and sat down heavily.

'What the fuck...?'

I smiled. 'Hi, Ed. Vanessa wanted the best caterer in London to do Hugo's party, so here I am.'

A young woman came in. She had perfect hair, clear skin,

make-up carefully applied to make it look as natural as possible, as if she needed any anyway, and the attitude of one who has grown up with money. Julia, Ed's daughter.

'Daddy, have you seen Mummy? I can't find the guest list to give the security people.'

'I have it here,' I said, handing her the paper. Ed was still sitting, open-mouthed, looking at me with hostility.

Julia took the list without a thank you – if she were mine she'd have better manners – and left us alone again.

'What do you think you're doing?' Ed hissed.

'My job.'

'But here? How could you? How fucking dare you?'

'Ed, calm down. It's okay. Vanessa doesn't know anything about us. I'm just the caterer.'

'Oh no you're not. It's been "my caterer this" and "my caterer that" for the last month. She's practically dependent on you for breathing these days.'

I smiled and thanked God for the rich who think of everyone else as staff with no name. Without realising it, she had kept my secret for me brilliantly.

Ed was breathing heavily and I suggested he sit down and poured him a drink. Whisky on the rocks.

'Ah, you've met,' said Vanessa as she swept into the kitchen. 'This woman is my saviour,' she added.

Ed grunted and sipped his drink.

'Now don't go having too many of those, Edward. You need to be sober to make your speech after dinner.' He rolled his eyes and made no response.

'The guests will be here in half an hour, is all in order?' she asked me. I pointed to the food stacked in its heated trays. 'All present and correct. The waiting staff are ready to receive the guests and pass around drinks and finger food. The band is setting up, the rain has held off. It's going to be a perfect night. Relax and enjoy it.'

She smiled distractedly as we heard the thud of someone rushing down the stairs and the birthday boy himself burst into the room.

'Hugo, I wish you wouldn't–'

'Thunder down the stairs. I know.' He flashed his mother a heart-stopping smile, flicked a glance at his father, ignored me completely and left again muttering something about needing a hair of the dog.

'Right, well, I'll go and see to Mummy and Daddy. They're sitting quietly in the lounge and say that's where they'll stay. Mummy doesn't feel up to the party. I wish I hadn't insisted on her coming.'

'Can I help?' I asked. 'I'm quite good with older people and she may respond differently to a stranger.'

Vanessa looked at me as if I'd offered her the Nobel Peace Prize and ushered me out of the room. I felt Ed's gaze on my back as I left and couldn't wait for later when I would make sure we had a few minutes alone.

Mrs Gordon-Jones was easily persuaded to sit in a quiet corner of the marquee when I promised her I'd make sure she had a sherry and a plate of food beside her throughout the evening, so I helped her to her seat and motioned for one of the waiters to see that she got what she needed. Mr Gordon-Jones said he'd be quite happy to mingle with the guests and check back with his wife every so often. I could never understand why people like Vanessa found these things so hard.

As the party got underway, I watched Ed moving between groups of guests, chatting, laughing, eating the food my people had prepared. When dinner was announced, for a while I was too busy to do anything but plate up and send the food out, so it wasn't until the plates were being collected, rinsed and packed into our crates for washing back at the catering kitchen that I had a chance to look for him again. The guests had risen from the tables and were chatting in groups. Some had even taken to the dance floor. He was talking to a short, dark-haired woman with breasts bursting out of a skimpy dress. She was looking up at him with ill-disguised lust and he could hardly take his eyes off her tits.

'Mr Bannerman,' I said, approaching them, 'could I have a word about the cake-cutting and the toasts?'

The woman put her hand on Ed's arm as if to stop him, but he turned away from her with an apology and led me out the back of the marquee.

'Have you forgiven me?' I asked.

'I'm thinking about it.' He looked me up and down. 'No one'll find us here,' he said. 'Don't you find it a turn-on that here we are together, a few feet away from all these people? I know I do.' He moved towards me, took my hand and pressed it to his crotch. He was already hard.

I snaked my arms around him and drew him to me, kissing him deeply. He threw his crutches to the ground and held me tighter, kissed me down my neck, slid one hand up inside my bra and rolled my nipple as he pulled my skirt up with his other hand.

'You're wearing panties,' he said.

'Of course, I didn't know we'd be doing this,' I gasped.

We made love against a tree in his back garden in the middle of his son's twenty-first birthday party with his wife and all their guests on the other side of a flimsy wall of canvas. Peals of laughter and snippets of conversation accompanied the snatches of our breath as we climaxed.

Once the cake was cut and handed out, the speeches made and toasts given, we packed up as much as we could, and Gavin drove the van back to my catering kitchen. I stayed behind with two waiters to serve drinks, but people were leaving and Hugo's friends were preparing to go clubbing. By eleven thirty, there was nothing more to do.

'I can't thank you enough,' said Vanessa, flopping onto a kitchen chair and watching as I wiped the counters down. 'It went brilliantly, and everyone commented on the food. You'll be inundated with requests from now on.'

'I'm glad it went well,' I said. 'Now, you look exhausted, so why don't you go to bed and let me finish off down here?'

'Oh, would you mind? It has been a very tiring day.'

Alone in the kitchen, I poured myself a large gin and tonic and sat waiting for Ed who was having a last drink with one of the guests. Sure enough, no sooner had I heard the front door closing than he was here.

'So?' I said.

'I'm still actually pretty fucking angry with you, Kirstie. This was a set-up,' he said in a low voice.

'I know about that fucking bit, but why angry?' I asked in my best butter-wouldn't-melt manner.

'You know what I mean. It was a dangerous thing to do. Anyone might have discovered us.'

'It was your idea to make love behind the marquee. Anyway, nobody found us.'

He frowned and then pulled me to him. 'I can't tell you I didn't enjoy it – you know what you do to me. I think you were as excited by the situation as I was – the fear of discovery added something, don't you think?'

I saw his pupils dilate and knew what was coming next.

'Vanessa's gone to bed and the youngsters have gone out. Shall we adjourn to the marquee, or would the bathroom be more your thing this time?' he asked, taking my hand.

We took our leisure this time. Lying on the grass behind the marquee, he dripped whisky onto my breasts and licked it off and I dipped his cock into my gin and sucked it. Afterwards, he started laughing.

'You're mad, you know that, don't you?'

'We're mad,' I said. 'For each other.'

He sighed, and I knew he agreed with me. He loved me with all his heart, as I loved him. We would find a way to be together forever.

Did I feel at all guilty about Vanessa? I can honestly say that at the time, I did not. She didn't register on my radar except as an obstacle to Ed and me being together. That's the honest – and the terrible – truth.

17

EXILE

It was odd waking up in someone else's house. I stayed with Ishbel for the first few days she was home to fill her freezer with meals and help with all the things that are so difficult when crutches and leg braces are involved, like getting in and out of a chair and showering which normally we take for granted. Once I'd given her a stern talking to she became an easy patient to look after, her good nature and optimism shining through.

I was the one who found our enforced companionship difficult. I had lived alone since my first disastrous flatshare in London. For more than half my life I had answered to no one, had established my own routines. I'd never thought about the give and take of sharing space nor had to look after anyone but myself.

Hard though I found it, it was me who insisted on staying. I felt it my duty but also a pleasure to be able to offer my time and support and although I was itching to get away after a couple of days, I also enjoyed the company and Ishbel's stories, of which she had many. Not only tales involving family members I was now meeting but the local folk tales and myths. My Shetland education was deepened by the time spent with her. My mother must have known them all, but she had never told me any of them. The books she read to me when I was young were of English children behaving well or suffering terrible consequences for their disobedience. Stories meant to terrify children into meek submission.

And, of course, while I was busy at Ishbel's, thoughts of the man on the ferry were more easily pushed to the back of my mind. I was afraid that as soon as I had more time, he would take front and centre stage. Even with the distraction of looking after Ishbel, I would find myself thinking about him at times and have to drag myself away from the fantasies of happily ever afters. But the fact that I *could* disentangle my thoughts from him made me feel hopeful I was finally starting to conquer my illness. I played the words of one of my therapists over and over in my head – *you are not your illness, you are bigger than it, you can be the one in control*. Maybe, at last, I was discovering the truth of it.

Duncan, Ewan, Una and others came to visit daily. I made tea and coffee, offered cake, sometimes lunch. Tavis, Catriona and Lorna came home from their holiday at the weekend and popped in. They didn't stay long because Lorna had started crawling, getting into everything and it was clear we needed to toddler-proof the house before she visited next time. I borrowed Duncan's car again and drove into Lerwick to buy a stair gate and while I was there, picked up a couple of books to keep Ishbel occupied.

Each time I went to Lerwick felt like a test and sitting on the ferry back to Yell I congratulated myself on the fact I had made it and was managing my feelings. If anyone had been watching me they would have observed a woman who sat quietly, hands in her lap, just occasionally biting the inside of her lip and letting her eyes flit around the other passengers. Usually there were few others, mostly groups of women who, like me, had been shopping and complained loudly about the terrible prices of everything.

I longed to see the man who had offered me water, and I fervently hoped I wouldn't.

After fitting the stair gate and making sure Ishbel had everything she needed, I gathered my belongings and moved back to the croft. She could manage now without a live-in companion. I continued to visit every day but had time to myself again, to walk, think, write, read and potter about doing the chores. I thought about the ferry man less and less until, after a week or so, he no longer intruded at all. I had been shaken by the experience but shedding all thought of him felt like a victory. It also made me feel that perhaps my whole life – since my first obsession anyway – had been one long failure. Surely if it had been this easy to prevent a full-blown episode I should have been able to do it before. Had I been so weak, or so desperate to be loved, that I had allowed my fantasies to rule me so completely?

I couldn't let myself go there. What was the point? If it was true, and I had been weak, I was stronger now. If I had needed to be loved, now I was. And not in the dramatic, high-stakes way that had stood in for true love. Admittedly, I was sometimes lonely, but I felt like I had my life back. It may have been a small life, but I was content.

The next time Dougal came with my groceries I told him that from now on I would do my own shopping. I was confident there was no one in Mid Yell who was going to trigger my obsession, and I wanted to be more involved in the community. He nodded as if he'd been expecting it and turned away.

'Thank you for delivering my food for the last few months,' I called after him. And then ran after him as he got into his ancient car. 'Here, this is for all your help.'

He looked at the money I'd thrust into his hand, pushed it into his pocket and drove away without looking at me. I watched him go, smiling to myself. Funny old bugger that he was.

Duncan came by later that day and asked if I was ready to hear more about Morag's life in England.

'I'm thinking you should read this for yoursel' instead of me telling you,' he said as he placed a letter on the table.

My fingers itched to close around the envelope and rush outside to read it in the golden afternoon sun, but I made myself sit. Since telling me about the first letter he'd been sharing his memories of her but now I'd be hearing what happened after she left.

'Yes,' I said. I didn't know how to go on. I had been thinking about it for the last month. In her first letter my mother had essentially told him he wouldn't be seeing her again but wanted to keep in touch to make herself feel better. That was my understanding of it anyway. I was angry with her for being so selfish. If Duncan had wanted me to soften towards her, what he'd told me of her parting had, in the end, had the opposite effect.

I was about to tell him so, but I looked at him, so at home at my table, and realised I wanted him to be happy and one way I could contribute to that happiness was trying to be more positive about my mother.

'I felt sorry for her, leaving the way she did,' I said. 'And for you, the one left behind.'

His started tapping his fingers gently on the table, a sign I recognised as the expression of painful feelings, or the attempt to quieten them. Duncan sat, breathing evenly, looking out the window, back to me, out the window again. I let him settle himself while I made tea, poured a tot of whisky into each cup and sat again.

''Twas easier for me than for her. I still had my friends and my family while she had no one. The lady she lived with was kind 'tis true but a stranger can no take the place of family. I felt aafil for her, and there was not a thing I could do. I thought about going to England to look for her but I didnae know where I would start. I reckon if someone wants to be lost, they can stay lost, mebbe even these days with th' internet and everyone with their eyes stuck to their phones.'

Duncan was loyal, thinking only about her and how she felt. I loved him all the more for it but still couldn't help feeling that his love for her was misplaced. It seemed to me she wrote to him to have some sort of connection, however slight, with her home and she offered him a glimpse into a new life she didn't want to share with him in person.

When he'd gone, I sat for a while thinking about my mother and her journey south. There was a part of me that didn't want to know any more, that wanted to hold on to my anger and disappointment in her as if they somehow justified what I had become.

Curiosity got the better of me, of course. I opened the second letter and read. It was dated 12th December 1957, and written in girlish rounded handwriting, nothing like the elegant hand I knew my mother to have.

Dear Duncan,

I think I left you on the train south. Not you, literally, of course, but that was the last bit I wrote. I've so much to tell you!

I didn't know where I was going to end up, all I knew was that I had a ticket to London and would see what happened there. Well, I escaped with my life but only just – or at least, that's how it felt at the time. London is HUGE. Ten times bigger and noisier than Edinburgh, which seemed ten times bigger and noisier than Aberdeen which was a hundred times bigger than Lerwick. ENORMOUS. I walked out of the station thinking I might find somewhere to stay, and almost got run over on the first road I tried to cross. There were cars EVERYWHERE. And buses and taxis and people. Oh, my, the people! Rushing along the pavements without looking where they were going, as if they had to get to the most important job in the world OR ELSE.

I realise I've used a lot of capital letters – but that's how London made me feel – like everything was big and important and there was no room for anyone new. Especially someone who didn't know what they were doing and might cause a delay for one of the insiders. And it was grey and forbidding too. Not a welcoming place at all. I felt a pang of homesickness for the village where the stone may be grey but you can still see the sky over the top of the buildings and the land and the sea beyond. I couldn't imagine living a life without being able to see the sea. So I decided I had to get on another train and find the coast.

Well, that wasn't as easy as it sounds. I went back into the station to buy a ticket but before that, I found a map of England in a newsagents and decided to keep heading south – it was the closest way to get to the sea. So, I asked for a ticket to a south-coast town, and the ticket man said I couldn't go from that station, I had to go from Victoria Station, a bus ride away. I must have looked as scared as I felt at the idea of getting a bus in London, because he very kindly told me exactly where I had to wait, how much it would cost, and to ask the driver to put me off at Victoria. You'll be pleased to hear, and I hope, proud of me for getting there in one piece. London has two huge stations – Victoria was easily as big as King's Cross, with platforms for trains going here, there and everywhere. But I managed to get on the right one, and after a relatively short journey, arrived in this town. As soon as I walked out of the station I knew I had been right to get to the coast. Although it doesn't smell the same as home because there's no peat or heathland, at least the sea is still salty and there's a sharpness to the air that was missing in London. I sat in a bus shelter on the waterfront, gazing at the water over the pebble beach. Yes, that's what I said. Pebbles! Can you imagine a beach covered in stones instead of sand? I could hardly believe my eyes.

I smiled. I grew up there and pebbles on a beach were normal, but everything was new to her, and she wrote as if her experiences made her breathless with excitement and wonder, a young woman on an adventure. I turned back to the letter.

Anyway, I sat there, too tired to make another decision but knowing I had to find somewhere to stay and worrying my money would run out before I got a job. And then, my guardian angel appeared.

Her name is Ronnie, short for Veronica, and she sat right down beside me on the bench. She had a scarf on her head, but it was tied up at the front, above her forehead not under her chin, and it made her look daring somehow. She lit a cigarette and blew the smoke out of the side of her mouth and smiled at me.

'You waiting for the number 42?' she asked.

'I don't really know,' I said.

She narrowed her eyes at me. 'You're not from around here, are you?'

'No, I'm from the Shetland Isles,' I said.

'Where are they, then?'

'North of Scotland – a long way away.' I almost started crying then. I had to dig my fingernails into my palm to stop myself.

'Explains the funny accent then,' she said.

'I thought it was you who had the funny accent,' I said, and she laughed and that's when she told me her name.

'I'm Morag,' I said, and had to repeat it because she'd never heard it before and didn't get it first time.

'Where are you staying, Morag the Scot?' she asked.

I told her I'd been travelling for two days and I hadn't anywhere to stay. I wasn't even sure if I'd stay in this town or carry on to somewhere else.

'Oh, you should stay here – it's a great town. There's lots of jobs and cheap places to live, cinemas, clubs – lots to do for a girl like you.'

I wasn't sure how Ronnie knew what kind of girl I was but I needed a job and liked the idea of the cinema – you know I've never been to one, Duncan. I was annoyed when you went and didn't ask me, do you remember? You saw 20,000 Leagues Under the Sea and told me all about it when you got back. Anyway, I thought it would be good to live in a town with a cinema, and I liked Ronnie, so I decided to stay.

A trolley bus approached, and Ronnie jumped on. I followed her because I didn't want to lose her. We sat at the back behind an old man with a hacking cough and a large swelling on his neck. I sat right back on the seat, keeping as far away from him as the space allowed.

Ronnie asked me what I was going to do, and I said I needed to find a place to live and get a job.

'What kind of job?'

I told her I didn't have any experience and would try anything, and she got all thoughtful for a moment and then *said she'd speak to her manager about finding me some work. Then she got up and jumped off the bus. I had to follow, because she hadn't told me how to find her, and if she was going to get me a job, I needed to see her again. She wrote down her address and told me to come and see her that evening. Then she entered a big shop and disappeared. I looked up and saw a tall sign: J Sainsbury written in gold letters. The front windows were being cleaned on the inside by a man in a starched apron, and beyond, I could see display cabinets and counters with people in crisp white uniforms standing behind them. Ronnie appeared and waved, then turned to say something to the woman next to her. I didn't know if this was the manager she'd talked about but I didn't stay to find out. I badly needed a job and certainly wouldn't get one looking the way I did. I had to find a place to stay and have a bath and get into my clean clothes before I let a manager see me.*

I passed a post office along the street and went in to get a thruppenny stamp for this letter to you, (I meant to write much sooner – forgive me!) and wondered briefly if I should let my family know where I am. But I decided not to, and you're not to either – promise. I'm still not decided how I feel about my mammie but I don't think she deserves to know anything about me since she said she never wanted to see me again. As I left the shop having bought my stamp, I saw some cards in the window. One caught my eye.

'Room for rent in quiet house in Hove. Only women need apply.'

There was a telephone number underneath but I've never used one, so I memorised the address and decided to go round there immediately. The lady in the post office was very kind when I went in again to ask the way.

I was exhausted, and nervous as I stood on the

doorstep, and it took me the last of my courage to knock on the door. An old lady opened it. She had a blue rinse and round glasses that made her eyes look big, like one of the short-eared owls at home. Her lipstick didn't quite follow the outline of her lips but when she smiled at me, I thought the sun had come out.

'I've come about the room,' I said.

She asked me in and offered me a cup of tea. I could have kissed her right there and then.

The house is large and bright with a living room at the front and a kitchen at the back and a tidy garden overlooking a railway line. I don't seem to be able to get away from trains!

Miss Harris asked me a lot about myself, almost like an interview but I didn't mind because she kept smiling and nodding and handing me slices of sponge cake.

In the end, she said she liked me, and had heard a lot of good things about the Scots, and the room was mine if I liked. I hadn't even seen the room, but I knew I wanted it, that I would be happy with Miss Harris, who is a funny old lady but has a big heart.

My room is at the back of the house over the kitchen. Miss Harris apologised that it isn't very big, but she hasn't seen the alcove off the kitchen I used to sleep in. And I reckon the whole croft would fit in my bedroom and the bathroom next to it. Yes, an indoor bathroom! With a deep bath with hot and cold taps, and a toilet and a wash-hand basin. My bedroom has a big window with cheerful curtains, a bed with a colourful bedspread, a bedside table, a chest of drawers and a wardrobe. I have two sets of clothes, a hairbrush and a notebook for writing in and nothing else, so I don't know what I'll use all the furniture for. My clean dress looked lonely hanging in the wardrobe when I put it in there. I think I'll have to get more clothes when I have a job.

I stopped again, a tear sliding down my cheek. My mother's excitement at an indoor bathroom with hot and cold water, the idea of her one dress hanging in a big, old wardrobe. I began to realise how brave she'd been, how determined. Wiping the tears away, I read on.

Oh, Duncan, you can't imagine how it feels to have such a big room, and all for me. I'm not sure how I'll ever get used to sleeping without hearing Da' snoring next door and Mammie sighing and shifting in the night.

Anyway, I had a wash and rinsed out my clothes, put everything clean on and sat gazing around my room for ages until Miss Harris called up the stairs that dinner was ready.

Three things became apparent that first dinner: Miss Harris is lonely and likes to talk; she can make the lightest sponge cake in England but overcooks everything else, and she is as kind as her smile is wide. She is charging hardly any rent because she knows anyone who lives with her has to put up with her burnt offerings at mealtimes. But what they lack in quality they make up for in quantity – I've never seen so much food. That first night the sausages were singed, the potatoes puddled on the plate but there was enough to feed all of Yell and more besides. Miss Harris doesn't seem to eat very much but I managed to eat six sausages while she looked on, smiling and talking about her terrible cooking!

'We'll get on just fine, I know it,' she said as I scooped up more potatoes.

She is such a dear.

I offered to do the dishes after dinner, and she tried to stop me, but I told her I'd always helped with the chores and it would make me feel less homesick if she allowed me to help her, so in the end she agreed. I washed up while she made another cup of tea for us both. It was just past seven when we finished, and dark outside but Miss Harris likes to keep the curtains open. She said she spent so much time in an air-raid shelter in the war she can't abide being closed in anymore. The light from the street lamp outside glowed warmly into the sitting room as we drank our tea, and I had the thought that one day, this will feel like home.

I wondered if it ever had. She'd never mentioned it, or Miss Harris, to me.

A little later I showed her the piece of paper Ronnie had written her address on and asked her if she knew where it was – and it is only a few streets away, which is lucky. I told Miss Harris I had to go and see my friend as she was helping me find a job, but I wouldn't be in late. It felt good to know that someone would be expecting me home again.

It was raining, and although Miss Harris lent me an umbrella, my feet were soaking by the time I found Ronnie's address. As I shook out the umbrella on the doorstep I heard laughter coming from inside the house and then footsteps coming along the hall towards the front door. When Ronnie opened it, the smell of onions cooking wafted out.

Ronnie lives with her mother and two sisters, but her father ran off with another woman some years ago. Fancy that! I've never met anyone whose father did that, have you? No, of course you haven't, because we know all the same people. Anyway, they seem quite happy without a man in the house. Mrs Spencer, Ronnie's mother, had been to Stirling on a holiday once, many years ago. She seemed to find it strange that I didn't know it but I wonder if she knows every town in England? Anyway, she was nice enough and invited me to eat with them, but I couldn't fit another mouthful in, so I sat with them while they ate, squeezed around the kitchen table.

Maggie, one of Ronnie's sisters, wanted to know why I was there – not their house but that town, so far away from home. I told her I wanted to see the world, and she laughed and said I was hardly going to do that in their stinky old town. That's exactly what she said!

After dinner was over and Ronnie and her sisters had cleared away, we stayed in the kitchen while her mother and sisters went to read and do homework in the sitting room. I was bursting to hear what she had to say about a job by then and could hardly sit still. But Ronnie got in first and asked me if I'd found a place to stay. I told her about Miss Harris and her house, and she told me I was very resourceful finding a room so quickly. Then she said she might have found me a job too! So she became the second person that day I wanted to kiss!

She told me there was a job going on the cheese and dairy counter, and the manager would interview me the next day.

I was so excited, and nervous, and homesick I couldn't sleep that night. The noises in the house were unfamiliar and every so often a train would clatter past. I lay in my bed under the colourful bedspread and prayed I would get the job and Ronnie would become my friend, and that you and everyone at home were all right, although I still don't want to think about Mammie.

In the morning, Miss Harris made me eat a full breakfast even though I thought I might be sick, and she told me I looked very presentable. She walked me to the bus stop and waited until the bus came and told the driver where to put me off, which I was grateful for because I don't know if I would have recognised the place.

Mr Johnson was waiting for me in his office when I arrived. I didn't know what to do, so I curtseyed, which made him smile. He asked me where I'd worked before, and when I told him I hadn't, I thought I'd lost the job but then he asked what I'd done at home – had I helped around the house, and I could tell him all the chores I used to do, and he offered me the job! Then he took me to the counter with Dairy written in bold letters on the wall behind it, and introduced me to Miss Chalcott who would teach me what I had to do.

When he'd gone, Miss Chalcott taught me how to cut the different cheeses – we have Cheddar, Wensleydale, Red Leicester and Stilton, which stinks. She also showed me how to cut, weigh and pat the butter into neat rectangles with special wooden paddles.

I laughed out loud at that. My mother using wooden sticks to pat butter into shape! It had never occurred to me until then that it didn't come ready-packaged. It made me realise how much the world has changed in a short time and that for her, everything was new, yet she seemed to approach it all eagerly.

It's not taxing work but it's a job, and I'll be making my own money. Ronnie works on the Tinned Goods counter, fetching and bagging items for the customers. I didn't know so many different types of food came in tins – fruit, vegetables, fish and meat. It's very sophisticated.

I started work the very next day, and now I've been there nearly two months (sorry again this letter's taken so long!) I can hardly believe it. Life has settled into a routine, and I am enjoying it, mostly. I still get lonely but Miss Harris is good company, and I see Ronnie at work and sometimes on

Saturday afternoons we go to the pictures – there are two picture houses here, the Gaiety and the Duke of York, so there's usually something on that we want to see.

Weekdays I go straight home. Miss Harris has lent me her bicycle so I can save the bus fares. We're not idle in the evenings; there always seems to be some mending to do and she likes knitting and I've crocheted myself a new tam-o'-shanter as I lost my old one somewhere between Edinburgh and here. We listen to the wireless if there's a play on but otherwise talk or sit in companionable silence.

So, Duncan, that's my life. I know I've told you a lot but I want you to be able to imagine what I'm doing, as I can imagine what you're doing. I know that in the mornings you'll be cutting peat or seeing to the sheep, or perhaps out on the boat with the other men catching fish, or mending nets. And now, you can imagine me patting butter, riding a bicycle, going to the pictures. What you can't imagine is how different this place is to Yell, and it would take a whole book to tell you that.

I hope you are well. I miss you all and will write again soon,

Happy Christmas,

Morag x

I wondered what Duncan would have made of the letter. Would he have been hoping for her to say she was coming home, that she was missing him in particular? If so, he must have been severely disappointed.

I read it over and stopped again at the bit where she wrote about her room at Miss Harris's. She'd never had a room all to herself before, having slept throughout her childhood on the truckle bed in the kitchen at the croft with Robbie and Alasdair on the floor beside her. I couldn't shake the image from my head of her single dress hanging in the wardrobe. It seemed to sum up, so perfectly, her life then and now. She had never accumulated objects. She was not a mother who kept first drawings, school reports, handmade gifts. Perhaps that was more a result of her life on the island though, the lack of money, the lack of space to store anything, the lack of a need for such things when life was lived in a community of living memory rather than inert keepsakes.

I wondered what had happened to Ronnie. I'd never heard my mother mention her. But then again, it wasn't such a surprise. Like possessions, she had no room for more than one friend at a time. A life pared down to the necessities. One husband. One child. One friend.

I couldn't imagine her working in Sainsbury's either. Patting butter. How boring it must have been to stand cutting cheese and butter and packaging it up for the women, some of whom probably came in every day, not having a fridge at home. How exhausting, to stand at a counter for hour after hour. The mother I knew would have found it humiliating and taxing, having to be pleasant to customers who prattled away about nothing. But she didn't sound bitter about it and if she struggled with her role in any way, it didn't come across in the letter. Was she painting a rosy picture for Duncan, or had she actually enjoyed her new life? What would her alternative have been had she stayed in Mid Yell?

As I thought more about her, it began to dawn on me that in many ways she had done better than me. I may have had more dresses in my wardrobe, but I had no husband, no child, and until I arrived here, few people I could call true friends. My life had lurched from one obsessive liaison to another. And the people I had counted as friends in London – who had been good, loyal friends – we hardly kept in touch now, despite all the promises.

18

THE CONFESSION

After Hugo's party I had little reason to contact Vanessa, but over the next few weeks I dropped in occasionally with a meal for her to take to her parents, good friend that I was.

So I was there the day a letter arrived for Ed. And not just any letter – perfume wafted from the pale-pink envelope as Vanessa held it in her hand, looking at the loopy, feminine handwriting. I saw a shadow of suspicion pass across her face and then she put the letter on the kitchen table between us and slumped into a seat.

Taking some deep breaths, I calmed the roilings in my belly.

'Looks like a young person's writing,' I said, staring at it, feeling my lips tighten against further words.

'Yes. Probably someone's idea of a joke,' she said but the way she also couldn't take her eyes off the letter belied her words. She was upset.

'Let's have a cup of tea,' I said, taking the kettle to the sink. 'I'm sure there's an innocent explanation.'

'Of course,' she said but a tear glistened in her eye.

'You can't think this is worth worrying over, surely?' I asked, putting a hand on her shoulder, a gesture which acted as a tap. She started sobbing, burying her head in my stomach and clinging on around my waist like I was a lifebuoy. I pulled her gently to her feet and walked her into the sitting room where we could be more comfortable. She drew a tissue from her sleeve, blew her nose and dried her eyes, rubbing the mascara from under them as best she could. When she looked up at me there were grey streaks across her cheeks.

'Do you think he's having an affair?' she asked.

I took a deep, steadying breath. 'I don't know, of course, but one letter doesn't mean anything, and wouldn't it be rather obvious to send it to the house anyway? I mean, these days there are much more secret ways to communicate if you don't want to be found out. I'm sure this has an innocent explanation.'

Vanessa brightened and squeezed my hand. 'You're right. I'm worrying over nothing. Ed will probably laugh at me for getting so worked up about it.'

'Why don't you just throw it away? What he doesn't know can't hurt him, and you can forget all about it as soon as it's in the bin. In fact, even better, I'll take it with me and throw it out so you don't have to see it again.'

She looked at me, gratitude written all over her face. 'Thank you, Kirstie. You're a godsend.'

'I'm just glad I was here,' I said.

I rang her a few days later to see how she was. She'd just intercepted another letter. Same handwriting, same perfume.

'Take some deep breaths and sit yourself down. I can be there in twenty minutes.'

'Oh, Kirstie, would you?'

'Of course. See you soon.'

On my way I practised my self-talk, one of the techniques I'd picked up from a book. Stay strong, stay steady. You are a worthwhile person.

I arrived to a blotchy-faced Vanessa. This was obviously worse than the first time. She let me in and collapsed into my arms and if I hadn't been prepared for it, we would both have ended up on the floor. I managed to get her into the lounge and onto the sofa. She had the open letter in one hand and proffered it up for me to read.

Darling Ed,
I ache for you. My bed is still warm from your body but already I want you here again. I can't wait until we can be together forever. Please say it will be soon.
Your ever loving,
Hot Bod xoxoxo

She watched me read it, tears streaking her cheeks. Jaw clenched, I scrunched it into a ball and put it in my bag to dispose of later.

'No denying it now. He's got another woman,' she said and collapsed against the cushions sobbing noisily.

I considered for a moment. 'This still isn't proof–'

Her head shot up. 'How can you say that? Read the bloody thing again! She wants him in her bed as soon as he's left it. What more proof do you need?'

'What I mean is,' I said, taking her hand and unclenching the fist she'd made, 'this person may think it a joke. You know, just to get a rise out of your husband.'

'Sounds like she has already "got a rise" out of my husband – more than once.' She yanked her hand away from mine and crossed her arms. She sucked on her bottom lip. 'But why would he have an affair? It's not like we don't have sex regularly and I haven't become old and frumpy – I go to the gym and wear good clothes, make-up – and I do it all for him.'

I felt myself blanche. I couldn't bear to think of Ed having sex with anyone else. He'd told me he made love to Vanessa infrequently, so she didn't suspect he was playing around but here she was telling me they had a healthy sex life. My jaw hardened.

'What are you going to do then?' I asked.

Vanessa stared at me through bleary eyes and shook her head. 'I don't know. I really don't.'

'Look,' I said, 'perhaps the best thing is not to say anything yet. If this woman doesn't get a response from him maybe she'll stop. No use having a barney over nothing.' I put my arm round her shoulders and pulled her close. 'I'm sure there's an explanation for it.'

Oh, the Sisterhood!

Vanessa rested against me and I felt the fight go out of her. She wanted to believe me, and I could almost hear the battle going on in her mind to make herself do so. In the end, she sighed, wiped her face again and sat up.

'You're right. No use making a mountain out of a molehill. Take the bloody thing away, would you?'

It wasn't up to me to mention the letters to Ed and during the two brief meetings we had in that time he didn't say anything, so I assumed Vanessa had kept her mouth shut. When Ed and I were together it was as wonderful as ever – we made love, lay together afterwards, showered together, often having another quickie with the water streaming over our bodies. I couldn't get enough of him, and in between times, I had the memories of our time together to sustain me. I felt complete in a way no other man or relationship had ever allowed me.

A week later, Vanessa rang me. A parcel had arrived for Ed, the address written in the same handwriting as the letters. I could hear the anger in her voice as she asked me to come round and join her in the 'opening ceremony', as she called it. I thought of it more as bomb disposal.

We stood at the kitchen island, the small, brown-paper package between us. Under the outer wrapping there was a layer of pink tissue paper. Vanessa handled it like it might explode. I watched her face rather than her hands. She sucked in her lips and held her breath, staring intently at what she was doing, barely blinking. A muscle twitched in her jaw.

She held up a tube of strawberry flavoured lubricant and then dropped it in distaste.

I reached for it and the note taped to it.

'Want to read it, or chuck it?' I asked.

She shook her head. 'I have no interest in finding out what Hot Bod has to say. But I tell you what – if I ever find out who she is, I'll shove this bloody stuff so far up her you-know-what she'll never be able to sit down again.'

'Have you said anything about the letters to your husband?' I asked.

'No, but I can't let this go. If he's up to something, I'll know – he's terrible at lying.' She reached for the note I'd separated from the tube, and read it. Her hand went to her mouth and her eyes opened wide, then she threw it down and laughed.

'Read it,' she said, gasping for air. 'It's – I can't describe it.'

I picked it up and looked at it.

Hey, Big Boy,
Something for next time – we can save time on dinner, just have
each other with a strawberry dessert. I'm wet just thinking
about it.
Hot Bod xoxoxox

'Brief and to the point,' I said. 'It's almost comedic. I mean, people don't really say things like that to each other, do they?'

'Well, Hot Bod certainly does. If Ed is innocent in all this, he at least might know who could be behind it – a madwoman at work or a disgruntled employee. And if he's not – well, he won't know what's hit him.'

'Fighting words, Vanessa – what do you mean?'

She looked at me and deflated, sinking onto a stool. Tears welled in her weary-looking eyes, and I realised what a toll this was taking on her. 'I don't know what to do – tell me, Kirstie – please, tell me what to do. You're the only other person who knows about this, the only one I can ask.'

I bit the inside of my cheek and looked at the note, the pink tissue paper, the lube.

'I think you're right – this is more than a joke now, if that's what it was. You need to speak to your husband.'

'Then you think–'

'I don't know what to think but you need to know. Talk to him. Let him either explain himself or prove his innocence. You won't rest until you do, and you look like you need to sleep.'

She put a hand on my arm. 'I'm scared. What if it's true – what if he is planning on leaving me?'

'I'd say it's better to know than live like this, wouldn't you? Knowledge is power, isn't that what they say? Once you know what's happening, you'll know what to do. You're a strong, resilient woman.'

She took a deep breath and lifted her chin. 'You're right. I need to know. I'll talk to him tonight.'

'Good luck,' I said.

19

———

EXILE

In the morning, I ate some porridge – I'd started making it the Scottish way, with water and salt instead of milk and sugar – and put on my walking shoes. The summer had been wet even for Yell, and the ground was saturated. In the fragile light of the September morning, I started down the hill to check on Ishbel. And I wanted to have a chat with Una about what it had been like for a woman of her age – almost my mother's age – growing up on Yell.

Una could have won gold in a talking event for the Scottish Olympic team. I asked one simple question and there I was, several hours later and she had barely stopped for breath. Even as she replenished the teapot and poured cup after cup, so I was in danger of drowning in the stuff, she carried on. It was as if she'd been waiting all her life for someone to show an interest in her. Maybe she had. Everyone else in her life had known her since they were born, and who asks someone you've known that long about themselves?

My question had been, 'What do women do in the Shetlands if they choose not to leave?'

If Una was typical, the short answer was, not much. Not in

terms of career anyway. The choices were limited, the jobs scarce. Her first job had been at a fish processing plant, but she'd hated the smell and hadn't been able to eat fish since. She said she'd always wanted to be a florist but there was little call for it in Mid Yell, and she would have needed to go to Aberdeen to train, which she hadn't wanted to do. Most of her life she'd run a bed and breakfast for the birdwatchers and tourists who flocked to the Shetlands in the summer months, and in the winter she'd hand-knitted jumpers and socks to sell in a craft shop in Lerwick.

'Mebbe you think it wasn't an interesting life and I'm sure it hasn't been compared to many but it's had its moments. So many people come to us now, there's no need to travel to other places. We hear stories from all over and see the photos without having to endure the weather and the foreign food.'

Blessed with a vice-like memory, I think Una told me about every guest who'd ever stayed and what they'd had for breakfast each day. I was hypnotised by her voice and accent and after a while, let the rhythm of her words lull me into such a relaxed state that it took me a few moments to realise she'd stopped talking.

'Sorry,' I said. 'Did you ask me something?'

She laughed. 'Only if you wanted a wee bit of lunch? We've been chatting for so long I need to eat something before I faint!'

I made my excuses and left but promised to return to see her again before too long.

When I got to Ishbel's, Lorna was there.

'Catriona had to go to a meeting, so I've got the bairn,' she said. 'But it's harder than I thought to look after her when I'm less able on my feet.'

Lorna was pulling herself up on the furniture, swaying on unsteady legs before crashing onto her bottom again, burbling away and oblivious to everything around her as she focused on her task. We watched her for a while.

'Such concentration,' I said.

Ishbel laughed. 'Aye. I'd like a bit of that. I'm so bored I can't focus on anything these days. I hate this!'

Lorna started crying.

'Och, now look what I've done,' said Ishbel.

'Don't worry, she'll be okay.' I scooped Lorna up and went into the kitchen to make her some lunch. She sat in her highchair as I sliced cheese and gave her a stick of it to chew on, made toast and cut it into soldiers she gripped so tightly they turned to mush in her hands. She laughed as she dropped them, and I bent to pick them up. Such a fun game, her looking over her table at me on my hands and knees on the floor beneath her.

When Catriona had collected her and left, I sat with Ishbel who was looking weary and pale.

'You need to get out, Ishbel,' I said. 'It's no good being cooped up in here the whole time.'

'Don't I know it,' she said. 'I'm going quietly mad. I usually go into school during the holidays to get ahead in planning and tidy up the classroom but now I'm sitting here and worrying about being behind. Term starts again in three weeks, and I'm stuck here like a beached whale. I could scream.'

'How about I drive you into school? You could sit with your leg up along the back seat.'

'You'd do that for me?'

'Of course,' I said.

She turned to me and her face lit up. 'Really? You're fantastic.' She looked around the room as if making sure there was nobody else there. 'Of course,' she said in a low voice, 'you know I'm not meant to go out too much, don't you?'

I laughed. 'We'll have to fly under the radar then. It'll be our secret.'

'As you well know, there are no secrets on Yell. But thank you, Kirstie. You'll be saving my life.'

'Not quite,' I said. 'But I'll do it, and gladly.'

We set a date for early the next week when a colleague of Ishbel's would also be at the school and they could help each other getting their classrooms ready. I didn't stay long after that. I had to do some shopping and I wanted to get back to the cottage. I had been thinking about what Una said about the lack of opportunities for women of her generation on the islands and wondering whether my mother would ever have been content to stay. I knew her not as an ambitious woman but certainly one who needed to be busy. Would she have been content to work in a fish processing plant all her life? I couldn't see it. I also couldn't imagine her married to a gentle man like Duncan who had all he ever wanted on the islands, except for the woman he loved. My mother's relationship with my father had been clipped, distant and at times violent. He had treated her with disdain, and she had perfected the art of carrying on as if he wasn't there. Being in a room with them was like inhabiting a freezer with the constant threat of oxygen deprivation. Who would she have been if she'd stayed and married Duncan? Would she have turned him into a hard, aggressive man or would he have made her soft and loving? I wanted to see my mother more than I ever had in my life. I started a mental list of the questions I wanted to ask her and spent hours wondering how to approach them so she might give me some answers rather than her usual defensive silence.

When I got to the shop, Sheila, who was also the postmistress, handed me a postcard.

'It's from your mother,' she said. 'Looks like she's having a nice time. I havenae been to Cuba but I like the music.'

'Did she say anything else?' I asked.

Sheila, either not picking up on my sarcasm, or choosing to

ignore it, said, 'Only that she's going to come and see the old place when she gets back.'

I gasped. Coming here? Minutes ago, it had been what I wanted. Now, I realised, it was also what I dreaded. Or more accurately, I wanted to see her but not on the island. I had made this little part of the world mine, had claimed the people here for myself, and I didn't want her taking them from me.

'Are you okay, Kirstie?'

'Fine, thanks.' I took the postcard and escaped from the shop, forgetting I needed to buy food.

I walked fast, conscious of the card in my pocket but determined not to read it until I was in the safety of the cottage. When I got in, I leant against the door catching my breath, putting off the moment when I had to take the postcard out of my pocket and read the words my mother had written. But then my hand reached for it and my eyes ran across it several times taking in the words.

Dear Kirstie, I am in Cuba. It's dirty and primitive but has a certain appeal. The food is awful, but the nightlife is lively. I haven't danced so much in years, if ever. I am coming to Yell when I get back. I'll send dates nearer the time. Mother x

My first reaction was disbelief. My mother had never so much as twitched a hip to music in the time I'd known her, let alone danced a salsa. But this first response was soon overpowered by the second – I was aware of a deep disappointment but what more could I have expected? A sentence about missing me? Perhaps that she was coming to see me, rather than merely making a trip to Yell? And yet I knew she was coming because of me. Nothing else would have made her return after all this time. Coming because of me was not the same as coming to see me, however. I believe my being here had piqued her curiosity about the place and the people.

It was dated almost a month ago. I looked around me at the home I had made and wondered how much longer I would have it to myself. I couldn't imagine sharing it with my mother. We had never shared space comfortably and this cottage – and maybe the whole island – was too small for the two of us. My skin prickled at the idea of her sitting with me at the table and my insides tightened when I thought of waking with her next to me, of hearing her going to the outhouse, cleaning her teeth at the sink. I shrank at the image of her clothes drying next to mine by the range. The intimacies of daily life. I considered moving out and hated her for it.

For the next few days, I went around in a clenched state, my body and mind already defending themselves from the intrusion. I couldn't concentrate on reading or writing, I missed parts of conversations, forgot half the purchases I needed to make when I went to the shop. I walked for hours each day over the moorlands as if putting as much distance as I could between my mother and myself but one day I ended up on the Ness of Vatsetter, the place where it all began – the rape that made her run away into the arms of an unloving man and give birth to a child she found difficult and who eventually ran away from her. The circle of life. What a farce.

The day was unusually still. I sat looking out to sea, the sound of the languid waves caressing the rocks below me, the taste of salt in the air. The sun was low and washed the colour out of everything and even the birds seemed listless, riding the thermals lazily. In contrast, my heart beat fast against my ribs and my breath sounded loud in my ears.

'Why are you coming?' I shouted to the sky.

Why didn't you love me?

Why haven't you come before?

It was a Tuesday when Ishbel and I ventured into Lerwick for the first time. She sat regally in the back of the car, and we joked about me wearing a chauffeur's cap and calling her ma'am. Our banter sat lightly on top of my anxiety. I had agreed to take her to her doctor's appointment and from there to school. She needed a couple of hours, she said, and I'd blithely told her I would stroll round the town and look in shops until it was time to pick her up again. But as the day had drawn closer, I'd been having dreams about meeting a 'Mr Right' in Lerwick – dreams that were both exciting and terrifying.

The day was clear but there were grey clouds on the horizon. As we drove, Ishbel pointed out friends' houses where she'd played as a child. Several of them looked abandoned, poor, tumbledown cottages in need of a little love and attention.

'Of all my childhood friends only two or three stayed. The others are all spread out – Australia, Canada, England. Those of us still here sometimes wonder what our lives would have been like if we'd gone but I don't think any of us is sorry we stayed. There's a lot to be said for a community and no one can deny that we live in a beautiful part of the world.'

'The weather could be better,' I said. 'But this place has certainly got under my skin. I can't imagine living anywhere else now.'

'I'm glad,' said my passenger, and I smiled at her in the rear-view mirror.

I sat in the waiting area, nose in a magazine, while Ishbel saw the doctor. Even hidden behind a three-year-old *Vogue*, I gnawed at my fingernails. There were so many people around and half of them were male. I was relieved when Ishbel called my name, and I looked up to see her standing beside the reception desk with crutches crammed into her armpits.

'All good. I'm allowed to start weight-bearing,' she said. 'It's a red-letter day!'

The full leg brace had been removed and she'd been given a Moon Boot to walk in which looked about as comfortable as having a lump of concrete strapped to your leg, but she was all smiles and raring to go, tapping her way up the corridor and out to the car park. She was altogether more stoical about it than Ed had been with his. I forced my thoughts away from him to focus on Ishbel.

'Let's have lunch and then I'll be away up to the school, and you can shop to your heart's delight,' she said, so we parked outside a pub, went in and ordered their soup of the day, which turned out to be tinned tomato with a few basil leaves thrown on top accompanied by two slices of white bread and marg. Haute cuisine it was not.

I sat in the car once I'd dropped Ishbel off at the school and had helped her to her classroom. Did I dare go back into town? So far everything had gone well but would I be courting disaster to go to a few shops?

As I sat there, undecided, Ed and his Moon Boot limped into my thoughts again, and this time he was more difficult to dislodge.

20

THE CONFESSION

Of course it was me sending the letters. No surprise there. I felt the need to take things into my own hands and force Ed to move out. We hadn't talked about it. In fact, he'd never mentioned leaving Vanessa, and that was the point. I knew he wanted to, but he was too much of a gentleman to hurt her. It was one of the reasons I loved him. But enough was enough.

I sat with my phone in my hand waiting to hear from him all that evening, but it was Vanessa who rang. She sounded calm.

'I did it, Kirstie. I confronted him, showed him the evidence and he was genuinely surprised. I've known him for twenty-five years and I know when he's lying, and tonight he was telling the truth. He was outraged that someone would play a trick like this on us and swore to get to the bottom of it. I just wanted to say thank you for being there for me and encouraging me to be brave. It's funny, in a way I think this has brought Ed and me closer together again. We'd been drifting apart a little in recent times but – well, you know.'

I did know. 'I'm glad for you,' I said through gritted teeth. 'Look, I'm sorry, it's late. I was almost asleep.'

'Oh, yes. Apologies. I just thought you'd like to know.'

'See you soon,' I said, then hung up and hurled the phone across the room.

What the fuck was he playing at? I'd given him the out he wanted, all he had to do was hang his head in shame, admit he was in love with someone else, and leave. What was so hard about that? I'd done all the legwork.

I retrieved my phone and called Ed's number but his mobile was off. I couldn't risk calling the landline because Vanessa might answer and I needed to have a plan before I spoke to her again. I sat all night thinking about him. Was he a coward, or was he just too empathic for his own good? Had I not made it clear enough that I wanted a future with him, that he need never be alone?

In the morning there was a loud knock on my door. 'It's me, open up.'

Ed! He'd come to me after all.

When I opened the door he pushed past me and strode into the lounge, stood there with his back against the window, arms crossed. 'What the fuck do you think you are doing?' he shouted.

'Please don't yell, Ed. I did it because I love you. I did it for us, so that we can be together.'

He laughed harshly. 'For us? There's no us, Kirstie. I've never loved you. We just fuck occasionally.'

My hand flew to my heart. I felt like he'd stabbed me. 'But–'

'But nothing. Now I'll tell you what's going to happen. We're never going to see each other again and you'll stay away from my wife, or I'll call the police and tell them what a fucking crazy bitch you are. Understand?'

I took a step towards him. 'Ed, don't do this, you're upset I know but when you calm down, you'll see I was only trying to clear the way for you and me to be together. That's all I want.'

'You know what? You're pathetic. Get a life and stay the fuck out of mine. I've warned you.'

He started towards the door, and I tried to grab him, to make him stay and listen, to see reason, but he pushed me away. I lunged again and grabbed hold of his jacket, holding on tight, desperate not to let him go. I felt his hand in my hair and then a sharp pain as he pulled. He yanked his jacket out of my grasp and ran out of the flat. I heard the door slam and his tread on the stairs. Then nothing.

My knees buckled. Lying on the floor, my mind was racing. He loved me, he had to. And I couldn't live without him. We were meant for each other, I knew it.

But no matter how often I told myself all that, I couldn't drive the pain of what had happened out of my mind. Ed had said horrible, nasty things and told me he didn't love me, which had to be a lie.

I calmed down with the help of half a bottle of Glenfiddich. All he needed was time. He was upset. I should have told him what I was doing so he was prepared, then this would have turned out differently. It was my fault it had all gone wrong. I would do better next time.

What we had couldn't be denied.

21

EXILE

Two weeks after the first postcard announcing her visit, my mother phoned the shop and spoke to Sheila. The next time I was in, she said, 'Your mother arrives in three days. She'll need picking up from the morning ferry in Lerwick.'

I took a deep breath and leant against the counter, suddenly weak.

'You don't look so very pleased at the news, Kirstie.'

I consciously moved my mouth into a smile. 'I haven't seen her for a long time,' was all I could manage without telling a lie.

Once again I left the shop without half of my list, scurrying away as fast as I could back to my sanctuary.

I had three days to prepare but there was nothing practical to do. I had cleaned the cottage, washed the spare sheets, made meal plans. My mother was about to enter my territory and the thing I still had to get ready was my head.

I spent a sleepless night thinking about my parents, their relationship, my childhood. Round and round in circles, remembering the good bits – the holiday to Italy (which my mother had obviously not thought a *proper* holiday – possibly because we were self-catering rather than staying in a hotel). It had been when I was very little and my parents were still just able to be civil to each other. There were visits to Brighton Pier and eating candyfloss with my father. He used to bury his face in the huge cloud of it and come up with wispy pink whiskers stuck to his face. It made me laugh every time as I pulled the strands off and stuffed them into my mouth until all that was left on his face was a sugary tidemark which must have felt sticky and uncomfortable as it dried and tightened on his skin. There were ballet lessons and performances, with Mother bending over the sewing machine for hours at a time making tutus and other costumes, as I swirled about and told her about the ballerina I would become. She was always good at things like that.

But for every positive memory there were negative ones – arguments, hostility, walkouts and coldness. It wasn't just that my parents no longer talked to each other, they also stopped engaging with me most of the time, as if they had retired into separate corners and forgotten there was someone still out there in the middle of the ring.

Over the years I have tried to forgive my parents for their inadequate parenting. Self-help books told me that holding on to anger was only hurting myself, which, although trite-sounding, is probably true. And sometimes I *can* let go of the anger but when I do I am confronted by an ocean of sadness, fear, and self-loathing. At those moments, I am a vulnerable, unlovable child pretending to be an adult and trying to make it in the big wide world. A victim. And I never wanted to be a victim. I may not have had any control over my 'relationships' but I sure as hell wasn't going to end up like my mother. It has been my anger that's enabled me to do what I have done – to be as different from her as possible. To be independent, to make a career, build a business. Without it, I would have crumbled. Anger has kept me going.

And if I forgave her, I had to accept responsibility for my life. The realisation hit me, leaving me gasping for breath. The cold, hard truth.

I tossed and turned in my bed and saw the sun rise over the rim of the world. Another day. One day closer to my mother's arrival and I was a basket case.

In the morning I went to see Ishbel. Unable to calm myself, I had to talk to someone. She was more mobile with every passing day and insisted on making the tea and buttering a piece of fruitcake for me.

'I won't have any myself – I already feel like a hippo I've put on so much weight from sitting around for so long. So, Kirstie, you look like you just had a tooth extracted, I've never seen you look so down in the mouth. Is it because of your mother's arrival?'

The Mid Yell telegraph had been in action. It was impossible to keep a secret in this community. Duncan would already know, and I kicked myself that I hadn't gone straight round to tell him, the one person, apart from me, with the most invested in the event.

'Yes. I don't know how I feel about it.' I took a bite of the moist cake, taking a moment to savour the rich flavours of fruit peel and alcohol. Ishbel waited for me to continue. I'd been hoping she might do the talking, telling me how I should feel so I could have something to rail against.

In the end I broke the awkward silence. 'We're not close, as you know, and haven't shared a house for many years. I have my habits and no doubt she has hers.' I faltered. This was what happened when I sat thinking on my own, I'd get sidetracked by the practicalities and skirt around the crux of the matter.

I took a deep breath. 'I'm afraid she's going to spoil this place for me.'

There, it was said. I held my breath.

Ishbel took my hand and held it gently. Tears welled in my eyes and spilled down my cheeks.

Before she could say anything, I continued, 'She turned her back on this place and the people she knew, and I've made it mine. You know how hard I found it to feel safe here and to begin to make friends. Now she'll swan in and take it all away again.'

Ishbel took a deep breath and let it out with a sigh. 'You do know, don't you, Kirstie, that it is possible your friends here have big enough hearts to love both of you. It doesn't have to be either/or.'

I sniffed and lifted my gaze to hers. 'But she's from here, she belongs.'

'And what's that got to do with the price of fish?' asked Ishbel, laughing. 'She may have been born here but as far as I'm concerned you belonged here from the moment you set foot in that cottage of yours and made it your home. This place is in your blood and there's nobody can take it away from you unless you let them.'

I sighed and my shoulders released. Ishbel was right. I had carved out my own place in this community, had built my own friendships. There was no reason to feel threatened, and I had to admit that part of me was interested to see if my mother could make herself at home here after all these years.

'Have you seen Duncan?' I asked.

She nodded. 'He came by yesterday. He was the one who told me.'

'I should have told him. I'm sorry he heard it from someone else. We've been talking about her, you know. I think he still loves her, or the woman he thinks she is. I hope he isn't disappointed.'

'I didn't know that. See? You certainly belong here when you know people's secrets.'

'I shouldn't have said anything. I assumed it was common knowledge. And he hasn't said as much, it's just a way he has when he's talking about her, a softness in his voice, and the way he drums his fingers on whatever is to hand. I might be wrong.'

'I doubt it. You're a good judge of character – you chose me to be your friend!'

'You had to persevere at first though. I never did thank you for not giving up on me and for insisting that everyone else gave me the space I needed.'

Ishbel reddened. 'Well, now,' she said, 'I have to ring Una and thank her for the stew she dropped off for me. Oh, and I'll ask someone else to take me into Lerwick next time so you can spend time with your mother.'

I laughed. 'I'll need the break and an understanding person to talk to, so please let me take you. Just let me know when.'

On the day of my mother's arrival, I borrowed Duncan's car and was at the port in Lerwick at 7.20 in the morning, standing in a shroud of fog, hands in my pockets, neck pulled well into my jacket collar. Watching the ferry from Aberdeen pull into the quay, I felt a mixture of hope and fear – or perhaps it was the anticipation of disappointment. I wondered how our relationship might change now she was home and whether the islands would gather her unto themselves again and allow her to soften.

I saw her before she saw me. My guts clenched. Her hair was blowing in the stiff breeze. She raised a hand and I returned the wave, but she was just flattening her hair down. I watched her approach and thought how thin her legs were, like little sticks in their practical brown tights. Had they always been like that? She walked with small, neat steps, looking at her feet as if worried there might be an obstacle to trip her. And the stoop, surely that was new?

And then she was right in front of me, the line of her mouth thin-lipped and downturned. That wasn't new.

'Mother, welcome.'

She raised her head and looked into my eyes. There was no smile, no hugs or kisses, just a nod of the head as she handed me her suitcase and we walked together back to the car. Her hair was greyer than it had been when last I saw her, and thinner. The creases of her face deeper and despite a slight tan, she looked drawn. She was in her late seventies and showing it.

As we drove north towards the Yell ferry, I snuck glances at her. She sat looking straight ahead as if the scenery was of no interest to her at all.

'How was the trip?' I asked.

'It was long. There was some trackwork on the line and we sat outside Manchester in a field for hours. Good thing I'd left plenty of time between my arrival in Aberdeen and my departure. I had thought I would get some dinner. As it was, I had to buy food on the ferry which was salty and expensive. Still, I'm here now.'

'Are you excited to be back?' She didn't look it, but I had to ask. She wasn't a demonstrative person, so she might have been jumping up and down on the inside, desperate to get her first sight of her birthplace.

'Not especially. I thought I might as well come and see what you've done to the croft.'

She had her handbag on her lap, and now opened it and took out a packet of mints with fingers that trembled slightly.

I had to stifle the urge to shout or swerve the car or tell her that Duncan still held a torch for her – anything to get a reaction from her, it didn't matter what. It was like sitting next to a robot. She had to be feeling something about her return – anxiety, fear, anticipation, hope? Anything but this seeming indifference. And yet, this was her. When I was a child I thought she didn't have any feelings because she never showed them. Whatever was happening, she was calm and distant. Sometimes it was helpful. Mostly not. Much of my more outrageous behaviour when I was younger was an attempt to get her to react – even if her reaction was to slap me across the face. She never did. It was as if she couldn't even spare the energy to chide me and, in the end, I gave up. I'd run out of stamina and ideas to get her attention. Now I suspect it was depression making her behave like that.

In the car, the silence was becoming uncomfortable – for me, anyway. My mother seemed quite composed.

'I love the view from here,' I said as we crested a hill and the northern half of the mainland spread out before us.

My mother stared straight ahead, her jaw clenched.

I gripped the steering wheel so tightly my knuckles whitened.

'Is there anyone you particularly want to see?' I asked.

'No.'

'Well, Duncan and Ewan are looking forward to seeing you, and their cousin, Una – she was just a wee girl when you left – she's excited to meet you. And Ishbel, of course. And I'm sorry to tell you that Andrew Tulloch died a few years ago, and as I wrote, your brother, Robbie died earlier this year.'

'I've come here for a quiet time. I'll not be rushing around making social calls.'

Her accent, which I'd always thought was strongly Scottish,

sounded almost English in comparison to the others on the island.

I smiled to myself and decided not to tell her she didn't have to go anywhere – they would all come to see her as soon as they knew she'd arrived, which would be the minute we drove through the village.

I was wrong. There was no welcoming committee. They must have decided to give her time to settle in. We skirted round each other, uneasy companions. She looked around the cottage with the eye of an estate agent, not someone who had lived there for the first seventeen years of her life. Detached, almost disinterested.

'So, what do you think? What's it like being back?' I asked when she'd looked about.

'I think you don't keep a very neat house, is what I think. Look at the muck around the sink.'

It was true, the grouting around the old porcelain sink was grubby and when I'd tried to clean it some had crumbled away. I'd stopped noticing all the jobs that needed to be done around the place, instead enjoying it as it was. When I was a child the house had always been a sterile place, not a speck of dust, nothing out of place. It never felt like a real home – cosy, lived in. In contrast, the cottage with its uneven floors and windows that didn't quite fit, the door that stuck in wet weather, crumbling grout and animals in the roof was comforting.

I took a deep breath. And then another. And I remembered this had been my coping strategy when my anger got me nowhere. Breathing slowly and deeply was the way I stopped myself from being sent to prison for matricide.

'Anything else?' I asked, smiling tightly.

'What else do you want me to think?'

'I don't know, Mother – how about curious to see the old place and people, or scared, or – well, anything, really?'

'I don't know what you want from me, Kirsten, but you'll not get it by losing your temper. I'm going to lie down. It's been a long trip and I'm not as young as I used to be.'

I bit my lip and picked up her suitcase. 'I've put you in the bedroom, I'll take the truckle bed while you're here.'

'As you wish.'

I started chopping vegetables for lunch but was distracted by a strange sound from the bedroom. It took me a while to identify what it was: my mother was crying. I stood at the table, unsure what to do. In the end I decided to leave her. I doubted my mother would appreciate me barging in on this private moment. Any clumsy attempts on my behalf to console her would either be extremely awkward for us both or rebuffed outright. At least, that's what I told myself as I went outside to breathe in the crisp air.

Standing there, looking out towards the sea, I felt sorry for my mother, and knew she would hate that. I resolved not to mention what I'd heard, and to give her time.

When I went back inside, she was sitting at the kitchen table holding her father's violin. Her cheeks were wet and her eyelashes glistened with tears. She sniffed and wiped her eyes when she saw me, put the instrument down and went into the bedroom again, closing the door behind her.

My resolution went out the window. I paused in the kitchen, and then followed her.

'I'm sorry, Mother. It must be hard for you, coming back here after all this time.'

'I'm fine, Kirsten, really. Just tired.'

'It's okay to be sad, you know, and worried. How could you not be? You were driven away from this place and–'

'I'm going to have a sleep now,' she said, and lay down, turning her back on me.

'We'll talk later then,' I said, and closed the door.

The whisky bottle was on the shelf. How tempting it was to take a swig to dampen these feelings. But I had sworn before she came that I wouldn't take to drink on her account. Steeling myself against my impulse, I left the cottage again and went to the shore.

A female otter and her cubs were shimmering in the shallows, swimming in and out of the seaweed, chasing each other and I could swear they had smiles on their little faces, enjoying the game and each other. A family at play.

That evening I cooked a simple dinner and waited for my mother to appear, but she didn't and when I knocked on the bedroom door there was no answer, so I ate alone and washed up quietly.

The next morning, Mother got up early. Lying in the truckle bed behind the curtain I could hear her moving about the room, cleaning out the grate, going outside to get some peat blocks from the stack near the door, lighting the fire. She filled the kettle and set it on the heat. I had promised myself I wouldn't let her do anything while she was here but now that seemed unfair. She needed to be busy, to be in control. I could let her feel herself to be in charge – perhaps it would help her open up. So I didn't interrupt her as she went about her work, familiarising herself once again with the chores she must have carried out in her childhood. And then I heard her start to sing.

Amazing Grace, how sweet the sound
That saved a wretch like me.

She faltered on the words and hummed the next few bars in a reedy voice, and then finished strongly.

Was blind but now I see.

We used to sing it at school, and I had to hold my breath so as not to join in. I knew she needed privacy in this moment.

I lay until my bladder forced me up and to the outhouse. When I came back in, the table was set, porridge bubbling on the stove, and the teapot in pride of place in the centre of the table.

'Good morning, Kirsten. Porridge?'

'Thanks. Did you sleep well?'

'Like the proverbial log. It must be the sea air. I slept well on the cruise as well. Better than I have in years.'

'Yes,' I said, 'how was the cruise?' Perhaps we had to start on neutral topics.

'Fine. We went to some interesting places. I sent you a postcard.'

'Yes, from Cuba. I couldn't imagine you dancing.'

'We started in Florida and went to the Bahamas, Cuba, Jamaica, the Cayman Islands and Mexico,' she said.

'Did you have a favourite?'

'There were lectures on the ship about all the places we went to, it was all interesting and very well organised.'

It was as if we were having parallel conversations. I tried again.

'You enjoyed all the places?'

'Hans said he'd never been on such a well conducted trip.'

'Hans?'

'Yes. I met him on board.'

'Was he your salsa partner by any chance?'

Did I notice a blush creep up my mother's neck? She certainly turned away abruptly and busied herself with the porridge pot. Tempted as I was to know more, I didn't push it.

We had had a conversation of more than two sentences, and I didn't want to jeopardise our tenuous connection.

'Was it one of those enormous floating hotels you went on?'

'Och, no. It was a yacht. A big one, mind you. A superyacht I think they called it.' She turned back to look at me, the blush gone. 'There were twenty passengers and ten crew. Very comfortable. I thought if I was going to have a holiday, I'd have the best one I could. I don't fancy those big ships at all.'

I smiled. 'I'm glad you had a good time.'

She sat to eat her breakfast, spooning the porridge into her mouth, eating like a bird in tiny mouthfuls. I bolted mine down and refilled the teapot.

'What do you want to do today?' I asked.

'A walk, I think. I'd like to stretch these old legs.'

'Shall we go together, or would you prefer to be on your own?'

She didn't answer immediately, so I prepared myself for a rejection but after a while she said, 'Yes, come. I'm not sure I'll remember the way on my own.'

'The way to where?'

'You know, Kirsten. You know.' She stared at me.

I did know, of course, but my stomach turned at the idea. 'Are you sure?'

'I'll put my stout shoes on. I'll be ready as soon as I've pulled a comb through my hair.'

The day had dawned clear and bright, the dazzle of the sun on the sea almost blinding. My mother stumbled a couple of times as we made our way slowly towards Vatsetter, and I linked my arm through hers to steady her. I felt her stiffen but she didn't pull away. When was the last time we'd touched? How long had her arm been so thin I could feel the bones even through a sweater and a quilted jacket? It was as if she was performing some sort of vanishing act.

We walked in silence. I didn't know what to say, how to broach the subject of the rape. I wanted to know everything about this old woman who was my mother, before it was too late. But I realised I might as well discard all my questions – she was only going to tell her story when she was ready, if at all. I thought about asking Duncan for the rest of the letters so at least I could learn more about her early years in England but that seemed ridiculous when I had the woman right next to me. I had to be patient and hope the weight loss and lack of appetite were not the result of some horrible disease that was going to take her before there was time for us to learn more about each other. And I had to hope she would want to tell me about her life.

We stood leaning into the wind gusting from the north. I watched her taking in the scenery, biting her lips as if even now, all these years later, she needed to choke back the words she had wanted to scream at the time.

The wind blew my hair around my face and the smell of damp moss and salt water filled my nostrils. Next to me I heard my mother's jagged breath. And then she started shouting.

'You bastard. I hope you rot in Hell!' Her hands were balled into fists, her arms rigid by her sides. I stood next to her, not knowing what to do, what to say, but glad, in a way, that she was angry. And expressing it.

She stopped, stood still. Together we looked out over the grey North Sea, the waves crashing on the rocks below us.

'Are you okay?' I asked eventually.

She pulled her coat more tightly around herself, adjusted the scarf at her neck. 'Aye, Kirsten, I'm fine now. It was a long time ago.'

'But it was the reason you left – it changed your whole life.'

'It did, but who can say whether it wasn't for the better?' She lifted her chin and turned to me. Her eyes were hard but there were bright dots of pink on her cheeks.

'I–' I stopped myself. I had been about to ask how on earth the life she had lived with my father could possibly have been better than staying on the island, marrying Duncan or someone else, having the dozens of children she had supposedly wanted. But I realised it was the only thing she could believe, that made sense of the choice she'd made. It was either that, or risk being crushed by the weight of regret. Was that what her tears had been about the day before?

'We'll not talk about that event anymore. It's done.'

'Did you miss home?' I asked gently. I couldn't let it go.

'Of course I did, at first, but slowly I settled into my new place with Miss Harris, made a friend, went to college. I couldn't have done that if I'd stayed here.' She looked out to sea again, at the islands of Hascosay and Fetlar to the east. 'I was a good teacher. If I'd stayed here I would have missed out on that.'

'What about Duncan – he wanted to marry you?'

'Is that what he says? It's a long time ago, I think he is misremembering.' Her mouth lifted into a thin smile.

'Why should he? He seems to remember other things clearly enough. Maybe it's you who's got it wrong.'

She whirled round and snapped at me. 'If you're going to take everyone else's side against mine, I may as well leave now. If you choose to believe him over me, there's no point in talking about any of it.'

'I'm not choosing sides. I want to know the truth. You've never talked about this place, these people. They're my relatives too, you know, and you kept me from them. All I know about your childhood is from them.' I hadn't meant to raise my voice, but the words came out hard, accusing.

'It wasn't important. It probably still isn't. This isn't my home anymore, and nor is it yours, however hard you try and fit in and make a place among these people. You should pack your bags and go home, get back to work.'

I felt her words in my solar plexus, was winded and wounded by them.

'And what the hell would you know about fitting in, eh?'

The words were out there before I could stop them, those words that could only drive the wedge between us ever deeper.

She started walking away, watching her feet and stepping carefully. I was torn between shouting at her, demanding that she stop and talk, and my usual act of caving in to her refusal to engage with me.

Old habits die hard.

Hands balled into fists in my pockets, I followed her, far enough away to preclude talk but close enough to catch her if she stumbled. At the croft, she carefully untied her shoes, hung her coat on the peg and went into her room, shutting the door quietly behind her. I went outside and kicked a tussock of grass until my foot ached and the blades of hard, grey-green grass were strewn all around.

She didn't appear again until dinner which she picked at before declaring herself full.

'I'm sorry about earlier.' I almost choked on the apology, but I was the one with the vested interest here, the one who wanted to understand, to know her story as a way of making sense of mine, while she seemed to need nothing from me.

'We'll say no more about it. Thank you for dinner.'

'Was it okay? You haven't eaten very much.'

'I've had plenty. I'm not used to such rich food.'

It was only pasta with a simple tomato sauce, nothing rich about it. It felt as if not eating my food was my mother's way of proving yet again she had no need of me or my offerings. I'd felt the same whenever she'd put away the drawings I did for her as a child, the gifts I'd bought her from my saved pocket money. I was so peripheral to her life, nothing stuck.

Deep breaths, I reminded myself.

'Would you like to meet Ishbel tomorrow? We'd have to go there – she's broken her leg and can't get about very much at the moment.'

'Remind me who she is?'

'Your niece – Robbie's daughter.'

'Ah, yes. Robbie.' She closed her eyes as if to catch a memory of him, and a faint smile lifted her lips.

'I'm told he used to meet you from school with Ned, the pony, and let you ride home.' It seemed a safe recollection to start with.

'Aye, he did.' She opened her eyes. They were bright with tears. 'Fat little pony he was in spite of all the work he did around the place, pulling the cart full of peat cuttings, delivering them to the houses about here. Your grandfather used to make sure all the folk had plenty. And he'd take the milk and cheese and butter to the old 'uns too. Your grandmother used to curse him for giving away so much food, but he'd just smile and tell her they'd be rewarded in heaven for their acts on earth. And it's not as if we went hungry.'

I took note of the fact she'd spoken about the pony rather than her brother, and that she'd referred to her parents as my grandparents, but I'd rarely heard so many words come out of my mother's mouth. Never seen her looking so relaxed. Maybe Yell was working its magic on her as I'd hoped.

'Were there girls your age around when you were a child?' I

realised I'd never heard anyone talk about them if there were – Una was quite a lot younger than my mother.

'Girls? Yes, there was Fi Galdie, and a year or two younger, Ailsa Leask. We were all in the same class at school. Well, we all were – there was only one class! Duncan and Ewan, Andrew Tulloch, Bram Jamieson.' She came to an abrupt stop. 'Well, enough of them.' She brushed some imaginary crumbs off her lap and got up to take her plate to the sink.

'I'll do the dishes, Mother, you sit. I'll make some tea.' I wanted to prolong the moment. It was the most information I'd ever got out of her.

'I'm not used to sitting, Kirsten. I'll make the tea.' I relented and sat watching her. Once the kettle was on the range she leant against the sink and looked out the window over the moor that descended to the shoreline and the ever-changing sea. She was so still it was as if she'd become a statue, caught between the past and the present. And then she took a deep breath, pushed down on the edge of the sink to stand taller, and said, 'I remembered the cottage being closer to the sea. But I was always in a hurry back then, so everything seemed closer I suppose. Although the croft feels smaller than I remembered. How did five of us live here without getting under each other's feet all the time, I wonder?'

We sat either side of the range, drinking our tea. My mother was quiet after her revelations and appeared to be lost in her own thoughts but then her chin dropped onto her chest, and she let out a little snore. I let her be for a while, observing her like I would watch an animal in its natural habitat. Her once thick hair had thinned and silvered. She wore it in a short bob with Kirby grips holding both sides away from her face. It was a style that could so easily have looked childish but with her narrow face, small, neat nose and high cheekbones, she looked almost elegant.

The sleeves of her cardigan had inched up her forearms and I noticed scars on her wrists. I took a deep breath and held it. At that moment, my mother woke up, adjusted her sleeves in what seemed like a habitual movement, and, saying goodnight, went to her room.

She'd been here less than two days and already I was all over the place. She'd tried, at some stage, to kill herself. But when? They were old scars, but how old? The scars and her obvious distress earlier had shocked me, had made me realise that the hard carapace she'd spent a lifetime building wasn't as strong or as impenetrable as I'd thought. Although I wanted to know her, I also wondered if I was ready to hear what she might say. I felt caught in a dance with her, falling into step briefly, which felt new and hopeful, and then pirouetting away again, back to our old habits.

I did what I was good at. Turned my thoughts away from what was in front of me, back to the past. Ed and our unhealthy 'dance'.

Did it start when I realised my parents could not, or would not give me the love I craved, so I set about finding someone who could love me, who would want to be with me and me alone? Is my illness, my 'love obsession' explained away as easily as that? A lonely child-woman desperate for love? I can't believe it is, but I also can't imagine what more it is. When I feel loved I am complete. When I am not, I live in a dark swirl of despair. Or have until now.

I now know Ed didn't love me. There was none of the romance I craved. We had sex, a lot of it, but I mistook it for love. He wasn't capable and, maybe, neither am I. I fooled myself into believing that what we had would develop into what I wanted, but it never did and never would. Yet I long for companionship, for the give and take of a healthy relationship.

I was buoyed by my recent success at resisting the man on

the ferry. I can only hope it was the beginning of a new future for me. On this small island in the middle of the North Sea, I am held in a web of friendship, and feel no need for more. Can I say I am cured, that I will never again fall into the mire of delusion?

I couldn't sleep, so in the end I got up and carried on with my confession.

22

THE CONFESSION

After my efforts to get Ed away from his wife he stayed away from me. I waited for him at the station, watched the house but never saw him. I wondered if he'd left Vanessa after all and was expecting me to come to him. I rang Vanessa to ask how she was, and she invited me round for coffee. His things were still there. Vanessa said he'd started taking the car to work because the trains were full of loonies and he couldn't stand it anymore. They were planning a trip to Italy, just the two of them, as a second honeymoon. Ed was being very attentive and loving, she said.

She had a sated look about her. And a smugness. She had stared into what might have been a chasm in her marriage and found it was merely a ditch.

I wanted to hit her. To swing a heavy object at her and watch her head cave in. Lucky for her I remained just rational enough to realise that if I killed her, I would be separated from Ed forever. Instead, I left.

I am so ashamed. I was so ill. And yet, so rational. Is that possible? Even at the time I watched myself do these things and part of me was incredulous, shocked, but a larger part was impressed at my own ingenuity. I would find a way to be with Ed. It was my goal, my guiding light, my reason for being.

I was waiting for him in the underground car park when he finished work.

'How the fuck did you find me?' he asked. Not quite the reception I had hoped for but at least he'd acknowledged me.

'I had to see you, Ed.'

'Get away from me. I told you, you're nothing to me. Whatever we had, it's over.'

'It can't be. It takes two to make a relationship and two to break it, and I refuse to let you break it. We're meant for each other; you have to stop denying it to yourself.' I had prepared the speech and was rather proud of it.

'You're mad.' He stepped back as I moved towards him.

'I know you have to pretend, Ed, and I respect you for it, really I do but there's no one else here.' I swept my eyes around just to make sure and then dropping my voice to a sexy whisper, added, 'And I'm wearing those panties you like so much. I'm wet just thinking about you making love to me here in this car park, right now.' I might even have licked my lips. I knew how to make him notice me. Need me. Love me.

His pupils dilated when he was aroused and there was a minute change in the pattern of his breath. I opened my coat to reveal myself, dressed only in the crotchless knickers, licked my finger and started rubbing my clitoris. My nipples hardened and suddenly his mouth was on one of them and his hand brushed mine aside as he took over, caressing my clitoris, making me shudder in anticipation. I undid his belt and slid my hand around his hard cock and guided it into me as we backed up against a pillar, groaning, kissing, nipping.

'That wasn't fair, Kirstie,' he said afterwards, wiping my lipstick off his mouth. 'It doesn't change anything.'

'Of course not,' I said, knowing it changed everything. He couldn't keep his hands off me. He loved me. I needed no more proof. On my way home I delighted in the sensation of his semen trickling down my thighs.

23

———

EXILE

I was sure that my mother wouldn't tell me how she got the scars on her wrists if I asked. Like everything else about her, I had to wait until she was ready to tell me. If ever. I determined to wait it out and behave as normal. After all, it was just one more thing she hadn't told me about.

'I've invited Duncan up for dinner,' I said the next morning. I hadn't yet but he was never busy, so I was sure he'd come.

Did my mother blush? She did, but whether from anger or from anticipation, I didn't know.

She said nothing.

'I'll need to go shopping, and I'll pop in to see how Ishbel is. Do you want to come with me? I know you'll like her, and she's keen to meet you.'

'I can arrange my own affairs quite well, thank you, Kirsten. I will stay here this morning and write some letters.' She stared at me with her mouth tight and her eyes cold in the way she used to when I was young and had done something she didn't like. I had to remind myself that I was forty-four years old and didn't need her approval, nor had I done anything wrong. Duncan often came up for a meal.

Admittedly it was usually lunch, but dinner had somehow seemed more appropriate for his first meeting with my mother in sixty years.

'Want me to get you some stamps?'

'Stamps?'

'Yes – you said you were going to write some letters,' I said.

'So I did. Yes, two first class.'

'Who are you writing to?'

'That's for me to know and you to keep your nose out of. I can do what I want, I am an adult, after all.'

She sounded rather petulant and I wondered what she was hiding. Perhaps she was in communication with her Cuban dance partner, Hans, or whatever his name was, and didn't want me to know I might be getting a new father. I smiled to myself. Wild imagination. The idea of my mother with a man was outrageous – I mean, I'd never even seen her and my father touching each other. Most of the time they didn't even talk. I used to think I must have been an immaculate conception.

I hummed to myself as I walked down to the village.

I went to see Ishbel only to find her lying on the sofa with a wet flannel on her forehead and the curtains drawn.

'Migraine,' she said. 'Sorry – terrible company today.'

'Can I get you anything – tea, a cold pack for your head, drugs?'

She held the cloth out to me. 'If you could just dampen that again I'd be grateful.'

I left soon after, having made her promise to send for me if she needed anything else.

Sheila nodded to me as I entered the shop, and asked after Morag.

'She's still settling in. I'm sure she'll be down this way in a day or two,' I said.

Sheila shrugged as if she wasn't desperate to meet my

mother, as if people returning to Yell after sixty years were two a penny.

I bought the stamps and the food I needed for the dinner and headed over to Duncan and Ewan's. I wasn't sure whether it would be rude not to invite Ewan too, but as it happened, he was going out to his folk club anyway and said that as he was playing fiddle in the band, he couldn't really pull out. I promised to have him up another time.

'So, Duncan – are you ready to see Morag again after all this time?' I asked.

His weathered face took on a rosy flush and his eyes wouldn't meet mine. His hands, usually so steady, shook slightly on the arms of his chair, and he sucked in his lips before answering.

'Aye, 'tis time,' he said. It was, but he looked shell-shocked rather than pleased at the idea.

'Come up any time you like. We'll eat at seven.'

He could decide whether he came for a drink and chat beforehand, or came dead on seven, ate and left. At that moment, I'd have put money on the latter.

I spent the afternoon getting everything ready – a crate with a cushion on top to make a third chair, the table scrubbed, glasses polished, vegetables cleaned and chopped. I stuffed a salmon with a crushed walnut, preserved lemon and parsley mixture and wrapped it in foil ready to go. My mother dithered. I'd never known her so agitated. She sat at the kitchen table and watched, then moved to the other chair and took out her writing case, put it down again, went out for a breath of (very) fresh air, came in all rosy-cheeked and sat again, pulling at the sleeves of her cardigan.

'Are you okay?' I asked when I thought I'd go out of my mind with her restless wanderings.

'Perfectly. I'm just not used to having so little to do.'

'Why don't you go for a walk then?'

She looked out the window and pursed her lips. 'No. No, I think I prefer to stay here. I'll read my book. It's very good. Have you heard of it?'

'I don't know – you haven't told me what it's called.' I shook my head and laughed.

'There's no need to get uppity with me. It's quite a new one – *The Girl on the Train*.'

I thought about it. I had read it and hated it. I thought the plot implausible, and the protagonist was completely obsessed, drunk half the time and thoroughly unlikeable. She reminded me of myself, and it made for a highly uncomfortable reading experience.

She went into the bedroom and closed the door. I took a deep breath, ready to carry on with my preparations but the door opened again and there she was, like the proverbial bad penny.

'Mother, what *is* the matter?'

She stood, wringing her hands and looking as if she was about to cry.

'What's he like these days?' she asked.

My chest suddenly didn't feel big enough for my heart. I took one of her hands and sat her down. 'He's kind and gentle and the most loyal friend anyone could ever hope for. And he's missed you.'

She sighed and her shoulders relaxed but then she jumped up and muttered something about old fools and wonky memories and getting ready. This time, she didn't reappear until after six. She'd put some make-up on and had clips in her hair with little blue bows on them. They could have made her look like mutton dressed as lamb but in fact she wore them with dignity. They matched the colour of her cardigan which brought out the deep blue of her eyes and made her look younger, softer. She accepted a small glass of whisky and sat, breathing steadily, staring out the door, which was open to the lowering evening sun.

At a quarter to seven, Duncan appeared carrying a bunch of flowers in one hand and a bottle of home-made elderflower wine in the other. He'd had a haircut since the morning and was wearing his best suit.

'Come in, come in, make yourself at home,' I said, and then tried to make myself scarce so he and my mother could greet each other privately after all this time but in such a tiny cottage, it was impossible to get away.

Duncan put the wine on the table and held the flowers out to my mother.

'Stargazer lilies. I grow them in my garden. They were your favourites.' His cheeks were bright red, but his eyes were steady as he looked at my mother.

She took them, buried her face in them, and then lifted her gaze to his. 'And they still are. Thank you, Duncan. Won't you sit down? A glass of whisky for you?'

She flitted around like a little bird, needing to be busy, playing the hostess. He sat and watched her, a look on his face like he'd just arrived home after a long journey.

I served the salmon and invited them to help themselves to vegetables and crusty bread, and we sat around the table in an awkward silence.

'Well,' I said after a while, 'to reunions!' and raised my glass. We had opened Duncan's wine. If it was anything like the stuff he usually made, it would soon loosen their tongues.

'Friends and family.' My mother raised her glass. Her eyes were moist.

Duncan seemed unable to speak, so he just held his glass up and nodded.

'It's been a while, Duncan,' my mother said, not quite meeting his gaze.

'Aye, that it has,' he said, staring at his plate.

We sat there so still I could hear my watch ticking. I looked from one to the other. My mother was biting her lip, Duncan clasping and unclasping his hands in his lap.

'I'm sorry I stopped writing,' said my mother suddenly.

'Aye. You were busy I 'spect.' Duncan looked at her and down at his hands again.

They lapsed into silence once more and concentrated on pushing the food around their plates. Duncan usually had a healthy appetite and an interest in food but beans on toast would have done for all that was being eaten. I wondered whether to try and start a conversation or leave them to it and decided on the latter but when I got up to clear the table, they both looked at me in mute appeal, so I sat down again. They weren't ready to be alone with sixty years of absence between them.

I filled their glasses and smiled at them.

'So, Mother, have you told Duncan about your salsa dancing in Cuba?'

I knew she hadn't. They'd hardly spoken more than ten words to each other, and I'd heard every one, which, if she were feeling more comfortable, my mother would have pointed out to me in no uncertain terms. But I thought it would be easier to start on something recent and impersonal than launching straight into the distant past.

'Get away, he doesn't want to hear about that,' she said, blushing.

'Och, but I do,' said Duncan eagerly. 'Ye still like dancing, do ye?'

She nodded. 'Aye. I still do. Though I haven't danced a reel since I – well, for a long time.'

'But this salsie – it's similar or what?'

'It's Latin American – not quite the same but fun anyway.'

I noticed she didn't correct him, and I was glad. If it had been me, she would have jumped on my mistake. She was different with Duncan; gentler, kinder, softer.

'So–' Duncan stopped again.

'You haven't told me much about your cruise, Mother, so come on, spill the beans.'

She beamed at me as if I'd single-handedly stopped the *Titanic* from sinking, and started telling us about the places she'd been, what she'd seen, the food she'd eaten, even a couple of funny stories about the people she'd met, one of whom had been terrified of drowning and had gone on the cruise as some sort of immersion therapy. No pun intended, she said. Duncan and I laughed and drained our glasses. The wine was all gone and it was time for the whisky to come out again.

'Not for me,' said my mother, covering her glass with her hand.

'I'd best be going,' said Duncan, getting up.

'Well, just a small one then,' said my mother quickly. 'Won't you stay a little longer, Duncan?'

He sat again, gazing at my mother as if she'd just proposed to him. 'Aye then, a wee while longer.'

I poured the drinks and cleared the table. 'I'm just going to get some more peat for the fire and then I'll get dessert,' I said, and picking up the basket, I left before they could stop me. It was time they had a few moments to themselves. Time to talk to each other.

The sky was darkening over the sea and the birds were flying home to their nests in the cliffs. I heard the lapping of the waves on the shore and was overcome by a sense of peace, of things slotting into place. Of course, there were still all sorts of things I wanted and needed but they didn't feel important right then, and anyway, I trusted they would take care of themselves. I had seen my mother in a new light, and although the beam hadn't been aimed at me, it gave me hope that it could be cast wider to include all those around her.

I heard laughter on the still night air and closed my eyes, imagining the two old folk reminiscing.

Half an hour or so later, I was covered in goosebumps, and thought they'd probably be wondering what had happened to me, so I made my way back to the cottage. As I walked in, they both hastily retrieved their hands and put them on their laps. I noticed that the level of the whisky had gone down a fair way.

'Am I interrupting?' I asked.

'No, no – we've just been chatting about the old times,' said my mother.

'Aye. Old times.' Duncan cast a look at my mother, and she smiled and either forgetting I was there or not caring, held out her hand to him. He took it, completely enveloping it in his big, strong hand and stroking it with his thumb.

'Anything you can share?' I asked.

They looked at each other like a pair of love-struck teenagers and shook their heads. 'Nothing you'd be interested in,' said my mother.

I wasn't so sure. Everything about my mother interested me these days but I didn't push it.

'Stewed fruit and cream?' I asked, gesturing to the bowl of apples and blackberries.

'Just a wee bit, thank you, Kirstie,' said Duncan.

'None for me, thank you,' said my mother. 'I've to think about my waistline these days. I don't get about as much as I used to.'

'I think you're perfect as ye are,' said Duncan and she blushed and looked away.

'So,' I said, passing Duncan his dessert and sitting down. I glanced from one to the other, but they were smiling at each other. I felt like a third wheel.

Soon after he'd finished eating, Duncan got up to leave. My mother saw him to the door, and he bent his head to kiss her on the cheek and then walked off into the night, humming to himself. Turning back towards me, I saw my mother's blush, and she smiled at me.

'Silly old fool that he is,' she said and dropped into her seat again.

'How was it, seeing him again?'

She looked past me, out into the darkness, back into the past, and nodded. 'It was all right. Aye, it was all right.'

'Just all right?'

'What do you want me to say, Kirsten?' Her eyes hardened.

I shrugged. 'You seemed to be enjoying yourselves, that's all.'

She softened again and slumped slightly in her chair. 'He hasn't changed. All these years, and he hasn't changed one bit.'

'And you?'

'Och, I'm not the same at all. Leaving here, England, your father – they all changed me.'

I sat very still, breathing slowly, fingers crossed. Would she start telling me her story?

'Leaving here was the hardest thing I've ever done.' She stared into space, and I thought that was all I was going to get but then she went on.

'You know why I left, and you know where I ended up.'

'I know a little more than that, actually. Duncan showed me one of the letters you wrote to him.' I bit my lip, realising what I'd said.

Her eyes flashed in the low light, and her jaw clenched. 'What on earth gave you the right to ask him about me?'

I took a deep breath. Interesting that it was my fault for asking rather than his for telling.

'You're my mother. I know nothing about your life because you've been so bloody secretive. Don't you think it might have had an impact on me?'

'There's no need to shout at me, Kirsten.' She patted her hair as if my outburst had somehow messed it up, then clasped her hands in her lap. Minutes passed with no sound but the scratching of a mouse in the roof.

'All right. I accept you felt a need to ask.'

Round one to Kirstie, I thought, and felt my shoulders release a bit.

'I can't believe the silly old fool kept them all these years. He was always a bit soft in the head.' But she didn't sound angry with him. She sounded pleased, flattered that he cared enough to hang on to whatever he had of her.

'I know about Miss Harris and your job in Sainsbury's on the butter and cheese counter.'

'Aye, that was me. What I couldn't do with a pair of butter paddles wasn't worth doing.' She laughed, briefly. 'It was such a long time ago. I thought I was the bee's knees, living in England, having a job, digs, friends. For a while it was enough. I found myself thinking less and less about home and what had happened and started enjoying myself, going to the cinema and tea dances and the like. Always with my friend, Ronnie. I never wanted a boyfriend. I didn't trust men anymore.'

A thought struck me. 'How did your mother find out about what happened? Duncan said he never told.'

She clenched her teeth and stared at me, nostrils flared. 'I got my monthly as we were doing the washing one day. I was so relieved that I said something.'

'You told her?'

'Of course not.' She gazed past me, took a sharp breath. 'I made a comment about being glad to get it. I'd always had terrible periods, so she quizzed me. I never admitted to anything, but she made up her mind that I was fallen and wouldn't have me under her roof. She was a God-fearing woman. I begged her to change her mind.'

'Understandably,' I said, but she didn't seem to hear me.

She drew herself up and swallowed hard.

'She arranged for me to leave; told everyone I was going off to learn to be a secretary.'

I shook my head. 'But if you'd told her a man forced himself—'

'It would have made no difference. It would have been my fault for being so keen to be a birding guide.' She closed her eyes for a moment and then looked at her hands. 'Anyway, Ronnie went and got married, and Miss Harris suggested I try out for teacher's college and my life changed again. If I hadn't gone to college, I never would have met Lydia.'

'Lydia?' I'd never heard her mentioned before.

My mother looked at me and her gaze sharpened again. 'That's enough for tonight. You've always been a nosy one, Kirsten. I need to go to bed.' And off she lurched, on slightly shaky legs.

Nosy? Perhaps, but it hadn't got me very far. I sat at the table wondering about all my mother had told me, and about this Lydia and why the mention of her had pulled my mother so abruptly out of her reverie.

My mind was busy, and sleep eluded me again. In the small hours of the morning, I took out my notebook and continued with my confession.

24

THE CONFESSION

We didn't see each other very much because Vanessa was still suspicious and we had to be careful, but Ed left his cufflinks on my bedside table one time, and I knew it was a sign.

I still sometimes stood outside the house and watched. I know he knew I was there, and he'd signal that he loved me – a light on in the bedroom window, his silhouette against the light in the lounge. I would go home and fantasise about being with him.

He wouldn't talk about the future and I started getting impatient. I wanted him to myself, as much as I knew he wanted me. I loved him for his consideration of his family but it was our turn. I realised that although it had made him angry before when I had intervened, I would have to take the initiative again. It was the only way.

I hadn't seen Vanessa for a while. Not because I felt guilty but because there had been no reason. It was time to get reacquainted. No letters this time, no subterfuge.

I invited her out for dinner. She was pleased I'd got in contact again and apologetic that she'd not been in touch. I arrived early at the little trattoria I had chosen and watched as she came in, glancing around to find me. She was wearing a little Johnny Was number. Apt, I thought. A bit of a cliché. But that's what she was. A wealthy, dull housewife who wore designer clothes and had a bored husband.

I rose as she approached the table and when we sat, made small talk for a while and drank red wine. We ordered, osso buco for me and a salad for her. She said she was watching her weight and laughed self-consciously.

I wondered what he'd ever seen in her. Yes, she was attractive in a Home Counties sort of way, but she had little to say for herself and no opinions about anything. I found myself trying not to yawn as we finished our food. Well I did, as she'd pushed hers around the plate for a while and then given up.

I couldn't wait any longer. She had to be told.

'Vanessa, there's something you need to know.'

She looked at me and I saw fear in her eyes. She took a sip of wine, her hand shaking.

'Ed is having an affair. Those letters were real.'

She gasped and put the glass down heavily, sloshing wine over the tablecloth.

'What do you mean? How do you know? We're good – I mean – we're getting on better than we've been for a long time.' She slumped, tears welling. 'How do you know?' she repeated.

I put his cufflinks on the table between us. 'He left these at my flat.'

Vanessa gazed at them for a long time. She was absolutely still.

'I gave him those for our tenth wedding anniversary,' she said quietly.

I waited.

She looked up. 'You?' she went on. 'Are you telling me it's been you all along?'

I nodded. 'We're in love, have been for over a year.'

Her hands flew to her throat. A guttural sound escaped her mouth.

'Look, I know this is hard for you, but we want to be together,' I said.

'You wrote the letters?'

She leant across the table, eyes narrowed. 'You fucking bitch. You low-down conniving slut,' she hissed.

I stayed absolutely still, watching her.

'I thought you were my friend.'

Still I said nothing.

She got to her feet, snatched the cufflinks off the table and left.

She stopped with one hand on the door, turned to me, lifted her chin and screamed, 'Bitch!'

The other diners stared. I shrugged, shook my head as if I had no idea why she was behaving that way, then paid the bill and left the restaurant, happy in the knowledge that Ed would soon be mine.

As I approached my front door a few minutes later I heard footsteps hurrying along the footpath. I turned to see Vanessa running towards me, her face blotchy and tear-stained.

'Don't do this – please, don't take him away from me.' She sniffed and smeared snot across her face with the back of her hand. 'I'm begging you to–'

'It's not up to me, Vanessa. Ed and I can't help that we're in love. We didn't ask for it to be this way, it just happened.' I felt calm, in control. It was Vanessa who was making a fool of herself.

'I'm nothing without him. I *have* nothing without him. Please, Kirstie, please.' She reached out a hand to me, trying to clutch at my sleeve. I moved my arm away and her hand fell by her side. She looked beaten and as if the veil of obsession parted for a moment, I could feel what she was feeling – the rawness, the desperation, the fear. And then I thought of Ed and me and the moment was gone. We were meant to be together, and Vanessa would have to accept it.

'You'll get over him.' I said it as kindly as I could, but it wasn't what she wanted to hear. She took a deep breath.

'How dare you – how fucking dare you?' she shrieked. 'I thought you were my friend – but it was all pretence. You're a lunatic, a fucking lunatic.' Spit flew and her hair had escaped from her velvet hairband. She launched herself at me and we both fell to the ground. Winded for a few seconds, I lay there, Vanessa on top of me, and the only thought I had was that we were wearing the same perfume.

I rolled her off me, picked myself up and brushed myself down slowly, trying to breathe calmly. No wonder Ed wants me instead of her, I thought, she's a harpy. Poor man, having to put up with her for all these years.

She also made her way up and stood there, hands on hips, expecting an answer.

'Love is love,' I said and shrugged.

She threw herself at me again, but I was prepared this time and stepped sideways, so she stumbled and landed on the stairs up to the flat. And then she started wailing. Full-on wailing like she was at a funeral. I half expected her to start tearing her clothes and pulling at her hair. And for another moment I felt sorry for her, but I remembered what was at stake. She was keeping Ed and I apart and we needed to be together.

'I'll call a taxi for you,' I said, and shoved past her to go upstairs and take my coat off.

Next thing I knew, she was in my flat sweeping things off the shelves, throwing books around and still the awful wailing. I should have closed the door.

I threatened to call the police. Even that didn't calm her down. I had to shut myself in the bathroom to avoid getting hit by the objects being flung around. I admired her in a way – she was going down fighting.

In the end, she ran out of steam and I heard her footsteps on the stairs. Leaving the bathroom, I surveyed the mess she'd made of my flat. Shaking and full of adrenaline, I started shelving the books again and picking up the pieces of the broken ornaments and the glass from the coffee table she'd managed to shatter.

And as I worked, I realised it was over. Vanessa knew, Ed could leave, and all would be well. I started humming as I put my flat back together.

Ed didn't appear that night. I wasn't worried. In fact, I felt it only right he should spend a last night in the family home. No doubt Vanessa was begging him to stay while he packed up his clothes and the bits and pieces he wanted to keep. I didn't want anything from his house, I just wanted him, but he probably had a few items he wanted to bring with him, mementos he would look at after a few months and toss in the bin, wondering why he'd thought them special.

He didn't turn up the next day either. I rang the landline, his office, his mobile, tried all the messaging apps I could think of. I tried to calm myself with the idea that he would come when he was ready, when he could take me in his arms and thank me for doing what it took for us to be together.

After a week I was going insane. I had been to the house and there was no one there. I stayed all day and most of a night and nobody went in or out, no lights came on. The place was deserted.

The next day I went to his work but was told he'd taken some time off and wasn't expected back for a month. I didn't believe them, so I waited outside there all day too, and all evening until even the cleaners had left the building and the security guards put the lights out floor by floor until only the foyer was lit, spilling its yellow light out onto the pavement.

Somehow I managed to make it home and searched for a drink. There was the last third of a bottle of vodka. I downed it in one and then went to the off-licence down the street and bought more. A lot more. Enough to drown myself in. I sat on my floor and drank. Where was he? What was going on? Why hadn't he come?

I felt one of my eyes being prised open and focused enough to see Yasmin kneeling beside me. She stared into my eye at the same time as putting two fingers on my neck, checking for a pulse. I groaned and rolled over, vomiting onto the Persian rug.

'Thank God. What the fuck have you been doing, Kirstie? You haven't answered your phone for two days, and now this – you stink of booze and piss. Thank Christ we didn't have any jobs on. What's the matter with you? I'm calling an ambulance.'

'No – please don't. I'm okay now. Just get me some water.'

She looked me over and then nodded. 'So why are you in this state? No – don't tell me, I know.'

'Ed,' I managed to whisper. 'He's gone.' And with that admission, I started sobbing.

Yasmin had every right to be very annoyed with me but, to give her her due, she was great – she held me until I quietened down, marched me into the bathroom and ordered me to have a shower. I looked at my body as the water fell over me, and realised I had bruises all over from falling around in my drunken state.

Yasmin made coffee and sat me at my kitchen table. 'No man is worth this, Kirstie. Believe me. No man.'

I wanted more than anything at that moment to be left

alone, so I agreed with her, drank my coffee like a good little girl and told her I felt better.

'Thanks for coming,' I said as she headed down the stairs.

'See you tomorrow,' she said, looking up at me when she reached the bottom. 'We have a partner's lunch to do at that swanky new law firm. I've done the prep.'

'See you then,' I said, closing the door and sinking against it. What was the point? I didn't care if the partners got their lunch or not, or if anyone ever ate again.

I couldn't get rid of an image of Ed and Vanessa together. And then I realised she must be holding him captive, that somehow, she had managed to whisk him away and was poisoning him against me. It was all her fault and I had to find them and put a stop to it before it was too late and he never got away from her.

All this against the backdrop of a deep and deafening silence.

25

———

EXILE

My mother was taciturn when she got up the next day. It was clear there was no point in trying to get her to talk more about Lydia or what had happened the night before. It was so frustrating having her there but also having to march to the beat of her drum. It had always been the same and I found myself reacting like a teenager, letting her know of my displeasure by the clatter of a saucepan on the hearth and the careless strewing of the cutlery on the breakfast table. For a precise woman like my mother, who at home always set the table for breakfast before she went to bed, this amounted to open warfare. Yet she bit her tongue and pecked at her porridge and even said thank you when she'd had enough.

'Ishbel's expecting us at ten,' I said. She wasn't, but she'd be in.

'Is that so?' Her eyes narrowed and I thought she was going to refuse to come but she didn't. Instead, she disappeared into the bedroom and came out after a while having combed her already neat hair and put her clips in.

We walked slowly, in silence. I thought about her ease with Duncan and balled my hands into fists in my pockets. My mother stumbled and I didn't try to catch her. Instead, she caught hold of my arm, stopped for a moment to settle herself and then hooked her arm through mine and carried on.

'I can understand you've a lot of questions, Kirsten.'

She must have felt my body stiffen in surprise because she stopped again, let go of my arm and stepped in front of me so we were facing each other.

'We've not been close, not seen much of each other, I know.'

'Rather an understatement, don't you think?' I realised too late how antagonistic it sounded, how stuck in this way of relating I was.

She pursed her lips, looked past me.

'Sorry,' I said.

'What's done is done.' She looked briefly into my eyes and then her gaze slid away again.

Something in me broke. Rage bubbled up from deep in my guts. She may not care about our lack of relationship, but I did. I bit on a knuckle to try and stop the words, but they came anyway.

'I think I deserve a bit better now than a "what's done is done".'

She stepped back. I loomed over her, easily six inches taller than her. My chest was heaving.

She put her hands up in defence and said, 'Shouting won't get you anywhere, Kirsten. Calm down now.'

When has being told to calm down ever worked? It just made me all the angrier. I wanted to hurt her the way she'd hurt me. I wanted to care as little as she did.

'I might as well go home right now,' she said, turning away.

'Oh, right, off you go. Let's not talk about anything, we'll just keep sweeping it under the carpet for another forty years, shall we?' I took some deep breaths and called after her, 'You'll have to get a taxi to Lerwick.'

She stopped, looked in my direction again, and said, 'I'm not leaving, I'm going home to the croft. I'll see you when you're calmer.'

Home. The croft.

It was my home, not hers. How dare she claim it back. Hot tears streaked down my cheeks. It was as I had expected. This place wasn't big enough for both of us but she had the prior claim. I watched her walk carefully back up the track, half hoping she'd fall and break her neck.

I didn't go to see Ishbel. I wasn't in a fit state to see anyone. Instead, I marched across the hills to stand on the cliffs of Vatsetter, letting the wind whip my hair around my face and listening to the waves crashing on the rocks below. I yelled at the sky until I was hoarse, giving voice to the injustices heaped upon me.

'It's my croft! She's taking Duncan away from me – she turned her back on him sixty years ago and now she's claiming him too!'

And then I sank to my knees, rocking back and forth.

I don't know how long I stayed there. I was shivering with cold and hugging myself for warmth when I started taking in my surroundings again. But I felt calmer.

Walking home slowly I thought about how I was going to approach my mother but when I got to the croft she wasn't there.

I checked in the bedroom, wondering if maybe she'd left after all, but her things were still around. I looked through her drawers, picking up the ugly thick stockings, the serviceable tops. I opened her night cream and poked a finger deep into it then rubbed it into my face slowly. I used her hairbrush, pinned my unruly mop back with her clips. Her face powder and lipstick next, and then peering into the mirror I tried to find a trace of her in me, but we looked nothing alike. I took more of the night cream and wiped the make-up off with it, pulled the clips out of my hair, ran my hands through it to free it from any likeness to her neat bob.

She didn't come home until I was in bed that night. I didn't acknowledge her. I heard her close the bedroom door and move around the room, undressing, combing her hair, getting into bed, all the time humming. She was happy.

We were coldly civil to each other for the next day or two, spending as little time together as was possible in a small space but with few other places to go. On the third morning, I could stand it no longer.

'I'm going to see Ishbel.'

'I'll come too – I would like to meet her,' said my mother.

I stared at her, took a few deep breaths, and said, 'Come on then.'

She got her coat and stood outside the door waiting while I damped the fire and laced my boots.

I was halfway out the door when she started, as if the idea of going to meet Ishbel made her feel the need to talk.

'Motherhood didn't come easily to me, Kirsten. You've a right to be angry. I didn't mean we should forget the past but maybe we could draw a line, start again.'

I was about to respond but she held up a hand to stop me and went on. 'I probably don't deserve it, but I'd like us to know each other a wee bit better.'

My jaw dropped. I know it did because my mother told me to shut my mouth before the flies got in, just like she used to when I was little. Only this time she wasn't scowling.

I blinked. Know each other better? How wee, exactly? Enough to make her more comfortable living in my cottage?

Enough to have the occasional lunch together if ever I went back to Brighton? My lips began to tingle with words unspoken. I took a deep breath.

'I don't know what to say.'

'You don't have to say anything now. I know you were far from over the moon at me coming, and we've scratched around each other ever since I got here.'

She was right. And she was offering me what I thought I wanted – to get to know her more, better. She wasn't one to make overtures, to enjoy intimacies. I knew she'd seen Duncan again in the last day or two, so had her conversations with him caused this change? Could it have been so easy?

'Okay,' I said, and forced a smile. I was about to start walking again but stopped, one foot forward. 'What are the parameters of this arrangement – just to be clear?'

My mother gazed off into the distance, her eyes squinting against the glare. 'How about we start trying to be civil to each other? You can tell me about your life.' She smiled, expectantly.

No bloody fear, I thought with a shudder.

'You make it sound like we're two strangers who have just met.'

'In many ways it feels like that's what we are.' She shook her head. 'It's my fault, I know. I'm sorry.'

I nodded, the sudden lump in my throat making it difficult to speak. I knew this was hard for her. She wasn't one to lay her feelings on the line. I should be grateful she was offering me what I wanted.

It was a pivotal moment – my mother wanted to know about me. She didn't usually ask for anything. In fact, she was the world's biggest denier of self. She'd put up with my father for over fifty years, watching him have affairs but still looking after him and his needs.

She was looking into my eyes. Actually into them, rather

than past my shoulder, waiting for a response. And although I had waited to be seen by this woman for most of my life, in that moment her eyes felt like lasers cutting deep into long-held secrets and dreams. I shuffled on my feet, tucked some stray hair behind my ear, broke our gaze.

'Okay,' I said. I couldn't do more. Couldn't hug her, or even squeeze her arm. For now, okay had to be enough.

Our visit to Ishbel's was awkward after that. We should probably have gone home instead but the idea of being alone together, of sitting at the table and talking, of saying things that mattered and the fear of derailing the whole process by beginning in the wrong place, was too much.

So, I introduced my mother to Ishbel and left them in the sitting room while I went to make tea. Returning a few minutes later, I found them chatting about the past.

'Shall I pour?' I asked, too brightly. They nodded, smiled, and resumed their discussion of the local school and Ishbel's memories of it.

'It sounds exactly the same as when I went there all those years ago. One teacher, one class, all ages. I loved it,' said my mother.

That was news to me.

'So, what was it like for you growing up here, Mother?' I asked. I'd heard Ishbel's stories of little Morag and her big brother, Robbie, but her own memories would be different. She gazed into the distance, took a sip of tea and sat back in her chair. Ishbel sat forward in hers, leaning her elbows on her knees.

'It's been such a long time since I've thought of any of it,' she said. 'I remember having to help my mother with the chores around the croft and being jealous of Robbie and Alasdair who got to be outside with our daddy. And I remember roaming the hills and the beaches with all the other children, playing hide and seek or acting out the Border Wars between the Scots and the Sassenachs complete with murderous shrieks. Or we just ran for the sheer pleasure of it.' She stopped and looked out the window which held the view of the hill and the vastness of the sky. Her face softened as if she was watching her young self, running around with her friends, playing games, picking wildflowers, watching the birds soaring in great flocks against the blue. Then she turned back to us and there were tears in her eyes.

'Just a normal childhood, I suppose.'

Ishbel nodded. 'Mine was the same. My parents used to tell us to get out into the fresh air whatever the weather!'

My mother cleared her throat and turned to Ishbel. 'Robbie was a kind older brother. I expect he was a good father. You must miss him.'

'Yes. We all do. He was, as you say, a kind man, and loved having his family around him. I know he missed you being in his life.'

'Yes, well...'

Ishbel sucked in her lips. 'I didn't mean that as a criticism. I'm sorry. I only meant that he loved it when there were lots of people around making noise and telling stories.'

'He always was an extrovert,' said my mother.

'He talked about you. He missed you,' Ishbel said.

My mother's face hardened in what I was beginning to recognise as an attempt to deny the feelings welling up in her.

'Let's go, Mother,' I said, getting up. As my mother went into the hall to put on her coat, I apologised to Ishbel.

'She's sad and a bit touchy, as you can see. If we're ever to have any sort of relationship, we have to work towards it slowly.

Small steps.' I smiled tightly. It may have looked more like a grimace.

She put her arms around me and whispered into my ear, 'She's struggling with being back, I expect, but I see what you meant about her now. She's built a protective wall around herself.'

Releasing me, she said in a louder voice so my mother would hear, 'Come back soon, both of you. You're always welcome.'

My mother nodded to Sheila when we went into the shop to pick up some items for lunch but the look on her face put off even the shopkeeper. She'd spent so little time around other people for so many years that I guessed her conversation with Ishbel had worn her out. Sheila sniffed and raised her pencilled-in eyebrows to me but kept her mouth shut.

Trudging back to the cottage, Mother was tense, her hands fisted by her sides. We walked in silence. As we approached the croft, Duncan waved and called out and she immediately brightened up again. She was all four seasons in one day – the promise of better weather, the crisp cool of autumn, the cold of winter, the warmth of the sun. Well, that might have been putting it a bit strongly but here she was, once again, her softer self. Perhaps, over the years, she'd forgotten how to be with other people. Then again, hadn't she said she'd met people on her cruise, had even hinted at a dalliance with the dance partner? Or had I read too much into it, wanting her to be normal and listening for confirmation of it?

'I came away to see ye, my lassies. I hope I'm no in the way.'

I cringed and held my breath, waiting for my mother to turn on him and tell him that she was no one's lass, thank you very much, as I had heard her berate my father once for calling her his best girl. I must have been very young, because they were still talking to each other, and she had rounded on him.

'I am not your possession. I am not a girl, and I very much doubt that I am your best anything,' she had said.

Had I been older, I might have understood the full import of those words. I might even have cheered her feminist ideals. As it was, I thought my mother was just being horrible to my father, so I took his hand and squeezed it.

Now, my mother smiled, and her step quickened.

'Lovely to see you, Duncan. Come in, why don't you, and have a cup of tea.'

'I was actually hoping to walk with you, if you'd like. We could go and see the puffins.'

She looked at me and I shrugged and nodded, still too surprised to say anything.

'We'll no be long,' he said.

'Off you go. Take your time. I'll make some lunch.'

Duncan offered his arm and my mother took it, giggling like a schoolgirl. Duncan's tread was sure, my mother's less certain as they picked their way along the crest of the hill and started towards the cliffs.

He'd never taken me to see the puffins.

As I watched them go, I wondered yet again what my mother's life would have been like if she'd stayed among people who loved her. And I wondered what, if anything, I should tell her of my life. I couldn't imagine confidences. Broad brushstrokes perhaps. I knew I would have to say something in order to get her to open up too.

I was still following their progress as the truth crept up on me. I didn't want her to know anything about my pitiful life. I only wanted to know about hers. I wanted a relationship but on my terms. I wanted control.

Duncan stayed for lunch and he and my mother told me about the pod of orcas they'd watched in the channel between Yell and Fetlar, playing in the currents. I listened with half an ear, more interested in observing the way they played in the currents of their relationship. There was an ease between them I'd never witnessed between my parents. My mother would say something, and Duncan would smile, put a hand on her arm, lean in a little. My mother blossomed under his attention, and I felt a stab of envy.

He stayed until late in the afternoon, only leaving when he remembered he'd promised to look in on Ishbel before dinner. When we'd waved him off, my mother put the kettle back on the hearth and spooned tea into the pot. As we waited for it to brew, we allowed a silence to stretch between us, heavy with anticipation.

'Seems like you and Duncan are getting on well,' I said eventually.

She sighed and shrugged her thin shoulders. 'He hasn't changed.'

'What did you really come back for?'

She looked at me and then made herself busy pouring the tea. I thought she was going to ignore the question and I felt my guts start twisting. It was always like this, the distance, the dismissiveness. I was about to get up, to march down to the shore ranting about my passive-aggressive mother when she sat down again and looked me in the eye.

'To see the old place. To see you. I know you've struggled in your life and I'm sorry for it.'

I had to take some deep breaths before responding.

'I think we've both struggled, Mother.'

'Och, call me Morag. Mother sounds so formal, and we're

both adults. I've hardly been a mother to you for the last thirty years anyway.'

'And the rest,' I said before I could stop myself. 'I'd have loved a childhood like yours – running about carefree instead of trying to contort myself into the child I thought you wanted me to be. Was I so difficult?'

My mother shook her head and stared into the flames. 'Not you, no. Circumstances.'

'Father?'

She drew herself up and sat with a straight spine, which made her look like a child about to see the headmistress rather than the old woman she was. Vulnerable, sad.

In a small voice, she started talking.

'I realised not long after your father and I married that it was a mistake. We weren't suited to each other in any way. We had no interests in common and not much interest in each other after the first few months. We tried to do things together – walking at the weekends, going to the pictures, that sort of thing. We didn't have a lot of money but we both liked dancing, so we decided to take some ballroom lessons. He was a wonderful dancer, your father, light on his feet, graceful. He danced his way into bed with most of the ladies in the class, I learned later.'

'That's awful. I'm sorry–'

'You really must stop apologising for things that have nothing to do with you, Kirsten,' she said sharply, and then continued her story.

'I was so naïve in those days, I never suspected a thing until out of spite, Gladys Pocock told me what was going on. She'd been one of his earlier conquests, but he threw her over for Finula O'Riordan who had fat legs but danced a mean foxtrot.'

She paused, took a sip of tea. My hand hovered between us, wanting to rest on her arm, offering comfort in the way Duncan did, but not wanting to break the thread of her story I put my hand back in my lap.

'I was so ashamed. I knew it must be my fault he needed to look elsewhere. Things weren't – well, you know – what had happened here had put any notions of romance out of my head, if you know what I mean. Your father was a man with needs, and I was not the person to fulfil them. I wanted to leave but didn't have the wherewithal, and people like us didn't divorce in those days, it just wasn't done. So, I stayed, and he continued to stray.'

'I'm sorry–'

'Don't be,' she said, sounding exasperated. 'It wasn't your fault, it had nothing to do with you. You weren't even born.'

I bit my lips. This was the mother I knew, the one who was incapable of accepting comfort, of letting anyone in.

The sun slanted in through the door and a wind started rising. I stoked the fire and pulled my cardigan more tightly around me. My mother wrapped her hands around her mug and closed her eyes.

'I went back to work, teaching in the local school. Your father had made me stop when we married, saying it looked bad that he couldn't support us both. Going back caused tension between us but I no longer cared. I needed something to do to take my mind off everything else, and I was a good teacher, I knew that. Years we carried on, hardly talking, living our own lives. I'd saved a bit of money and had gathered the courage to leave. I was thinking about coming back here, although I think the courage might have failed me when the time came. I'd been away too long.'

'What stopped you?' I asked. 'Why did you stay?'

'I found out I was pregnant. Because even though he had any number of other women, he still occasionally wanted me.' She clenched her jaw. 'I couldn't leave then. I was too afraid. I didn't think I could bring a child up on my own. And when he found out I'd been saving money, he took it, so he had control of the finances. He didn't really want me, but he didn't want the shame of losing me either.'

I slumped in my chair, the weight of her decision compressing my lungs and squeezing the wind out of me. She had felt compelled to stay with a man who didn't love her and for whom she had no regard. To remain in a relationship that was dead long before I came along.

She got up and closed the door, throwing the cottage into twilight. It felt claustrophobic and I started to sweat.

'I think I need some air,' I said, brushing past her and out into the light, taking deep breaths as I strode to the beach. My parents' lives weren't my responsibility. I kept repeating it to myself. I wasn't to blame for their decisions. If my mother had been braver she could still have left, borrowed money, taken me with her, maybe come back here to family. Instead, she'd stayed and became more and more unhappy.

I marched along the hard sand, hands fisted in my pockets. Why couldn't I just forgive her and get on with my life?

The orcas were still there, surfacing and diving, their tall thin fins sinister as they carved the water. I watched them until I felt calm enough to go home.

The cottage was in darkness by the time I returned. Lighting a lamp, I pulled out my journal. It was time to write the last chapter of my confession. Now I suspected I was writing not for Ishbel after all, but for my mother. She'd said she wanted to know me, after all.

26

THE CONFESSION

I don't know how I survived. I probably wouldn't have if it hadn't been for Yasmin coming in regularly to force some food into me and make me wash. She also kept the business going. I didn't deserve her.

I didn't go out. Didn't even open the curtains or put the lights on. I couldn't go near the bed where Ed and I had made love, where I had planned and fantasised and dreamed of him. I lay on the floor or paced the flat, cursing myself, love, God. I slept when I was exhausted, only to wake to the nightmare again. What was she doing to him? How was she keeping us apart? I wanted to kill Vanessa, rescue Ed and bind him to me forever. I had never felt so desperate nor so powerless.

And then one night, there was a knock on my door. I knew it wasn't Yasmin, because she had a key. My heart fluttered in hope. I peered at myself in the mirror and was horrified. Quickly pulling a comb through my hair, I squeezed toothpaste into my mouth and rinsed it. Straightening my clothes, I spoke into the entryphone.

'Yes, who is it?' My voice sounded hollow, unsure.

'Open the door.'

It was him! Ed had come at last. I buzzed him in and rushed back into the bedroom to squirt some perfume on my neck and between my breasts and then stood at the top of the stairs watching him.

Something was wrong. He looked up towards me and I saw the greying stubble, the dark rings under his eyes, the receding hairline. There were deep lines connecting the sides of his nose to the downturned corners of his mouth. His breath was laboured.

I backed away as he reached the top of the stairs. This wasn't my Ed, the man I loved, the one I'd suffered for. This was an old man with a paunch and body odour.

'Kirstie.' He nodded at me as he walked past and into the sitting room.

I leant against the wall. I couldn't move. All the air had been sucked out of me and I was a deflated, withered shell. I had fallen out of love before, sometimes quickly, sometimes not, but always completely.

It was as if a switch was tripped and that was it.

'You could at least offer me a drink,' he wheedled. I was on my guard as I poured him a whisky and handed it to him. He knocked it back in one and held the glass out for a top-up.

'So, I expect you're pleased with yourself. You've really done it this time.' He looked at me with cold eyes.

'I–'

'Shut up!' he shouted. He rose onto his toes, hands by his sides, almost rigid with anger. 'Don't try and deny it. You've ruined my fucking marriage, messed up my life, left me with nothing.'

He loomed over me, bulkier than I remembered him being. Flabbier too.

'So now I'm all yours. My wife has thrown me out. My

children won't talk to me. Here I am, just like you wanted. Let's fuck, shall we? After all, that's all we ever did.'

That was a lie. He loved me. And I had loved him.

He pawed at my blouse, trying to undo the buttons. I pushed him off and he fell back onto the sofa, knocking his drink over as he went.

'Now, now, Kirstie. Play fair. I've made the effort to come and see you, so now we do fucky-fucky.'

'No.'

He lunged at me and grabbed my arm. 'What do you mean, no, you mad fucking bitch? You have given up the right to refuse me. You wanted me so badly you told my wife I was going to leave her, that we'd been planning it for months. Nothing I did could persuade her to forgive me. Can you imagine what that's even like? Having the woman you love treat you like shit, ignore your pleas, give all your clothes to a charity shop and turn your children against you? No, of course you can't because no one has ever loved you, have they? You haven't been able to dupe anyone into staying with you that long.'

His words pierced as surely as a razor and a calmness came over me, just as if I had cut myself. I stood my ground, looked him in the eye and shrugged.

His hands curled into fists, and I thought he was going to hit me. I steeled myself for the blow but he just put his face close to mine and said in a low voice, 'And Vanessa has tried to kill herself. Is that what you wanted? She thought you were her friend.'

I gasped, my hands clutching my stomach. 'I'm sorry – I–'

'Shut the fuck up. Your words are empty. All you can do is lie.'

I looked away, took a deep breath.

'Take your clothes off,' he said.

'No.'

He tore at me then, ripping my clothes and pulling his own off. Tackling me to the floor, he threw himself on top of me and tried to thrust his cock into me, but he wasn't hard enough. Again and again he tried, pulling my labia apart and trying to push himself in. I lay still, staring up at him, willing him to fail.

And then I started giggling. I couldn't help myself. It was almost like I was on the ceiling looking down on this pathetic man scrabbling around on top of me.

He started hitting me, punching me in the chest, the stomach, the ribs. I curled into a ball on the floor and he continued, slapping me around the head, kneeing me in the kidneys. At first, I took it, thinking of what I'd done to Vanessa. And then I snapped. He had been complicit. He may not have been planning to leave his wife, but he had been playing away from home. I wasn't the only one to blame. I started hitting back and he laughed. I bit and scratched, pulled his hair, kicked out, landed a punch on his cheek which hurt my hand. And I screamed. God, did I scream.

We ran out of energy. He started crying. Real tears. He felt sorry for himself. I gave him a tissue and sat watching as he blew his nose and wiped his eyes. All the bravado was gone. All that was left was a pathetic middle-aged man with his pants round his ankles and all the buttons ripped off his shirt.

'I've got nothing left. Nothing at all.'

'You've got your job,' I said. 'You can start again.' I was exhausted. Why wasn't he leaving?

'I've nowhere to live.' He looked around the flat, raised his eyebrows and looked at me.

Was he expecting me to offer him a bed, a place to stay? Perhaps he was the one who was mad.

'You'll find somewhere.'

'Kirstie, Kirstie,' all friendly now he needed something from me. 'Just a few nights, for old times' sake.'

'Not even one. Get out.'

He took a deep breath in and I thought he was going to start hitting me again but instead he spat in my face, tucked what was left of his shirt into his trousers and left, slamming the door behind him.

For hours after he'd gone, I sat, my mind blank. And then thoughts started intruding. I paced the flat, tears falling. Not for Ed. Not for me. Now I was no longer interested in him, I could hardly understand why I had acted as I had. It was as if I had been under a spell and now it was broken, nothing I'd done made any sense. I remembered every word and deed but not what had driven me to it. The obsession was over, and all that was left was shame, remorse and self-loathing.

And I was haunted by the idea of Vanessa taking pills, washing them down with gin or vodka or white wine. She was the innocent in all this. I wanted to make amends but there was nothing I could do to change what had occurred.

I felt very calm as I ran the bathwater, got a new razor blade out of its packet, undressed. Easing myself into the warm water, I lay back and closed my eyes, allowing myself momentarily to enjoy its comfort. Hot tears fell down my cheeks. A pain started in my chest and radiated through my body, making my back arch and twisting my limbs. Opening my mouth, I gave voice to the pain, the shame, the remorse. It was an ugly sound.

27

———

EXILE

A fine mist covered the island the next morning. My mother and I stayed near the fire and drank cups of tea. It should have felt cosy, but it didn't. I couldn't push aside the guilt I felt that she had stayed with my father because of me. I wasn't ready to hear more of her life with him, so every time she opened her mouth, I got in first, asking her if she had any plans for the day, whether she wanted more porridge, if she'd slept well.

'Kirsten – stop. It's like you've got ants in your pants this morning. What's the matter?'

Tell the truth, I said to myself. Tell her.

'Tell me about Lydia,' is what came out of my mouth.

'Ah, yes. I thought you'd ask about her.' She nodded, looking down at her neatly manicured hands. She seemed to be trying to come to a decision. I waited.

Finally, she lifted her gaze, although she didn't quite make eye contact, and said, 'All right. I'll tell you about what happened. I've never told another soul, not even Miss Harris who I was living with at the time.' She took a gulp of her tea, put the mug down again and started.

'I was at teacher training college in Brighton when I met her. She was in the year above me, but I came upon her one day in the library. She was crying, so I offered her my handkerchief. We got talking, and it came out that the reason she was upset was because her sister had just told her in confidence that her cousin, Gerald, whom she adored, had forced himself on a friend of hers when he was in college. Her sister said she'd known about it for months but couldn't keep it to herself any longer. Apparently, he'd even bragged about it to her, said he could have any girl he wanted, anytime. He was a birdwatcher in more than one sense of the word.'

My mother spoke in a monotone, as if keeping as much distance as she could between herself and the story she was telling, but I gasped.

'But that's–'

'I believe so, yes. It was the same Gerald who... well, anyway, you can imagine how I felt on hearing what she had to say. Or maybe you can't. At first, I didn't know what I felt myself, to tell you the truth. I was transported back to that day, and the outrage, shock, anger I felt then.'

I put my hand on hers and she let it rest there. We didn't say anything for a few minutes. The mist had lifted but a steady rain had started falling, streaking the windows salty white.

'You don't have to go on if you don't want to,' I said.

'No, it's fine. Now I've started I might as well continue. I'll make it brief.' She sucked in her lips and then carried on.

'I got over my initial shock quite quickly and pushed my own feelings aside. I'd become quite good at that. What was left was a desperate need to know all about the man who had changed my life forever. I became friends with Lydia, invited her to the pictures, for dinners, walks at the weekends. Sometimes we even studied together in companionable silence. I didn't like her; she was self-absorbed and insular. All she cared about was her family and her dogs. She never asked a thing about me, except to ask where I came from because she'd noticed I had an accent. I said Scotland, and that was enough for her.'

'But you had a plan?'

'Oh, yes, I certainly did. After a few weeks, I started asking her about this cousin of hers. What was he like, what did he do? She loved talking about him. I hardly had to mention his name and off she'd go. He was an engineer, she said, and had moved to somewhere in the north for work. He hadn't kept in touch with the family because he'd been engaged before he went but broke it off just before the wedding, leaving his fiancée distraught. His parents were angry with him, as the girl was the daughter of family friends, and his change of heart had caused them no end of difficulty and disappointment. I got the feeling that he was the black sheep of the family in a big way.

'I said I agreed with his parents, it was a horrible thing to do to someone, but Gerald could do no wrong in her eyes. I think she'd managed to block out the fact he'd forced himself on someone. She was in love with him even though he was her cousin and several years older than her.'

'It happens, I suppose. I mean, cousins can legally marry.'

My mother frowned at me. 'You're not getting the point, Kirsten. She was besotted. And I felt a growing desire to tell her what he was really like; that her parents and sister were right. The more I heard about him, the more my anger grew, and I wanted to destroy him in her eyes. I wanted to tell her what a despicable human being he was, who had no care for anyone or anything but himself. He was an animal. Worse than an animal.'

'Mother! Did you – what did you say?'

She shook her head and grunted. 'I said nothing. Oh, I had fantasies of telling her that her precious Gerald had raped me and had me thrown out of my home with nothing when I was seventeen. But what good would it have done? It wasn't her fault. But I did stop seeing her. I was afraid I would say something in an unguarded moment. I can't say I missed her, and she didn't try very hard to contact me. I felt a sense of liberation having made my decision, like something inside me had been released.'

I knew the feeling.

'You said before that your life changed again because of meeting Lydia,' I said.

'Aye. It did. I began to trust myself around other people again. I started believing I could control what I said in company, after all, I'd told her nothing. I grew in confidence, made a couple of new friends. Not that I wanted to talk about what had happened but until then I'd always been worried I'd let it slip out and then people would blame me and tell me to leave, as my mother had.'

I nodded.

'I also found myself less wary around men. I had met her brothers and they were kind and gentle. They made me realise that one black soul didn't have to colour the whole of mankind.'

'So did you have boyfriends before Father?' I almost laughed at the thought.

'One or two. Dancing partners, really, nothing more.'

'I bet you broke their hearts,' I said, feeling warmer towards her than I had until then.

'I don't know about that, Kirsten. More tea?' she said, lifting the pot and making a pouring motion.

'No,' I said. 'I'm drowning.'

She smiled. 'You can never have too much tea.'

'Did you never regret staying away – before you met my father, I mean?'

She looked at me and gave a sad little half-smile.

'I reckon you and I are alike. Too stubborn and proud for our own good.'

I nodded and she continued.

'I remained angry with my mother until I heard she was dead, and then it was too late to do anything about it. I feel the guilt and the pain of my decision every day, but I can't undo it.' She looked at me then. 'But I hope we can get on better before it's too late.'

Proud and stubborn. She was right. We were both that. I squeezed her hand and we fell into silence.

Later I walked down to see Ishbel while Mother went to see Duncan. The rain had stopped but left little diamonds on the heather, glistening in the weak sun. I squelched along the path in my wellies mulling over what my mother had told me. Would I have made the same decision? The temptation to tell Lydia about the nastier side of her perfect cousin must have been almost overwhelming. I was proud my mother had acted as she had. There was nothing to be gained from causing distress but I had, in my time, caused a lot, and it still haunted me. In some ways, my mother was the better woman.

Ishbel was doing more every day, getting about in her Moon Boot. She made coffee and we sat at her kitchen table.

'How's Morag?' she asked.

'Fine. We've been doing a bit of talking.'

'That's good. You've got a lot of catching up to do I 'spect.'

I nodded, thinking about what my mother had told me. Every detail of her life I learned was another stitch in the tapestry of our lives. And yet the whole picture still felt a long way off.

'How are she and Duncan getting on?' asked Ishbel.

I laughed. 'They're like a pair of teenagers. It's sweet but also rather odd seeing her get flustered when he's around.'

'Ah, young love, eh? Now, I've been meaning to talk to you about his birthday party. You're still happy to do the catering?'

'Of course. When is it?'

'Two weeks. I hope Morag will still be here?'

'To be honest I have no idea. She hasn't said anything about her plans but I'm sure she won't want to disappoint Duncan.'

We spent a while discussing menus. I wanted to do something really special for him.

'Could I borrow your car? I think I'll go to the library and look up some recipes.'

'Of course, when are you going?'

'Now, if that's all right.'

'Great. Give me a minute and I'll come with you. I need to do a few things in town too, including picking up my computer from the repair shop. It's been there since before my accident.'

She hobbled out to the car and sat heavily in the passenger seat. 'I can't wait for this damn boot to be off – I feel like an elephant limping around in it.'

'Do elephants limp a lot?' I asked.

'You ken what I mean. It makes me slow and heavy. You must be bored of coming to see me. And I'm going mad getting out so little.'

I laughed. 'I could no more imagine getting bored of your company than I could swimming to Fetlar.'

'People have done that,' said Ishbel. 'Some years ago. Not locals, of course. They were from Edinburgh. Students. I think it was a drunken dare. Two of them had to be rescued less than halfway there. The others made it but had to be treated for hypothermia.'

'Well, there you have it – I'm not likely to be so stupid. Tell me some more stories about the goings-on here.' Ishbel's store of folklore and local news was immense and kept us going all the way to Lerwick with me needing to do no more than nod and smile occasionally.

'You can drop me here,' she said when we got to the centre of town.

'When shall I pick you up?'

She thought for a moment, looking around as if contemplating how long it would take to finish her errands. 'Would a couple of hours give you enough time for what you need to do?' she asked.

'Perfect, see you back here.'

I watched her limp off and then made my way to the library, excitement dancing in my belly. I hadn't touched a computer for nine months.

I logged on, went to the site of a favourite food blogger and looked at her recent recipes, printed off a couple, and then went on to various other foodie websites. The menu for Duncan's do was coming together nicely. I was about to turn off the computer, but my fingers started typing in my email address. Biting my lips, I watched as messages loaded up. Three hundred and thirty-seven of them. Not many for nine months, but then I had told everyone I knew that I was going off-grid and would be un-contactable. Most were, indeed, spam, which managed to get past my firewall but there were a few others. Yasmin had sent Christmas wishes, as had a couple of other people from work and some clients.

Sixty-three were from Ed. My heart lurched. Not because I harboured any feelings for him but from dread as to what he might say. I considered deleting them without reading them but curiosity got the better of me. The first twenty or so were short and abusive but after that the tone changed. The messages got longer and longer, rambling about his life, all he'd lost, including me, who he now realised he had loved and maybe still did.

Could we get together and talk about it – perhaps we had a future together after all? The last ones were back to the abuse, accusing me of destroying him as a man, his family, his life and calling me every name under the sun, especially the one that started with C. He liked that one a lot, using it as a noun and strangely, a verb and an adverb too.

I knew I had behaved badly but he had too. It wasn't me who cheated on his wife, although I accepted blame for a lot of what had happened. I felt sorry for him in a detached sort of way – he was a man who couldn't be faithful to one woman, who, when found out, blamed everyone else. If I were to apologise to anyone it would be to Vanessa. Although I suspected by now she was managing quite well without him. At least, I wanted to believe she was. She had lost the most in this charade, and through no fault of her own. Ed and I had played out our parts – the sex addict and the fantasist. She had done nothing to deserve what we did to her. What I did to her. If that made me the cold, hard cuntly bitch he accused me of being, there was nothing I could do about it now.

I packed my guilt away, deleted all the messages and breathed a sigh of relief.

When I got home my mother was there, stirring a pot of something that smelled delicious. She called hello over her shoulder, and then stooped down to pull foil-wrapped potatoes out of the fire.

'Set the table, would you, Kirsten?'

'Sure – just the two of us, or is Duncan coming?'

'Just us.'

I put knives and forks and glasses on the table, poured us each a glass of wine from the bottle I'd bought in Lerwick.

'Are we celebrating something?' asked my mother.

'No, I just thought it'd be nice to have a glass with dinner.' And loosen your tongue, I added to myself. There was something I needed to know.

We sat eating her very good mutton stew, the butter melting over the potatoes in golden rivers.

'I hear you're to cook for Duncan's party,' she said.

'Yes. I did Lorna's christening; I think I told you. It went well, so he asked me to cater his eightieth. It's the least I can do for him. You'll still be here I presume?'

'Aye, he's made me promise. I'll likely be away soon after. There's things I need to attend to at home.'

I was comforted to hear her call somewhere else home. This was my place now. There was nowhere else I could imagine living, despite the weather, and I couldn't share it indefinitely with her. In the new year I would have to think about how to earn some money, perhaps offering catering, maybe opening a café in the tourist season. But all that could wait for another few months.

'What do you need to do?' I asked.

'See to my finances mainly. I've decided to sell the house. It contains too many unpleasant memories. I've been looking at flats in retirement villages.'

'Wow,' I said. 'And what would you do there?'

She paused a moment, fork halfway to her mouth. 'I don't know, Kirsten. But I'll think of something.'

She looked sad, lost. It was unnerving, and no doubt the reason my next question slipped out.

'You wouldn't think of coming back here for good?'

She shook her head. 'I dinnae think so.'

I smiled, relieved to hear we wouldn't be living too close to each other. A retirement village may suit her well.

'You're sounding like a local already,' I said.

'Och, haud yer wheesht!'

'I don't even know what that means.'

'It means stop your blethering.'

I nodded and got back to my food. We ate in silence for a few minutes. I refilled our wine glasses. Finally, I gathered my courage and asked the question I needed answered.

'Mother–'

'Morag, please. I've told you, you're too old to call me mother now.'

'All right, Morag.' The name sounded foreign on my tongue. 'Did you regret keeping me?'

She stared at me like I had grown a second head or sprouted blue fur.

'Why do you ask?'

I swallowed hard, feeling a tightness in my lips that always accompanied emotional conversations. 'You seemed to find motherhood difficult.' I was shaking and had to put my knife and fork down and clasp my hands in my lap.

'I'm sorry you felt that way, Kirsten.'

'Are you saying I got it wrong?'

She set her cutlery down very carefully, pulled a clean hanky out of her sleeve and wiped her eyes. For a long time I thought she was going to say nothing but then she took a deep breath, looked at me briefly, and then away again.

'I was angry when I found out I was pregnant. I felt stuck just when I thought I could leave. I wasn't brave enough to be a single parent and had no support around to help me. Your father was overjoyed about being a father initially. He even promised he'd turn over a new leaf, we'd be a real family. He started coming home earlier in the evenings and staying around at weekends. We went together to buy the nursery furniture and baby clothes. I came round to the idea of being a mother and even started looking forward to it. It really did seem like we could be a family.'

She moistened her lips and continued.

'When you were born, I thought you were the most perfect thing I'd ever seen. All I wanted to do was look at you, hold you, sing to you. Your father was besotted too – I'd never seen him like that.'

She had a faraway look in her eyes as if seeing it all again.

'And?' I asked. It was nice to hear they'd loved me so completely, but I needed to know what had changed.

She looked at me, took my hand. 'He was a great father to you – took you out in your pram, even changed nappies and on rare occasions got up to you at night. I struggled. I suppose they'd call it post-natal depression. I felt like I was losing myself, heading down a dark tunnel. I'd lie awake all night worrying you were going to die, that I couldn't keep you safe. During the day I'd go through the motions – you were always fed and changed but more I couldn't do. I thought you'd be better off without me. Your father couldn't understand it and wouldn't put up with it. He moved into the spare room and acted as if I didn't exist. He'd come home from work and give you your bath, your dinner, put you to bed and then go out again. At weekends, he took you out on adventures and you were always so happy together. When he was at work, if you hurt yourself, it was him you wanted. He started having affairs again and that made everything worse because then I knew I was a bad mother *and* a bad wife.'

'I had no idea you were so depressed,' I said, feeling the inadequacy of my words. And then the question I had to ask.

'Is that when you tried to kill yourself?'

My mother's head snapped up and her hands automatically pulled at her sleeves.

'No. Not then.'

I poured her another glass of wine and we drank in silence for a while and I knew she'd say no more about it. Not then.

'Dad used to take me on long walks and then to a tea room somewhere for a milkshake.' I felt a warmth toward him I hadn't experienced for a very long time.

'Well, I have to say, he was a good father.'

'Until he wasn't there anymore,' I said.

She sighed. 'It wasn't you he was staying away from, it was me. He loved you. You must remember outings with him even when you were older.'

'Yes,' I said. But I was also angry with him. The time I had seen him with the woman outside the pub still hurt after all these years.

Heart thudding in my chest, I said, 'I wanted *you* to love me.'

She raised her eyebrows at me, and I thought I'd blown it but then she sighed.

'I know. It took me years to get over the depression and, when I did, I felt there was no place for me. You and your father were so close, a sealed unit. You'd had to be, of course, and I was glad he'd made the effort, but I had no idea how to join in.' She fiddled with the salt cellar and pursed her lips.

'You're saying it's his fault?' I sat back in my chair, arms crossed.

She sucked on her lower lip. 'Your father had started getting physical by then – he told me I was useless and a terrible mother. I wanted to leave but I didn't have any money and knew I couldn't take you away from your daddy anyway.'

My chest tightened. I gripped my glass and reminded myself to breathe. 'But you didn't go.'

'No. I didn't. I was miserable with your father but I couldn't leave you when it came to it. I loved you but I was angry. So angry. With your father, with God, with my own mother who had thrown me out, with myself, and eventually, with you.'

'I didn't ask to be born.'

'No, I know. Anger isn't rational though, is it? I think, in my warped logic, you were partly to blame for keeping me there.'

I sat up straighter, ready for a fight, but my mother held up a hand to quieten me.

'I'm sorry, Kirsten. I know it doesn't make sense, and I'm not wanting to make you feel bad, I'm just trying to tell the truth. I've been sorely wanting as a mother but I'm so proud of how you've turned out. You're a strong, independent woman who knows her mind.'

I laughed then. In fact, I snorted. 'You have no idea about me,' I said, shaking my head. 'You only see what you want to see. My life has been shit. I suffer from obsessional thinking and have disastrous relationships.'

My mother gasped and looked away.

'Don't turn your head,' I said. 'Look at your strong, independent daughter who has completely fucked relationships with men and when they go wrong, drinks herself into oblivion.'

She was crying and I was too. 'I never knew. Oh, poor wee Kirsten. I swear, I never knew.'

'No. You were too busy looking the other way making sure the house was clean so other people wouldn't judge us badly.'

She sat, shoulders slumped, tears on her cheeks. My anger kept rising and I stoked it with memories of her turning away from me when all I wanted was a smile. I wanted her to feel as bad as I did.

And then in a terrible instant I saw her as she was – old and vulnerable. And I realised that from the moment her mother sent her away she had felt unloved, unlovable, and unable to trust anyone else enough to love them. Even her own husband and daughter. I felt myself deflating, all the anger being sucked out of me, leaving pity in its place. Pity for her, for me, even for my father. We'd been stranded in a tangle of feelings and circumstances none of us was equipped for.

'Maybe I was too – looking the other way, I mean.'

'Can you ever forgive me?' she asked.

I looked at her narrow little face, her tear-bright eyes.

I was exhausted from all my conflicting emotions.

'To be honest, I don't know. I hope so, for both of us, but one conversation doesn't magically make everything right.'

She nodded. 'Of course.'

'But at least we're talking.'

'Aye. At least we're doing that.'

I didn't sleep that night. One phrase kept circling through my mind. "You're a strong, independent woman." I had been quick to deny it. Often, I was not those things. But sometimes I was.

Duncan's birthday party was to be held in the village hall, and once again he and Ewan had offered their kitchen for the preparation. He'd let Ishbel and me choose the menu for the buffet and he'd organised the drink. He'd hired a band from Lerwick to play so Ewan could sit with his family and eat a meal, although he had borrowed Grandy's fiddle again, expecting his brother would want to play at some stage in the evening. My mother helped me during the day, cleaning and chopping vegetables, humming to herself. We were still being careful around one another but we weren't as awkward as we had been. A door had been opened and we were both dancing on the threshold.

In the middle of the afternoon she excused herself to go and get ready. She'd been all a-dither for quite some time by then, like a girl going on her first date, so I was happy to see the back of her. On my own I got into the rhythm of cooking for a large number of people. I'd planned everything down to the last sprig of thyme as always and enjoyed being in the kitchen as the autumn light faded outside.

Just before seven, Duncan and Ewan came to carry the food to the hall. A great pot of fish soup, crusty bread, a Moroccan lamb tagine with herbed couscous, salads, a birthday cake with cream and berries. They couldn't carry it all, so said they'd send Una's nephew, David, to fetch the rest.

'Ye've done me proud, lassie,' said Duncan as I wished him happy birthday and kissed him on the cheek.

'I hope you enjoy your evening.'

A few minutes later, a tall man walked in.

'I've been told to—' he said, and then stopped and looked at me. 'Are you okay?'

I was breathless. Speechless. It was the man from the ferry. In Duncan's kitchen. He was as good-looking as I remembered, and smiling at me.

'I'm fine,' I squeaked.

'I know you from somewhere.'

'A ferry some time ago.'

He laughed. 'Aye, that's right. You were seasick and then you disappeared. But maybe it's me that causes these attacks you have, for you seem all at sea again.'

I peeled myself away from the kitchen bench I was leaning on. 'I'm fine,' I said. 'Sorry. It was just a surprise to see you, that's all.'

'A good one, I hope.'

I nodded. It was. I was in a room with a handsome man, and

I wasn't imagining our lives together. I wanted to sing Alleluia at the top of my voice.

'Here's the tray for you to take. Take care not to let the soup spill.'

'I hope you'll have a dance with me later,' he said.

'I've got two left feet but if you want bruised toes, you're on. Now, off with you before the food gets cold.'

I watched him walk carefully over to the hall, admiring his neat bum. My heart was no longer thudding, but a quiet sense of anticipation warmed me as I turned my mind back to getting the last of the food to the hall.

Una had been in charge of the decorations and the hall was hung with birthday banners and multicoloured balloons. We set the food out on a long table along the back wall, smaller tables to eat at had red cloths on them, the band was setting up on the stage at the front. The guests were beginning to arrive when I drove Ishbel's car up to the croft to change, drag a brush through my hair and collect Morag. By the time we got back everyone was gathered, the band playing covers of old pop songs quietly so people could chat and drink and sit themselves around the tables to eat. Duncan met us at the door and led us to his table where Ewan, Ishbel, Una and David were waiting for us so the party could start.

And what a party it was. Everyone tucked into the food and ate heartily. The band turned up the volume after we'd eaten and changed from seventies' and eighties' pop covers to Highland folk. Soon the dance floor was heaving with people Stripping the Willow and being Gay Gordons, reeling away to their hearts' content. Duncan asked Morag to dance and off they took, spinning and skipping like a pair of thirty-year-olds. Gone was her stiff, arthritic gait. They moved well together, hardly taking their eyes off each other. I watched as sixty years of sadness lifted from my mother's shoulders. Her cheeks were pink, her step jaunty, and the smile didn't leave her face.

'She looks happy,' said Ishbel, sitting beside me, her Moon Boot preventing her from taking a turn on the dance floor.

'She does,' I said. 'I think coming back here has been good for her. I've never seen her like this.'

'And the two of you?'

I paused, a glass of wine halfway to my lips. 'It's going in the right direction. I'm beginning to understand her more but there's a way to go, you know?' I looked at my cousin and she smiled and squeezed my arm.

'At least you've started, and you haven't had to escape down to my house for a couple of days!'

The Eightsome Reel came to an end and the dancers returned to their seats. All bar Ewan, who took to the stage. The bandleader held out a microphone to him and he tapped it suspiciously and blew into it before saying, 'Can ye all hear me?'

'Yes,' we bellowed back.

He reddened and held the mic a little further away. 'Aye, well, you all know why we're here this evening and thank ye all for coming. I'm not one to do a lot of talking, so I'll keep it brief.'

There was a collective sigh of relief and then laughter. Ewan smiled, acknowledging the sentiment.

'Duncan has been my brother all my life as ye ken, and he's been a decent brother to have, looking out for me when we were peerie boys and ever since. He has always been honest, loyal and kind to everyone.'

He paused and looked over at his brother and Morag who were sitting shoulder to shoulder. Duncan smiled and blushed.

Ewan finished in a rush. 'I ken he'll be embarrassed about me saying this, but he's been happier these last few weeks than I've seen him in a long time.'

A few catcalls and wolf whistles from around the room.

Ewan patted the air in front of him to quieten things down. 'So, I ask ye all to charge your glasses and stand to wish Duncan a happy eightieth birthday!'

We all stood, glasses raised, and yelled, 'And many more!'

'Speech,' yelled someone from the back of the room, and they were joined by more voices.

Duncan laughed and walked up to the mic.

'All I can say is, thank ye all. It's been a grand life I've had here. There's only one thing I would have changed in all these years.' He looked over at my mother and held out a hand. 'It's been grand you coming hame, Morag. It was a sad day when you left but now you're hame, and it's like a loop's been closed and the world feels a'right again.' He paused, a blush creeping up his neck.

He rubbed his ear and glanced at Ewan before turning his gaze back to my mother. 'Morag, I was wondering if you'd do me the honour of being my wife?'

I gasped and looked at Ishbel. Her mouth was open in a large O, so she was clearly as surprised as I was. Several people called out, 'What's your answer, Morag?'

I turned to my mother who looked as if she'd been slammed back into her seat. Her eyes were wide, her lips parted and all the colour had drained from her face. Fluttering her hands in front of her chest as if trying to cool herself down, she slowly got to her feet. Then she practically ran from the room.

Duncan let the mic drop by his side, a look of utter desolation on his face.

I wanted to go and comfort him, but I also wanted to tell him that this was the mother I knew, the woman who was angry and scared, who pushed away the people who would be closest to her.

Instead, Ishbel pushed me towards to door.

'Go after her – she'll likely fall in the dark.'

I nodded. Glancing over to the stage I saw Duncan had been surrounded by his friends and family. I went out the door.

I was shocked and appalled at what had happened. Of course, she was surprised by Duncan's very public proposal, but her reaction seemed rather extreme. How could she do such a thing to Duncan in front of all those people, on his night?

It wasn't hard to find her. She was resting against a wall twenty yards or so away, hands to her face.

I stood in front of her until she looked up. In the dim street light I saw that her foundation was smudged and her skin blotchy from crying. She took a shuddering breath and stared back at me.

'I've done an awful thing, Kirsten,' she said.

'Yes, you have,' I said. 'Duncan's very upset.'

'No – I'm not talking about just now, although that's bad enough.'

'What then? What could be worse than humiliating the man who has been your most loyal friend all these years in front of his whole community?'

She covered her face with her hands again and started sobbing. I waited, a hand on her shoulder. My sympathies were with Duncan, my friend. And yet, my mother was clearly suffering too. I took some deep breaths and waited. Eventually she lifted her gaze to mine again.

'Why, Mother? Why are we out here with you sobbing? What's going on?'

'There's something I have to tell you. Duncan needs to hear it too. Would you go and see if he ever wants to talk to me again?'

'No. I won't be your messenger. If you want to speak to him, I think you should go in there and front up to him yourself. I'll come with you.' I stood back to let her pass.

She glared at me for a moment, and then slumped against the wall again. 'You're right, of course.' But she didn't move.

Minutes passed, neither of us saying anything. We both turned when we heard the swing of the hall door and footsteps approaching. The uneven gait announced it was Ishbel even before we saw her in the dim light.

'How is he?' I asked.

'He'll live,' said Ishbel. 'He wanted to leave but we persuaded him to stay for the cake.'

'I'm so sorry,' said Morag. 'I had no idea he was going to do that. I wasn't ready.'

I bit my lips.

Ishbel nodded. 'Clearly.' Her voice held no warmth.

'I need to go and see him, to explain.'

'I'd leave it until the morning if I were you. He's upset,' said Ishbel.

'This won't wait. It's been too long – I need to talk to him now.'

'Maybe Ishbel's right, you should give him some time,' I said. 'Let him be comforted by his friends.'

My mother looked like she wanted to slap me. 'I love him. That's why I can't marry him. I need to explain.'

Ishbel and I looked at each other. She raised her eyebrows and shrugged.

'Okay,' I said. 'But if you do anything more to hurt him, you'll have me to answer to.' As if she could do anything more.

Ishbel went in first but over her head I saw a cluster of people around Duncan. The band was back to playing covers from yesteryear, but no one was paying them any attention. Everyone stopped talking when we approached. I noticed a few death stares aimed at my mother, but other people looked at her with pity.

In a thin, shaky voice, she said, 'I'm sorry, Duncan. I need to talk to you, to explain myself.'

He looked up and although his eyes were glassy with tears, he smiled at her.

'Ye've no need to explain yoursel', I was being a romantic old fool. 'Tis I who should apologise, embarrassing ye in front of all these folk.'

She shook her head. 'Can we talk, please?'

He stood and his supporters edged back, still ready to surround him again if my mother said anything they didn't like.

'Can we go somewhere private?' she said.

'Of course, we'll go away hame.' He turned to the others. 'Please, keep drinking and dancing. I'm fine the noo.'

Morag raised her chin and Duncan offered her his arm even after what she'd done to him. As they walked out, my mother looked over her shoulder. 'You need to hear this too, Kirsten.'

I was glad to leave the hall. In that moment I felt I had been tarred with the same brush as my mother. If I could have put her on the next ferry to Aberdeen and never seen her again, I would have.

Back at his house, Duncan made tea. My mother sat at the table winding a hanky round her fingers and I leant against the kitchen counter.

With tea poured that none of us really wanted, Morag started speaking.

'I owe you an apology, Duncan. What I did tonight was unforgivable. You are a good and loving man. All these years you have been true to me and held my secret and this is how I repay you.' She stopped to blow her nose and wipe her eyes. Duncan held out a hand to her and she squeezed it then let it go.

'What I'm going to tell you has been eating away at me for sixty years. It has defined my life in many ways, none of them good. Because this one event has intruded into my decisions and my choices ever since, and you two are the ones who have felt it the most, for which I am sorry.' She paused again but kept looking at her hands, intertwined on the table in front of her, gripping hard.

'I've been working myself up to this moment since the letter you wrote, Kirsten, telling me that you knew the reason I'd left the island. I'd spent my life trying to forget that awful incident, but I knew then I never could and that it had affected more people than just me. That day – you know the one I'm referring to – it changed my life forever.'

My foot started tapping. We all knew what had happened, she didn't need to tell us again and try to justify her mean little life. I took a seat at the table next to Duncan, and held his warm, strong hand.

'I had shown other men to birdwatching sites before. He was no different, or so I believed. Well, you know what happened. He forced himself on me. I tried to fight him off but he was bigger and stronger than me, and kept telling me I'd enjoy it. When he'd finished, he stood over me laughing. I hated him like I had never hated anyone or anything before.'

She took a sip of her tea, her hands clasping the mug hard, and closed her eyes as if reliving the feeling.

'Ye dinnae have to say any more,' said Duncan.

She looked at him then, her eyes softening as they rested on his.

'Oh, but I do. I can't carry this anymore, and you need to know why I can't marry you, even though I do love you.'

Duncan took a breath as if to say something more, but she didn't give him time to react.

'When I got to my feet, he sneered at me as if I was worthless, which is exactly how I felt. He acted as if I should be grateful a man like him would want to do what he did with a girl like me. He was like a cockerel strutting amongst the hens.

Then he heard a bird cry and turned to look up. He held his binoculars up to his eyes and took a step towards the cliff edge–'

'I willnae hear another word,' said Duncan, half standing then sitting again and pulling at his sleeves. 'Not another word, ye hear?'

Morag ignored him and went on. 'I got to my feet and went towards him. He didn't acknowledge me in any way. He'd had his fun, now he was back to his birds. I shouted that I hated him, that he was a cruel brute.' She shrugged and shook her head. 'I was so angry, so upset. My whole body hurt. So, I pushed him. Hard. He went over the cliff.'

I stiffened. Had I just heard right? I screwed my eyes shut and took a deep breath. When I opened them again, Duncan was reaching for my mother's hand.

I looked at my mother, my tiny, bird-like mother, and saw her strength as if for the first time. I opened my mouth to say something but closed it again. I had no idea how to react, how I felt.

Duncan sighed. 'Och, Morag. Ye peerie thing, holding it te yersel' all this time.'

She looked at him and blinked a couple of times as if she'd been in a trance and was having to refocus. 'But you see, Duncan, why I can't marry you. I'm a murderer. I'm not fit for the likes of you.'

'Oh, my best lassie. I ken what you did all those years ago.'

She gasped. 'You knew?'

'Aye, I saw. But if ye hadnae done it, I would ha'. And then you said never to talk about it, so I didnae. It was our secret.'

28

───────────

THE CONFESSION

I fully intended to kill myself that night in the bath. What stopped me? Cowardice? Perhaps.

I rationalised it by telling myself that removing myself from everything I'd built in my life that meant anything to me was the better punishment. Exile to a lonely island. Isolation. My mother, on the other hand, left the island and lost herself in a city as her punishment, banishing herself from everyone who loved her.

The morning after that last fight with Ed, I dressed carefully to cover the bruises, made myself up and went down to the catering kitchen early, and was eating toast when Yasmin arrived. She smiled, relieved, I think, to see me up and ready for work. We sat, drinking coffee, planning menus and making lists of what was needed for upcoming events. She had kept the business running and I was going to reward her.

Later I went out to inspect a venue where we'd been asked to run an event. Ed's car was parked down the street. For a moment I faltered, glanced in and saw him lying on the back seat, his coat over him, asleep. Then lifted my chin and walked past.

The next few weeks were busy with work but also with my plans. I spoke to my mother about the cottage, gave many of my possessions away, offered the business to Yasmin at a knock-down price. She and Svetlana, another long-term member of the team raised the money and went into partnership. I still owned the property but asked for only enough rent to cover the mortgage. Yasmin was to move into my flat above the kitchen when I left.

I couldn't get Vanessa out of my head. Not a day passed when I didn't imagine calling, writing, going round to see her. I wanted to apologise, to beg for her forgiveness. What would she get out of any meeting we had? Perhaps she would enjoy shouting at me, but that wasn't really her way. The night she had followed me home had been so out of character for her.

The reality was, she needed nothing from me and what I really wanted was absolution, but I didn't deserve it. I had ruined her life and that of her family. I wanted to explain to her I was acting from within the grip of an obsession, that I had been ill but what difference would it make to her? The facts were still the same – her husband had had an affair and a woman she had thought her friend – who had actively worked her way into her life – had betrayed her.

I didn't see Ed again, but he wouldn't leave me alone. He called, sent texts and emails constantly. Mainly they were abusive, threatening revenge. Sometimes, probably when he'd been drinking, they were pathetic, self-pitying, rambling notes. I didn't respond but was still angered by them, as he must have been by mine all those weeks and months ago.

He had never truly cared for me; it was always about him and his sex addiction. I also realised I had never really cared about him. For me it was all about obsession. We'd been a match made in hell. It was a chilling realisation.

29

EXILE/HOME

After a sleepless night in which I went over and over my mother's confession, my reaction to it changing as fast as the Shetland weather, she knocked on my door. She'd been out all night.

'Can I come in?' she asked hesitantly.

'I'll put the kettle on,' I said. We took our places either side of the table with our cups of tea.

'I know it's a lot to take in. I'm sorry. I thought I might explain more, if you'll listen?'

I laughed. 'Surely there's no more? Are you going to tell me your name is actually Myra Hindley and you killed children and buried them on the Yorkshire Moors?'

'Kirsten, please. I know it's been a shock–'

'You could say. It's not every day you find out your mother pushed a bloke off a cliff.'

She gasped.

'Sorry. That sounded harsher than I meant it to. Thing is, I'm still trying to take it in.'

'Aye.' She sat in silence for a while, head bowed. The light rested softly between us. I wondered, as I had hundreds of times in the night, what I would have done in her shoes. Was she a hero or a villain?

The answer I came to was, both.

'I owe you more,' she said, lifting her eyes to mine.

I nodded but said nothing.

'I know nothing can change the years between us, the distance, the fear I felt. Everything I told you the other night about my life with your father was true but now you know what I did, I can add that I was terrified of being found out and losing you.' She moistened her lips, took a deep breath and carried on.

'I was always looking over my shoulder, waiting for the police to find me. I've lived my life like a coil sprung tight, dreading coming undone. It's why I've never made many friends, and why I never came back here until now. I thought someone might have guessed what had happened and call the police.'

'So, when you met Lydia–'

'Aye, he was dead, but I could hardly tell her, could I? She thought he was living in the north, having cut ties with his family.'

I looked at my mother, not quite knowing what to make of her and what she'd done. The secret she'd kept. The silence surrounding her early life.

'But you married – you must have been close to my father at one time, surely?'

She sat back for a moment and looked out the window. 'Your father was a charmer. Everyone liked him. I was flattered I was the one he chose. For a while, I thought we loved each other. But I realised we could never be close. I was too scared of letting my guard down. I could manage friendships but when you live with someone day in, day out, things might get said that ought not to be. I became quieter and quieter. Anyway, he needed more attention and adoration than I could give him. He soon tired of me, as you know, but I felt it was my fault. He started taking his temper out on me and having his affairs not long after we were married, and I believed it was my sentence, my punishment. I had deserved that life.'

I edged towards her. 'No one deserves to stay in a violent marriage.'

'I did. Killing someone is the ultimate violent act, don't you think?'

I was about to respond but she held up a hand. 'Would I do things differently if I had my time again? Maybe. I don't know. But it was the choice I made, and I was stuck with it. The only regret I have is that you came into the middle of all the hate and fear. No child deserves what you got – a mother too scared to love you, and a father who didn't want to be there.'

I bit my lip. 'You don't have to apologise for him.'

'I'm not. I'm apologising for me. I believe he still loved you, it was me he was staying away from but the effect, for you, was the same.' Her eyes were dry, but she wiped her hands over her face and sighed. 'I don't expect you to forgive me, Kirsten, but at least now you know the whole story.'

My head was full, my mind racing. I got up to fill the kettle just to give myself something to do apart from staring at my mother across the table.

'Apart from one thing. Your suicide attempt.'

She held up her arms, looked at the scars on her wrists.

'It was after I heard my parents were dead. The full weight of the decisions I'd made came crashing down on me. I'd let them die thinking I still hated them. That's a terrible thing to do to someone. I felt I'd created dead air all around myself – let no one in, not even my family and my daughter. I decided you'd be better off without me.'

I felt a tear slide down my cheek. 'Thank you for telling me,' I said, turning away from the hearth to face her again.

'It was time for you to hear the whole story. I'm getting on, and although I'm healthy for now, I don't have too many years left. I didn't want to die holding on to the secret that has dogged me all my life, and all that distance it's created between us. It's why I came back. I was working my way up to telling you but last night, when Duncan proposed, it threw me, and I knew it was time.'

'You're lucky he's such a forgiving man,' I said.

She smiled. 'Yes, he is, and I know how fortunate I am. But I've always loved you, Kirsten. Always. I used to go up into the spare room when you were at school and take out all the things you'd made me – pasta necklaces, pottery animals, the stories and poems you wrote. I pressed the flowers you picked for me and put them in my favourite books so I'd come upon them as I read.' A tear slid down her cheek. Its twin slid down mine.

'I never knew,' I said, sniffing and dragging my sleeve across my nose. My voice shook.

She didn't say anything. There was nothing she could say that would make a difference.

'I hated you.'

She sighed. 'I understand.'

'I said hated. Not hate. Now I'm sorry for all the wasted time.' I ran out of steam and sat, deflated, opposite her.

The silence lengthened and thickened the air in the cottage.

'You are definitely going to marry Duncan, aren't you?' I asked eventually.

Her lips twitched upwards into a smile. 'Yes. The silly man still wants me, and he makes me feel safe and happy. Do you mind?'

'Of course not. But if you hurt him, you'll have me to answer to. He's a good man – the best I've ever known. He's taught me a lot about forgiveness.'

'Me too, Kirsten, me too.'

The days shortened towards winter and the temperatures dropped from cool to cooler. The winds picked up, gales blowing across the North Sea at times, keeping everyone indoors and the fires banked up. There was a majesty in the brutal weather. When there was a let-up, I went to see Ishbel. I told her my mother's story knowing it would go no further but needing to hear myself say it, to hear the words out loud. She was shocked, of course, but quickly came to accept her actions.

'A spur-of-the-moment action, I suspect. I canna imagine her plotting it out given what had just happened to her. Who's to say what we'd 'a' done in her place. It's just a crying shame it affected you so,' she said gently.

And that was it. It was a crying shame. It wasn't a malicious act – it was a spur-of-the-moment reaction. And in the years that followed she was anxious and depressed and punishing herself for killing Gerald. I was the collateral damage. She hadn't set out to hurt me. She'd been blinded by the torment of her own demons – fear, shame, self-loathing.

An image of Duncan sitting at my table popped into my head, and a single word. Forgiveness. My mother hadn't been able to forgive herself, and I hadn't been able to forgive her either. But an old man who'd lived his life on a quiet island had taught us both something we'd failed to learn elsewhere.

I walked home to the cottage, gazing about me at the land I'd come to think of as my home.

A few days later, on a cold, early winter day, I sat on the damp sand looking out over the churning sea. Hearing laughter off to my right, I saw Morag and Duncan walking along the beach hand in hand, heads close together as he bent to hear something she said.

Watching them, I realised I'd been bound all my life by my anger, my pain and a desire to punish my mother. I didn't want to be ruled by those feelings anymore. I almost expected the sun to burst through the clouds and shine down on my epiphany – I could let go. I could choose love and forgiveness.

The settled feeling came and went. I struggled with letting go. I had been defined by my past for so long I had no idea who I could be in the future. Some days I still raged at what had happened. The old me was still too quick to lean towards hate and blame and punishment. But gradually those days were overtaken by more where I understood why my mother had behaved as she had and accepted that it wasn't because of me. And there were days in which I cried at what she'd been through and found a new respect for her strength.

Our relationship may never be easy, we have a lifetime of distance and hurt to overcome. Habits build over a long time and don't change just because we want them to. We can both take offence easily and our conversations stagger too often from gentle to jagged. But she's here to stay and we're making the effort.

'Do you remember all those dance costumes you used to make me?' I asked one day as we sat after dinner.

'Och, yes. Of course. Some of them were pesky things to sew – the acorn one springs to mind, it was so fiddly. But seeing you up there on the stage, dancing so beautifully, well, I was so proud.'

I laughed, remembering the day, the costume, the other little girls dressed as bluebells, daffodils, squirrels and dormice.

'Your teacher was creative, that's for sure,' said Morag. 'But you all loved her, and us mothers, well, we just did what we were told!'

That night I wrote in my diary.

Over time the picture I have of my mother as a cold woman in the background of my childhood is shifting to accommodate all the kinder memories I have and I am enjoying getting to know her more.

I don't know if I'm over my obsessions, I can't see into the future but I do know I have people around me who love me and whom I love in return. Among them I feel nurtured and accepted. And there is Una's nephew, David, who I met on the ferry and may see again. The idea scares and excites me in equal measure.

One evening, with the moon bright in the inky sky and the waves gently lapping the shore, I wrapped up warm and took my notebook to the beach. It was time to deal with the past once and for all. I lit candles in jars, made a circle of stones and filled it with the peat I had brought with me. Shielding the match from the breeze, I lit a fire.

I sat with my notebook on my lap and wrote. A single word on each page.

```
Hate
Anger
Blame
Self-loathing
Shame
```

I read through my confession for the last time and was, as always, horrified and ashamed. But I also felt a glimmer of something else: compassion for myself. I was doing my best. I was trying to change.

I wrote some more words.

```
Hope
Forgiveness
Love
```

I sat thinking about how they would change my life. How they were already changing my life.

At midnight on the longest night of the year, I started tearing the pages out of my notebook until only the last three were left. Hope, Forgiveness, Love. I added Compassion. Those I would keep.

Then page by page I fed my shameful confession into the blaze.

THE END

ACKNOWLEDGEMENTS

As always, I am indebted to my Writers Group and early readers for helping to shape this story into the book you hold in your hands. Also, my agent Michael Cybulski and associate, Sue Anderson and her panel of hawk-eyed readers. To all at Bloodhound Books and my editor, Ian Skewis, thank you once again for working your magic.

My husband, Neil deserves a medal for always listening as I discuss plot, character and story arc, and air all my doubts and insecurities while writing. This may be my fourth book, but the voice in my head that says no one will want to read it is still loud!

Lastly, to you, the reader. Thank you. I hope you find Kirstie's story interesting.

A NOTE FROM THE PUBLISHER

Thank you for reading this book. If you enjoyed it please do consider leaving a review on Amazon to help others find it too.

We hate typos. All of our books have been rigorously edited and proofread, but sometimes mistakes do slip through. If you have spotted a typo, please do let us know and we can get it amended within hours.

info@bloodhoundbooks.com